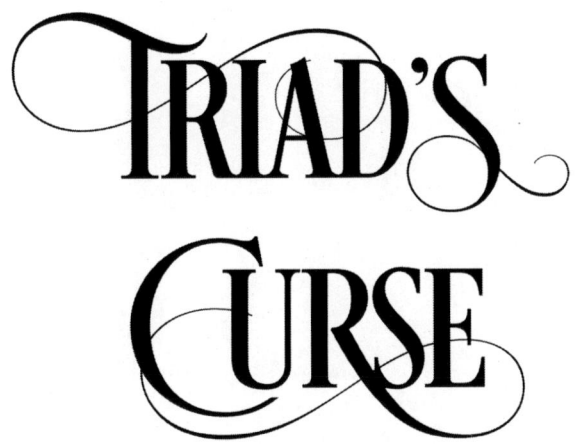

TRIAD'S CURSE

Mae Pierce

Edited by A Novel Idea

ISBN 9780645579512

Contents

Content Warning   VI

     VII

1. Cami   1

2. Cami   11

3. Cami   20

4. Cami   31

5. Fenar   36

6. Cami   47

7. Cami   53

8. Tallis   62

9. Cami   69

10. Cami   76

11. Wellyn   86

12. Fenar   91

13.	Cami	97
14.	Wellyn	122
15.	Shadow	127
16.	Cami	128
17.	Cami	136
18.	Eyke	140
19.	Cami	143
20.	Cami	159
21.	Fenar	173
22.	Cami	177
23.	Tallis	180
24.	Cami	190
25.	Fenar	198
26.	Cami	221
27.	Fenar	231
28.	Fenar	239
29.	Cami	248
30.	Tallis	262
31.	Wellyn	272
32.	Cami	276
33.	Eyke	295
34.	Cami	298
Epilogue		315
Glossary		327

Afterword   329

About Author   331

Content Warning

TRIAD'S CURSE contains depictions of:
- Blood (ingestion of)

- Blood kink

- Bullying

- Consensual sexual content

It also contains brief references to:
- Alcohol abuse

- Consensual sex under the influence of alcohol

Please note that this book end on a cliffhanger. Triad's Curse is part of a duet that will conclude in the next book, Triad's Cure.

To James
Who took a chance on a girl in a red dress. You gave
me courage from the first time we met, and these words
wouldn't exist without your belief in me.

Cami

THE HOUSE FELT LIKE a morgue when I walked in. The light from a lamp filled the space, an attempt to warm the deceased. My heart ached tenderly, knowing my mother likely switched it on before she left to take up vigil at the hospital again.

It was skirting two in the morning when I closed the door, my muscles aching from being used all night. The false smile had long slid off my face and my shoulders drooped down and forwards. I looked toward the hallway where my bedroom was but couldn't make the few steps there. I slid onto the couch instead and toed my shoes off with a hiss of relief. Next came my bra, which I flung across the room, cursing its very existence. I folded my legs up and tucked them under a threadbare blanket.

As I sank into the couch, my skin buzzed with an itch that no amount of twisting and turning could satisfy. Hot tears pricked my eyes, at the futility of it all. I had just finished a twelve-hour shift, my eyes dropping out of my head for the majority. Now I could finally sleep but my body scrounged up a speck of energy. It was enough to keep me staring wide-eyed at the ceiling.

The house was silent around me and I tucked the blanket closer. I never thought I would miss Dad's snoring, but the house seemed empty without the trumpeting from my parents' room.

Sleep must have claimed me eventually, because when I woke, the sun was streaming through the window and someone was slamming their fist on the door. I dragged myself from the couch, aching in places I didn't know I had. Shuffling to the door, I paused before checking the peephole. You couldn't be too careful in this neighborhood. Luckily, it was the elderly man who lived in the apartment next to ours. I opened the door a crack.

"Hey Gary, what can I do for you?" I asked, my voice rattling from the smoke of the bar last night. I covered a cough, clearing my throat while he brandished a thick envelope.

"Morning Cami. They've given me some of your mail again," he said and mumbled something under his breath about incompetent postal workers. I took the mail and gave him a tight smile. He was a grump but at least he didn't keep it. I'd lost a package a month ago and I swear someone had swiped it off the doorstep.

I thanked Gary and slipped back inside, turning the envelope over in my hand. I recognized the logo of an hourglass turned on its side. Legion Co. was a lifeline for me this past month. My fingers shook a little as I ripped the top open. I slid the papers out and forced myself to breathe as I read the letter to find the information I prayed was there.

Accepted.

I let out a squeal and bounced on my feet, the papers tight in my hand. I'd been impatiently waiting for a response ever since they took a sample of my blood, two weeks ago. They'd taken my blood two weeks ago and I had been waiting for a reply since that moment. After the news I received yesterday, I needed the money they promised more than anything.

I set the papers down and leaned on the kitchen bench, closing my eyes and taking a deep breath. I could do it. I could dig my family out of this mess. We could finally live together again in a house larger than a shoebox. Percy and Aaron could get the education they deserve, Ma would get a well-earned break and Dad would get the support he needed while he recuperated in hospital.

I sucked in another shaky breath as my throat clenched with pent up emotion. I could do this, I needed to do this. It was my fault our lives had imploded.

My phone buzzed in my pocket and I drew it out with shaky fingers. "Hello?" I said, not looking at the name.

"Morning Camellia, how was work last night?" My Ma's dulcet tones floated down the line, and cold froze uncomfortably in my chest. Hearing her say my full name always made me react that way. It reminded me too much of when things made sense, when the future looked hopeful for my parents. Dad had given a bunch of camellias to Ma on their first date and they were sickeningly romantic by immortalizing the moment by naming me after the flower.

"How is Dad?" I redirected, not wanting to tell her about the myriad of drunken creeps who had hit on me throughout the night, bold enough to grope my ass as I collected empty glasses. There was no point in saying anything when it happened. I just gritted my teeth and moved away, revulsion motoring me behind the bar. I would not complain and risk getting fired. We needed the money too much. Dad's hospital bills were already high enough, and Percy's care fees were due soon. The water bill I received yesterday had shocked me, the rates higher than I had budgeted for. I was going to head down to the hospital that afternoon, before another shift, but I wanted the confirmation that he was improving like Ma insisted he was.

"He got only a little sleep last night, unfortunately, so he's resting today," Ma said with a sigh. I could picture her sitting next to his bed, her hand cradling his diminished one. If Dad hadn't slept well last night, that would mean she probably hadn't either. She had been sleeping there since the boys had gone to stay with Aunty Dianne. It was against hospital rules, but the nurses allowed Ma overnight since she was technically staff and was using up her leave to be with him.

"How are you, Ma?" I asked, knowing her answer would be the same.

"Just fine, sweetheart, don't you worry about me." Her words shone like fluorescent lights, bright but fake.

"I'm going to pop in to see the boys and then I'll be over in the afternoon. I'll see you later?"

"Drive safely," she said before saying goodbye. I flinched, my fingers convulsing around the phone. My eyes fell to the papers, Even though it would hurt, I knew it was for the best. I could fix what I broke, no matter what it took.

Traffic was light and it only took thirty minutes to get to Aunty Dianne's neat suburb. Aaron and Percy were outside in Aunty Dianne's yard when I arrived. Aaron was eating a ham and cheese sandwich, a spread of UNO cards clutched in his free hand. Percy's carer, Blake, was laying down a red two when he spied me, a big grin eating up his face.

"Look who's here, boys! Your sister," he said, casting a warm look towards Percy, who seemed to brighten as I approached. His eyes were warm and his hand, curled in on itself, waved a little. He sat beside Blake in his special chair with pads around his waist helping to sit him upright. His hair tickled my cheek as I leaned down to kiss him. I breathed in his clean, crisp scent, knowing it was weird but needing to do it for my self-preservation. Aaron barreled into me, his arms squeezing around me as I lifted him up and swung him around.

"Cami! You're here!" He grinned as I put him down and sat on his chair, pulling him onto my lap. At seven years old, he was too big and almost at the point of being too cool for me to haul him into a cuddle, but I couldn't help myself. I needed to soak up both of their essences.

"How are my gorgeous bros today?" I asked, nudging Aaron to finish his sandwich. He gave me a gap-toothed smile and puffed out his chest.

"I've beaten Blake twice already. I'm an UNO master," he declared confidently. Blake sighed, his eyes twinkling.

"Percy felt like having a bit of sun this morning, so I thought a few games might make it even better."

Percy couldn't hold the cards as cerebral palsy made the movement challenging, but with Blake's help he could join in. Failing that, he loved to watch, and from the brightness in his eyes and the warmth in his cheeks I could tell he was having a great morning. He let out a few slow garbles and I nodded, knowing what he was asking me.

"I brought presents!" I pulled two soft toys from my bag. They were both wild for Pokémon and these had been my go to presents for them since they were old enough to care. I had a Snorlax for Aaron and a Psyduck for Percy. They were getting a little old for soft toys, but since these were the last ones I would be able to gift them, I didn't think it would matter too much. I tucked Percy's in his arm and he gave me a look of pure pleasure.

"Thanks Cami, Snorlax is so cool," Aaron said, bouncing his on the stack of UNO cards and making them scatter like the pieces of my heart. I wanted to get up and race from the backyard, but I made myself stay, memorizing the warmth of my brother pressed up against me with his small, wriggling form and big, exuberant smile.

The hours passed by quickly, ending with me asking Blake to take a photo of me and my boys before I left. I held back the tears until I was behind the wheel with the radio turned up loud enough for my sobs to sound less desperate. This was harder than I thought already, but I had no choice. My family needed me to do this.

The hospital was busy when I arrived, and I squeezed into an elevator to go to the second floor. Ma was reading a magazine when I walked in, her chair pressed up against Dad's bed. I gave her a hesitant smile, avoiding looking at Dad's sleeping form. She held her arms up and I sank into her embrace, resting my cheek on her shoulder for a moment before pulling away. Perching on the bed, careful not to disturb my deeply sleeping dad, I pulled out a chocolate bar and handed it to her.

"You look like you've been crying," Ma said, her forehead creasing. I gave her a tight smile and shrugged.

"I went to see the boys," I said, and she nodded.

"I understand," she whispered as her hand trailed over the bed to grip my knee and give it a quick squeeze. My heart clenched with the movement, enough that my breathing stuttered. This was agony. I wanted to soak up every second of their presence, but I also wanted to be gone, to get it over with.

Dad's black hair was slick and neat, his face clear of unruly curls. I knew that was Ma's doing. She kept him looking well-cared for, brushing his hair and even doing his nails for him. She cast a longing look at him with intensity like a magnetic force so strong that my he turned his head in his sleep to face her.

"I wish he was awake. He would love to talk to you." I clenched my teeth. I timed my visits to when I knew he was going to be sleeping. We hadn't spoken since he got the infection. I couldn't stand his injury, but with the infection added in, I could barely look at him. He should be striding into the kitchen with a cheeky smile, sipping a mug of coffee. His large hands, calloused and rough, should be shaping wood, not lying idle in a hospital bed. His veins were too pronounced, his skin too ashy and there were bruises marring it in strange places where needles and tubes had been inserted.

I pulled a folded piece of paper from my bag and handed it to Ma. "I brought this for him," I said, watching as she tucked it under the lamp on the side table.

"What's this one about?" she asked. She never read them before Dad, which made me feel pathetically grateful.

"A bear and wolf go to a bar," I summarized, and her eyes twinkled When I was younger, I noticed that Dad's favorite thing about reading the paper was the cartoons. He even had a collection of comics from when he was a child. I had made my own, silly little scribbles that made very little sense. But my dad adored them and requested I draw him more. Over time, it had become a tradition for me to draw him a comic for his birthday. After the accident, I had brought one in every time I visited, like the small pictures might allow me to atone. After I started avoiding visiting when he was awake, they were my way of communicating. To prepare for my departure, I had drawn a stack to put aside. I hoped they would make him smile in my absence.

My dad twitched in his sleep as I shifted on the bed. I didn't want him to wake up when I was here. I couldn't face it. Next Wednesday I would be gone, and my family would have everything they needed to build a better life. But I knew the security for their future would be a balm for my absence.

"I've got to get to work, Ma," I said, greedily helping myself to another hug. She clasped her hands in her lap when I finally pulled back.

"You work too much, sweetheart, you look so tired." She frowned and I sighed.

"We need the money and it helps me keep my mind off things," I answered, shouldering my bag. My nose wrinkled as I looked around the room, I wouldn't miss this smell, the searing stench of chemicals and underneath that, the miscellaneous scent of illness, of bodies trapped in beds, sweat laced tubes and lumpy mattresses. Mom's fingers dragged over dad's inert hand and her eyes flickered with pity as she sighed.

"It's not your fault, Camellia. I hope you don't think that," she whispered

It was.

"See you tomorrow. I love you, Ma," I hurried for the door before, smothering the tears that wanted to burst out.

I felt unhinged. I'd read through the contract and I was to present myself at Legion Co. next Wednesday with a small amount of luggage. Not that it mattered. I didn't care to take anything with me except my family, and that wasn't a possibility. But I could take photos at least.

The knowledge of what next Wednesday would bring was wreaking havoc on me. The enormity of what I was giving up pressed down on me. I had been drowning for so long, ever since that night when I made the worst mistake of my life. Now I could fix it, but it felt like the hardest choice to make. Stay and watch as my family lost everything? Or leave forever to provide for my family, and hopefully atone for my mistakes.

We could barely afford Blake's salary, even with a grant from the government. That was due to finish next month. Dad would still be in hospital for the foreseeable future, so his income was out. He didn't have employment insurance nd Ma only had so much leave she could take. The boys deserved to be with our parents without the threat of financial ruin hanging over their heads.

I almost wanted to have a drink to wash away the sense of unraveling I was feeling. Instead, I dressed and went to work where I endured spilled drinks, cleaned vomit from toilets and let gross drunk men paw my ass. I did it all because it was my fault we were in this position.

But I continued because I deserved the horrible things that happened to me. My family didn't.

Cami

WEDNESDAY CAME QUICKER THAN I expected. I had seen the boys one more time, leaving before Blake could interrogate me. He could tell something was up. It was obvious I'd barely slept and couldn't stomach more than a few bites of food. Barely managing a shower that morning, I left my face bare of any makeup. The bags under my eyes looked like bruises.

I stood outside Legion Co. for a good ten minutes, my lone bag heavy on my shoulder. I'd packed very few items of merit; an envelope of photos was the only sentimental item I allowed myself. I drew a shallow breath and walked through the door, my legs as shaky as a newborn lamb.

The receptionist met me with a brilliant smile and I shrunk a little in the face of her manicured beauty. Her skirt squeaked as she rounded the desk and outstretched her hand, her opalescent nails flashing in the light.

"Would you like me to take that for you, Ms. Perrin?" she asked, and I gave her a brief shake of my head.

"I've got it," I replied, hating how reedy my voice was. She waved her arm toward the elevator and smiled.

"Dr. Kerys is waiting for you on level five. You remember the way?" she said pleasantly, and I nodded mutely.

The bag felt like an anchor as I dragged my feet to the elevator but before I realized it, I was being ushered in front of Dr. Kerys. His hands were clasped were behind his back as he stood by the window, bathed in the light. A wide and welcoming smile grew over his face as I walked in. He had on a white coat, as he had the last time I'd met with him. Grey mingled with his dark hair, but he was a certified DILF, assuming he had kids. He had mentioned none in the brief time he'd dealt with me previously.

A woman sitting behind his desk rose, extending her hand for me to shake. Her cheeks were bright with heavy rouge and there was a hunger in her eye that I couldn't interpret. She gripped my hand with a hearty shake.

"Camellia Perrin, it's a pleasure to meet you. My name is Gloria Saure, I'll be overseeing the acceptance process and tying up the loose ends while we transition you." She motioned for me to take a seat and I slid in gratefully, feeling my knees wobble a little.

"I prefer Cami," I corrected. "Are you a lawyer?" She smiled and tilted her head.

"A little like a lawyer. I'll be working closely with you in the future," she said, finally. I pulled my bag closer to me and I fished around until I pulled out the contract. I hesitated, looking to Dr. Kerys, who nodded. I passed it to Gloria, my hand shaking slightly.

"It's all signed," I said. Gloria set it aside without looking at it.

"Did you read it all? You understand that this is a binding agreement. Your life will change after we leave this room. You will not see your family again. You will be privy to things that are too sensitive to allow you to live a normal life."

I had read the contract. Dr. Kerys had explained it all to me as well. They needed my blood for a particular trial. It would needed frequently and continually. I would have to move and cut ties with my family, not even able to tell them where I was going. Like witness protection, almost. The contract didn't even say where I would move, but I'd brought my passport with me.

The pay-off for these insane conditions? A ridiculous amount of money.

I nodded curtly. "I understand." Gloria beamed and held out her hand, her fingers waggling until I put my own in her grip. Her fingers clasped tightly around my wrist, pinching a little at the force of her hold. Dr. Kerys stood behind Gloria. He past my shoulder, avoiding my eyes.

"We can't divulge the nature of the task until you sign the agreement. You accept this?" He raised his eyebrows, and I nodded. Gloria opened her mouth, but I interrupted her.

"The money for my family, the cost of the house is included in that?" I fidgeted in the plush seat. Gloria shook her head, my hand still awkwardly gripped in her fingers.

"Of course not, dear. A mortgage for a house of their choosing and the five-million-dollar sum are separate. We also agree to provide a $650,000 bonus for each year you provide the results we expect from your blood."

"I didn't know that." I choked on my words, my eyes wide. Dr. Kerys nodded.

"We want to ensure we motivate you to succeed. Your blood, if successful, would be the key to a bright future for many."

I looked at my wrist stretched out and still in Gloria's grip. The blue veins pressed to the surface and felt words escape me. How could my blood be so important? For a moment I considered how absurd this all was, but swallowed any lingering doubts.

I nodded my acceptance again and Gloria gave me a sharp-toothed grin. Literally, her teeth flashed for a second and I thought they were sharp little fangs. Suddenly, there was a burning sensation on my wrist. I cried out and tried to yank it from Gloria, but she held tight. The burn prickled up my arm and over my body like a wave, filling every cell with tiny pops of pain.

Gloria let go of my hands and I fell back into the seat, perspiration dotting my forehead. The pain was gone as suddenly as it arrived. I pulled my hand up and saw a band of red welts around my wrist, slowly fading as I watched.

"What was that?" I hissed, glaring at Gloria and Dr. Kerys, who were blandly observing me.

"Just a Legion Binding Agreement." Gloria smiled and as her lips crept up, I could clearly see the sharp, angled edges of her fangs.

"Your teeth..." I sucked in a horrified breath, stumbling for the door, reaching for the handle as panic coursed through me.

"You won't come to any harm, Cami." Gloria soothed, but it only riled me up more. She turned to Dr. Kerys and spoke with him with muted tones, not even worried that I'd seen what she was hiding in her mouth.

"I am free to fill you in on the details now, Ms. Perrin," Dr. Kerys said, rounding the desk to perch on the edge. As he did, I saw a tawny tail flick up from behind him. Its end shaped like a rattlesnake, sending up a warning rattle as I furiously jiggled the door handle again. It wouldn't budge. I panted, walking backwards until I hit the opposite wall. Gloria cradled her head in one hand, examining her nails.

No, not nails. Claws. Sharp, blood-red claws that protruded further than any fingernail would. I eyed them both, my chest heaving forcefully. Adrenaline made my limbs tighten. My muscles screamed for flight but I couldn't move. I certainly couldn't speak, a fact that Dr. Kerys divined quickly enough. He nodded his head as if understanding my predicament.

"You can see I'm not quite human, Ms. Perrin. I apologize for the subterfuge." He said it so mildly I thought my brain would explode. He shrugged off the white coat and I watched as his tail swished languidly through the air. "I'm a Legion. The closest reference I can think for you would be demons, although we are nothing like them." He grimaced.

A hysterical bubble caught in my throat and I slid to the floor, staring at him in horror. Demons. I was dreaming, obviously. This had to be a hallucination. I let my shoulders slump, and I relaxed slightly, which Dr. Kerys took as an invitation to continue.

"Legion live on a different plane called Melbak, and we have been suffering from a crisis for the past two hundred years. Legion help maintain the health of the land through boosts, a special Legion whose blood provides power. They're the backbone of Legion society. Without them, there are no triads, no power to go towards Melbak. For an undiscernible reason, boosts have become rarer over time and now there are not enough to sustain every Legion. Melbak has suffered for it. The land is crying out for power. Resources are dwindling; the very land is bleeding for lack of boost blood."

"What the fuck?" I mumbled to myself, pinching my hip discretely. It hurt but I didn't wake up.

"Those in power have spent decades trying to discover why fewer boosts seem to present each year, but I believe the situation is too dire. We need a solution now, even if it isn't palatable to Legion society." He shared a loaded look with Gloria, who was all seriousness now. Knowing there were razor-sharp teeth in that mouth made me stiffen again.

"I have spent fifteen years searching for an alternative. I have traveled to more planes than I can remember, testing blood and hoping that we might find one that matches boost blood. In all that time, we have only found one. You, Ms. Perrin."

Dr. Kerys took a step towards me but halted when I curled into a ball. His tail swished as if my reaction agitated him, but his face was blank.

"Legion need you, Ms. Perrin. Melbak won't survive the next hundred years without more boosts. The Legion Heads granted me permission to conduct a trial. You will live in Melbak and become the boost of a triad. If you are successful, then more humans might be introduced, and we may save our land."

"What the fuck?" I said, my vocabulary reduced to those three words. I wasn't dreaming. I'd pinched myself three more times while he was talking, more frantic each time it failed to wake me.

"What is your true name? You're obviously not a doctor," I said, getting to my feet. My head was spinning. I needed a drink more than anything. I pinched myself again for the thought.

"My given name is Albion Kerys. I'm closer to a scientist if it helps. I have powers that help me to identify boost blood. It makes it very conducive for testing."

Gloria was looking at her watch, an almost comical sight if her hand wasn't half claw. I gulped as she looked up, her lips pursed.

"I know this is difficult, dear. I would like to give you more time to acclimate, but we need to go to Melbak before the portal closes. The Heads only gave permission for a day trip, otherwise, we'll have to wait for them to approve another trip."

She stood up and waved her hand, trying to usher me closer to her. Her eyes flashed when I didn't move immediately. Dr. Kerys—no, that's not right—Albion gave me a small smile.

"Ms. Perrin, if it would help you feel better, I will take a binding agreement to ensure no physical harm will come to you in Melbak. Would that allay some of your fears while we situate you there?"

I crossed my arms and frowned. Would it make me feel better? The only thing that would do that would be if I could go back an hour when I believed I was setting my family up for the future and would still be living on Earth.

"What does it do? I mean, if I come to harm, what happens?"

"If anything happens to you, I will take the damage."

I looked at Gloria now, who was shuffling nervously, her eyes darting to her gold watch.

"My family. I want proof that you will look after them." Despite this insane development, providing for them was still my priority. Gloria clasped her hands and nodded.

"Of course, dear. I'll be handling them personally. Their memories of you will alter so your absence won't cause them distres. As far as they know, you have accepted a job offer in Madagascar, too rural for phone coverage and reliable mail. The money they receive will come as a gift from you, but they won't question why they don't see you and I will create a block so they won't miss you. It would entirely defeat our purposes if they decided to make you a missing person!"

It was as if she'd punched me in the gut. My hand scrambled at the material covering my stomach. They wouldn't miss me. That was good. I hadn't left a note, only the stack of comics. I was most worried about how they would cope with me disappearing. Now that wasn't an issue. They would have everything they could ever dream of. My memories would remain; they would still wreck me, but that was fair.

I deserved it.

I could walk out that door and they'd still be paying for my stupid mistakes. I paled and jerked my head to look at Albion.

"What happens if I break my agreement?"

I shuddered when Gloria smiled pleasantly and answered for him.

"You can't leave, if that's what you're hoping. Everything you signed in the paperwork, agreeing to move, to cut ties with your family and allow your blood to be used for our purposes, is binding. You're physically unable to break it. If that door had been unlocked, you wouldn't be able to walk through it."

Albion sighed and walked to the door. He opened it with his keycard and swept his hand out in front of him. He raised an eyebrow at me, knowing I wanted proof. The hallway was lit by a dim fluorescent light. As my feet got closer to the door, I moved as if in mud. The air thickened around my limbs and immobilized me. My muscles pushed until sweat lined my brow. As soon as I moved to turn back, it released me. I could move freely and easily.

I glared at Gloria. "You tricked me."

She only shrugged and tapped her watch. "If it helps you feel better dear, you can certainly think that." She held out her hand, flicking her fingers with irritation. "But we are out of time, we must go now."

Cami

ALBION WALKED TO MY side and tucked my arm in the crook of his elbow. White flashed across my eyes as the walls disappeared and my skin crushed into my bones. The vocal chords of my neck froze, trapping the scream that wanted to escape. I was paralysed in a moment of agony, my lungs divested of air as the pressure mounted higher.

As suddenly as it started the weight disappeared and I was able to suck in a huge breath. The haze from the flash still permeated my vision as I tried to blink it away. Albion patted me on the back and pressed me onto a soft seat. I breathed deeply a few more times, my throat feeling hoarse as I blinked owlishly at him.

"Welcome to Melbak," he said smoothly, his hands linked behind his back. We were alone. Gloria was missing and as I looked around for her, Albion answered the question I was about to ask. "Gloria stayed behind to visit your family and organize the first payment. You will see her again in a few days. She is keeping a close eye on this trial for the Legion Heads."

I didn't answer him, slumping back in the velvet wingback chair I was sitting in. Stately furniture filled the room, the walls lined with books with spines marked in a language I didn't recognize. My feet carried me subconsciously to the three catherdral style windows, to give my my first view of Melbak. I gripped the windowsill, taking in a deep gulp of air.

It was a wasteland. Black veins coiled around the stunted trees. Fissures marred the ground in a haphazard web. Steam rose from darkened gaps. In the distance, I could see a large lake, or I assumed it was once a lake. What looked like oil slicked the surface, black and noxious.

"It's a beautiful day today," Albion sighed next to me and I shot him a look of disbelief.

"Bit different from Earth," I said. I was really in another world right now. A cloud of what looked like gigantic rats with wings shot into the air. I recoiled at the sight.

"Melbak didn't always look so grim. Gaer, the black substance you can see, has been slowly growing for centuries. It's sentient in a way, and seems impervious to any control. The Heads have tried all they can to stop it growing but all attempts have failed. When boosts dwindled, the Gaer spread. It even took the Lost Lake." He pointed to the water source covered in what looked like an oil slick.

"Can I even breathe here?" I asked, eyeing the steam curling from a fissure with distrust. Albion nodded and turned his back to the window, crossing his arms.

"Melbak is safe for breathing. You seem to be recovering from all the information I told you earlier."

I shrugged, training my eye on the horizon. The grappling terror I'd felt when I saw his tail and Gloria's teeth was still there. I was busy collecting memories and tucking them away in a box in my mind, they were part of my old life. I was here now. I had no choice but to move forward now. *You deserve to be taken to a world full of demon rip-offs*, a small part of me whispered.

"I would like to discuss your purpose here further and if you're amenable to it, introduce you to your triad."

I pushed my shoulders back and nodded, noticing my bag by Albion's desk. Thankfully, he'd thought to grab it as I'd been in too much of a state to think clearly. I walked to the plush chair and sat down, pulling my feet up underneath me cross-legged. Albion settled into the couch opposite me, looking almost giddy. I suppose this was exciting for him. I had something he'd been desperately searching for. If my blood worked the way he hoped, then Melbak might look less like an apocalyptic cliché.

"Your purpose is to be a boost for three others, your triad. Most boosts develop a romantic attachment to those in their triad, but it's not a requirement. You will live with them, become close and share your blood with them."

My eyes widened comically. "Ahh, like vampires?" I blurted out and Albion snorted.

"Not quite, although one of your triad has fangs. They will be required to ingest your blood, though. I understand that this will be a change, so I want to give you time to get to know your triad and acclimate to Melbak before being required to share blood."

"So generous," I said drily, the strangeness of this all making me feel numb. The door burst open, cutting off what Albion was about to say. Three men entered the room.

The first sauntered in, his shoulders drawn back as a hand carded through his dark locks with ease and nonchalance.His thick eyebrows drew together in confusion above his sharp, beak like nose.

The second man barreled into his back, sending him falling to his knees. Bright yellow hair, shorn close on the sides, like someone had gone over it with a yellow highlighter caught my eye. His head snapped to meet my gaze and I shrunk in my seat. He sneered as he perused me. I tried to swallow but found my mouth was dry.

"Move, Fenar," huffed a third voice. It's owner appearing with a mop of ruddy curls, he was willowy and pale, as tall as his companions, but seemed to hide in their wide shadows. His eyes widened as they saw me and as I saw the color, they were a dusky violet.

"Dad, what is going on?" the first guy asked Albion, his tail swishing furiously as he strode forward, ignoring me. Oh. I could see the resemblance; his tail was similar, with a rattle on the end. They had the same thick wavy hair and olive skin. Albion grimaced, shooting me an apologetic look.

I pulled my knees up close to my body, my arms going around them as if I could anchor myself the tighter I pulled them. Fenar stalked closer to me, dropping into a crouch as he got to the chair. He was eye level with me now and he slowly smiled. I couldn't help the squeak that escaped me as I saw what was in his mouth. Instead of a neat row of razor-sharp teeth like Gloria, he had four sharp fangs, two on the top and two on the bottom. Like a beast. A manic look leaked into his gaze and he tossed it back to his friends.

"Tallis, I did not mean you to be here until later." Albion sighed before snapping. "Fenar, leave her alone." Fenar rolled up on his long limbs.

"Can't help myself. I've never seen a human up close before," he said, flashing me an utterly wicked smile. "Whatever are you doing with this illicit contraband?"

"I had hoped to give you a little more time, Ms. Perrin—Cami—but this is my son, Tallis, and the members of his triad, Fenar and Wellyn."

Wellyn skirted around the perimeter of the room, barely blinking. He looked utterly terrified of me. A little bubble of laughter spluttered out of me at the sight. Albion's thick eyebrows bunched together at the sound and I waved my hand, dissmisively.

"Sorry, it's just a lot. I guess this is my triad?"

Wrong thing to say.

The room erupted into chaos. Tallis whirled on his dad, his hands suddenly bursting into flames. Albion started shouting a mile a minute as Fenar joined Tallis. I couldn't tear my eyes from the bright flames on Tallis's hands but with a gulp, forced myself. I wanted to cover my ears but settled for curling to the side. Right into the direct gaze of Wellyn. He was crouched by the side of my chair, his violet eyes wide and gorgeous, framed by thick, red lashes.

"H-hello," he said barely audible over the furious argument occurring in front of us. "My name is Wellyn."

A look of uncertainty spread over his delicate features as he slowly extended his hand. I couldn't help but smile. He had no sharp teeth or tails that I could discern. He looked more like a pixie than anything. Two fingers dragged down the side of my face, my skin erupting in goosebumps. I gave him a strange look, and he shrank, chastised.

"Sorry, that is how Legion greets another, I should have asked if it was alright. I know the human greeting though." His palm flattening towards me.

"Hello Wellyn, my name is Cami." I took his hand and gave it a quick shake, surprised at the coolness of his skin.

"You are our boost?" he asked. I leaned closer to catch the quiet inflection of his voice. Albion was no help, as he had his hands up in the air and was still arguing vehemently with Tallis and Fenar.

"I'm someone's boost," I replied, unsure on how to answer.

"Fine!" shouted Tallis as he threw himself into a seat, his arms crossed over his chest. His face was darker than stormcloud but at least he'd tucked his flame hands away. Obviously, my brain had short-circuited, considering instinct hadn't sent me screaming out the door. Fenar sat down in the opposite side of the room, his head landing in his hand like he hadn't been fiercely looming over Albion seconds before.

Albion sunk into his chair, a beleaguered sigh escaping his mouth. "My apologies again, Cami. My son needs to work on his manners."

Wellyn scooted a little closer to my chair, settling on the ground with his legs sprawled out.

"To answer your earlier question, yes, they are your triad."

"Dad, Cove has one more year to present. You know she is our boost," Tallis said, his voice straining a little as he cut me a wounded look.

"She won't." Albion tapped the side of his chair impatiently. "Her genetic markers haven't changed at all. I know you fancy yourself in love with the girl, but she isn't an option. You need a boost for your triad. I told you about the research I was doing. I thought you understood when I talked about a triad being chosen."

"I didn't think you meant me!" Tallis shouted, his hands flaring red. Fascinated, I watched, half expecting him to stamp his foot like a toddler in the middle of a tantrum. "Really? How could you think anyone would accept a *human* boost? You don't know what filth she could be harboring."

My back snapped straight at the disgust in his voice. "I won't do this with them if they're not willing," I spoke up, drawing their eyes. "If there is a triad who would be happier to accept me, I'd rather that."

Albion shot Tallis a dark glare before nodding in agreement. "Of course, of course, boosts are so rare that not all triads are lucky enough to have the chance. We shall take a vote. Those in favor of having Cami as your boost raise your hand."

Tallis's smug smile fell off his face as Wellyn's hand shot up and Fenar's followed, although reluctantly. I looked at the unnatural blonde with surprise and he replied with a sharp smile.

"I want a boost, even if it's under such unusual circumstances."

Tallis shook his head in disbelief, his mouth gaping open and his dark eyes filled with confusion. "But Cove, what about—"

"Tallis, you can still have a boost and a lover. It is rare but do as you must. You've been pining after the girl for years, not me. Wellyn can't even look at a girl without blushing," Fenar snapped, waving his hand dismissively. I looked at Wellyn and, as if on cue, his cheeks bloomed red.

"You can't do this to me," Tallis said to his father, "I won't forgive you," he promised fiercely, clearly meaning everyone was included in his promise. He darted to his feet and storming from the room.

"You'll thank me one day," Albion said. He sighed deeply.

"This is going really well," I said, arching an eyebrow at him. He gave me a thin lipped smile.

"This is the fix, I know it. Tallis will come around, especially when he sees the boost the others are benefiting from." He pinned the boys with a sharp look. "Cami is under my protection. She may be a human, but she is to be treated with respect. I made a binding agreement that she will come to no physical harm. She will also decide when to share her blood with you. Please tell my wayward son this."

Fenar snorted and shook his head "I trust you know what you're doing. I've got plans with a pretty face, so I'll leave you to it. But a human is going to have a hard time in Melbak, even if she is a boost. You know that, right?"

He didn't wait for confirmation, just shoved his hands in his pockets and headed for the door. His obvious dismissal of me didn't hurt; it only filled me with a further sense of foreboding. The situation was twisted enough without the added pressure of also being despised by my supposed triad.

"Wouldn't it just be easier to work with a different triad? One that would be more accepting of these unconventional arrangements?" I asked, and Wellyn let out a plaintive sound. Albion's tail lashed the air.

"It has to be this triad. The Legion Heads would only accept the trial if I put my legacy on the line. My only son, Tallis. There is a long history of distrust between Legion and humans, starting hundreds of years ago with a plague that was spread by humans. I went to Earth without permission, you know. We are strictly forbidden to visit your plane. If this doesn't work, he will be without a boost and suffer for it. Fenar and Wellyn are both wards of Melbak with no noble lines to taint if this doesn't go well."

Wellyn stiffened "Is that why they placed us together? Because it would be easier for you to experiment with our futures?"

Albion didn't flinch, his rattle stilling in the air. "Yes," he admitted. "I have been waiting for this moment for decades. I always knew they would tie Tallis up in my hopes and dreams."

"Yet you let him hope for Cove," Wellyn said, his voice filled with reproach. It sounded like Tallis had been holding a candle for this girl for a long time. I felt a pang of sympathy for the man. His own dad had been moving him around like a chess piece most of his life. I didn't want to be here anymore than he did. I couldn't fault him for his outburst. We were both pawns, it seemed.

A wave of fatigue washed over me and my head hit the back of the chair. It had been an absolute mess of a day. I was exhausted. My bones wanted to hibernate. I was strung out, a bow ready to propel an arrow forward, except I was the arrow as well and was being aimed towards a concrete wall.

"I think it would be prudent to table my misdeeds for the day. Cami needs to recover from her journey. Wellyn, can you situate her in your lodgings?"

The sweet-faced redhead took his lower lip and pressed it between his teeth. He nodded and stood, extending a hand to me.

"That's it? I'm just sent off to live with one guy who can't stand me, another who barely tolerates me, and one who..." I looked to Wellyn to see if he would fill in the gaps about how he thought about me. He gave me a beatific smile.

"Honored and pleased," he happily supplied, his cheeks dusting with pink. I couldn't help but smile back. At least I wasn't universally despised.

Albion sniffed and I could see the fatigue around his eyes. This day had been hard for him too, not that I forgave him.

"The sooner you settle in, the sooner we can see how successful you are as a boost. I don't see the point in delaying when you'll be required to live with them eventually."

The easy dismissal stung. Albion's gray eyes were flat and unfeeling. I wasn't sure what I wanted from him, except that he was the face that I'd known the longest and surely he must understand how jarring this was. Perhaps I hadn't been hysterical enough to warrant more time to adjust, but my nerves felt frayed. All he cared about what was running through my veins; the rest was an inconvenience, obviously. I could rely on myself, only myself. My family was my reason for doing this. It didn't matter what happened to me as long as I could care for them.

I stood on shaky feet, my knees knocking together as I willed my trembling muscles to hold up me a little longer. Wellyn shot up beside me, his fingers hovering near my elbow ready to help if I needed. I could feel a chill emanating from him. It made my skin erupt with goosebumps.

I gave Albion a tight-lipped nod and headed for the door, not knowing where I was going but too wrung out to protest any longer.

Cami

WELLYN BOUNCED AFTER ME, excitement evident in his wide-eyed look.

"Our apartment isn't too far from here," he assured me, pointing out the window to a wooded area. I followed the line of his slender finger, noting the dark-veined trees and pillar of what looked like buildings, rising beyond them in the distance.

We exited Albion's office and I was hit by a gust of warm air. Perspiration dotted my forehead immediately and I stumbled. Wellyn's hand curled around my elbow, steadying me. The coolness of his skin was so divine I let out a small moan.

"You're so cold." He snatched his hand back in surprise. A dark look passed over his features and I rushed to explain, "It's lovely, like a dip in a pool on a hot summer's day."

Wellyn still seemed unconvinced, not responsding to my comment.

"It's a good cold," I added, unsure why I felt the need to placate him. Something about him had crumbled at my simple words. I couldn't abide it. He seemed so open and sweet, and I wanted to keep it that way. Not to mention he was the only one who was even slightly kind to me. I was alone here, but it was nice to soak up some kindness. Especially as we walked through the woods and I got my first look at the black substance Albion had mentioned. It looked like sludge over the ground, tendrils hooked into its surroundings. It pulsated and the sight made me shiver.

"This is Gaer?"

"Albion told you of it?" Wellyn steered me around a crack in the ground, yellow gas puffing out of the black crevice.

"Just its name. I wasn't really ready to digest to much more information after he plucked me from Earth and brought me here." I shrugged, stepping a little closer to Wellyn as the fissure spluttered angrily.

"You did not know you were coming?" he asked, his violet eyes glinting in the sun's glare.

"I only knew I was saving my family."

"I'm sorry it has been such a jarring experience so far. Tallis and Fenar are like my family, and I know they didn't make the best first impression, but they'll come around." He offered me a hesitant smile.

We came to a building set upon four stone pillars. There was enough space to walk underneath without stooping. I raised my eyebrows at the strange sight. A building on stilts.

"The Gaer can spread across the ground and this stops it from entering the building easily."

At the top of the stilts was a metal cap.

"Does that stop it from climbing?" I asked. Wellyn nodded.

"It seems to avoid areas heavily inhabited by Legion, but it can grow. It never used to leave the woods and now it's spread all over Melbak."

I gave the dark throbbing mass a lingering look as Wellyn slipped his hand into an indented space in the wall. A set of stairs flickered in front of us like a holographic picture, except they were solid. I took a resigned step, my mind hazy enough that this didn't startle me as much as it should have. I felt like part of my brain had burnt off on the journey from Earth to Melbak. Or perhaps my mind had seen one too many unexplainable things and had shut down, no point in protesting when everything seemed remarkably crazy.

I followed Wellyn in silence, not knowing if he'd been speaking. If he was, I'd rudely ignored him, but he would have to cut me some slack. We walked down a hallway that was perfectly smooth except for small indentations that occurred a t regular intervals. Wellyn hovered his hand over one and a doorway appeared, cracked open. He ushered me in and I followed silently.

A small corridor opened into a wide open-plan apartment with a kitchen, a lounge and a small dining table. It was sparse; the only sign of being lived-in was a glass left on the side table, fingerprints marring the side. There was a pleasant view of Melbak, including a clear sight the path we'd just walked through the woods. I could see shifting dark lumps in the trees and wondered if they were more of those winged rats I'd seen earlier. Please, no.

Wellyn cleared his throat, and I was snapped from my musing. His hand came to cradle the back of his head as he ducked his gaze to the ground.

"Look, we did not know you were coming, so we had not set up a room or anything yet."

I followed him down a hallway on the opposite side of the room. He opened a door, revealing stacks of books, paper and other items I didn't recognize. There was barely any space to move.

"We will clean out the junk in here and set you up with a better room tomorrow. But until then, would you be happy to sleep in my bed?" I stiffened as he choked and added, "I will sleep on the couch, of course."

"Sure," I said, desperate to sink into anything soft right now. I wasn't above sleeping on a couch, so a bed would be a bonus. Wellyn looked relieved and he opened the next door and invited me in.

I don't know what I expected, but this wasn't it. The walls were dark and there was a damp undercurrent that I couldn't place. A light pulsed out blue waves, like the reflection of light on the ocean. It felt like a cave and something about the darkness flipped a switch in me. The exhaustion I'd felt from processing what had happened seemed to crash through my body. My mind had been working overdrive and my body had reached it's limit. I stepped toward the bed, crawling on all fours to the middle. It jostled, undulating with my movements.

"Is this a waterbed?" I just about screeched, flopping down and giggling as it moved underneath me.

"Yes," Wellyn confirmed, rubbing the back of his neck, looking sheepish. I wanted to reassure him again, that I thought it was a retro throwback, that my parents had one when I was younger. But my head nuzzled into a pillow that cradled my cheek and I felt sleep wash over me insanely fast. That I hadn't even taken my shoes off was my last thought before I slipped into a dreamless sleep.

Fenar

AFTER SEEKING SOME HARD drinks and company last night, not the date I had originally planned, I returned to our place early the next morning. I wrinkled my nose as I stepped through the door. It already smelled different. Our boost had a salty scent, not sweat exactly, but enough to make me thirsty. I wanted a taste, but I knew after that I would want to keep on tasting.

That was part of the reason I'd hightailed it out of Albion's office yesterday. She immediately intrigued my creature. The wolf had sniffed at her incessantly, prowling inside me until I couldn't take the frantic movement anymore. I had never seen a human in the flesh before, and she was cute with her dark hair a halo around her flushed cheeks. But she was a human and that would not work. I thought about the rumors regarding humans, how they'd spread disease and caused the Culling hundreds of years ago. I don't know how something so delicate could cause the amount of destruction that history heaped upon them.

Wellyn was hovering in the kitchen, opening drawers and cupboards almost frantically, seemingly unbothered by these worries of mine. Tallis had taken up his usual place in the window seat, the cushions stacked behind his back, and he turned to look at me when I entered.

"Took you long enough," he said, his face mulish. "I've been trying to reach you for an hour now."

I took my reader out of my pocket and saw the missed calls and pings in our group chat. I shrugged and threw myself down on the couch, piled with some of my collection of pillows and rugs. I tossed them to the floor below me and addressed Wellyn.

"Relegated to the couch already, hey?" I teased and snorted as his cheeks flooded a predictable pink. For a cold-blooded creature, he sure could blush.

"It was the least I could do. She did not ask for this or for you two to be such asses yesterday."

I arched an eyebrow at his mildly accusatory tone. Wellyn was anti-conflict. No matter what, he didn't want to fight.

"I couldn't care less if she had to sleep with the Gaer. She's not being our boost. It's not happening and I'll be telling my dad that this morning." Tallis fisted the material of the cushion he was leaning against.

"She's not?" I drawled, noting how disheveled Tallis looked. He had dark circles underneath his eyes and he had bitten his nails down to ragged nubs. He scowled at me furiously.

"Of course she's *sheking* not. She's a human for one," his face twisted with disgust, "second, I meant what I said yesterday. We will wait another year for Cove to present as a boost. It could still happen, anything is possible," he said feverishly, his eyes taking on a shine I didn't like.

"Tallis," Wellyn warned, chewing his lip, "I do not think your dad will budge on this. He—" Wellyn bit off with a curse, running his hand through his hair. "He basically admitted the Legion Heads placed us as a triad because Fenar and I are Wards of the Heads. There are no parental figures to protest a human being our boost. He said he has been planning for this likelihood for years. I cannot see him changing his mind."

Flames jumped in Tallis's hands, and I put out a placating hand, noting how his eyes flashed with the readiness to fight. I knew he still felt cheated about how our triad came to be, despite how successful we were now.

"Look, I'll come with you and we'll talk to your dad together. How about that? As far as the boost thing goes, it's better to have one than not, right? We won't get another chance, not with punks like Ambrose and his triad rubbing it in how good it is with their boost. Other triads would snap up a human in a second if it helped them become more powerful."

The flames winked out in Tallis's hands and the deep lines in his face softened a little. He looked towards the bedrooms and rolled his shoulders. Wellyn was shuffling uncomfortably, his eyes tracking Tallis's movements. I wanted to comfort the little guy, but Tallis needed us right now. Wellyn cleared his throat, and I gave him a look. This wasn't the time, but he opened his stupid mouth and spoke anyway.

"Have you declared these intentions to Cove? She might not feel the same way and I don't want to lose my only possible chance at a boost because you have unreciprocated feelings."

I could throttle him. I could hear the gulp he made from across the room. Tallis shot up from his seat, his back ramrod straight as he advanced towards Wellyn. He looked like he was about to burn him to a crisp, so I pushed in between them.

"She says she loves me," Tallis whispered through gritted teeth and, even though I knew it wasn't right, I interjected.

"She says 'I love you' to everyone, man."

I could feel Tallis's hands heating as he bunched a handful of my shirt in his fist, yanking me close enough that I could hear him snarl.

"It's different. We've known each other since we were children. I know we're made for each other."

"Is that what you tell yourself while you *shek* everything under the sun?" Wellyn asked, sounding steely. He wasn't giving the human up without a fight. It was strange to see Wellyn force this point, when he was normally the peacekeeper. Still strong as Tallis was seconds away from beating him to a pulp.

A small cough came from the hallway and I swung my head around to see the human watching us with wide eyes. She looked rumpled, creases on her cheeks and her eyes half hooded with sleep. Her skin was flushed, and it made imagine her thick, dark hair spread out beneath me, those cheeks pink for an entirely different reason. She fingered the hem of her nightshirt where it had fallen to her mid-thigh.

Wait. That was Wellyn's shirt, and didn't he look pleased about it. A stupid grin had slid across his face, his cheeks about as pink as hers now. Possessive *shekker*.

"Sorry to interrupt, but my stomach is about to eat itself," she said, looking like she wanted to run back to Wellyn's room.

"Morning. Did you sleep well?" he said, rushing over to bounce on his toes in front of her. I could tell by the way he vibrated his creature was close to the surface. That was interesting. Tallis noticed too, if the way he looked physically ill was any sign. She shot us a wary look before giving Wellyn a small smile and a shrug.

"That bed was so comfy, I don't know how you get out of it in the morning!" She stifled a little yawn, her fist coming up to cover her mouth. It was a shame her teeth looked so square; she'd look stunning with a pair of fangs. I shook my head and nudged Tallis from his death glare.

"Do you want to go track down your dad now?" I asked him, raising my eyebrows. He clenched his jaw and nodded, and I swept my hand in front of me, letting him lead the way. Tallis barked as he walked past them.

"Don't get comfortable, human, you won't be staying here another night. Don't touch too much, I don't want your germs spread around. Wellyn, keep her out of sight. I don't want people knowing they've saddled us with a human boost, even for a small amount of time."

Wellyn's face fell as if he'd been gut punched, but he hid it in seconds.

"It's Cami, not human. Good morning to you, although it looks like you've had better ones," she snapped back.

I raked my hand through my hair, choking on the laugh that wanted to bubble out of me. Tallis scowled and sniffed, turning on his heel and stalking towards the door.

"Morning, Cami," I said as I passed her to follow Tallis. I got a whiff of that sharp tang and my wolf raised its head in interest again. I didn't want to think about what that meant as I hurried after Tallis.

Tallis was silent the entire way to his dad's office, his shoulders rising further and further upwards until I thought they would swallow his ears. I tried to joke with him, telling him about how Ambrose had almost tripped at Vittori's last night and fallen into a pile of Gaer that had sneaked out in the lower light of night. He didn't respond, clearly locked in his mind. His hands clenched into fists at his side, his knuckles cracking as he unfurled and clenched over again.

He slammed his fist on the door of his dad's office and stalked in without waiting for a reply. Albion glanced up from his desk and looked to the ceiling, muttering under his breath as Tallis came to a stop in front of him. Sending a prayer to the powers that be most likely, he knew as well as I did what that look on Tallis's face meant. Barely contained fury required careful channeling, especially if he wanted to protect the ancient-looking tomes behind him.

"My son, Fenar, how can I help you this morning? Very early morning, I might add."

"I want to discuss your dumping a human boost on us," Tallis shot back, throwing himself into an armchair. Sliding into one as well, I gave Albion a tight-lipped nod. I was here to make sure Tallis didn't explode, but I was interested to hear what he had to say.

"Do you know what your mother loved doing more than anything?" Albion asked, leaning forward to Tallis with an intense look on his face. Tallis stilled, but I knew underneath that blank mask, he was an inferno. He couldn't bear the thought of his mother. Albion knew this, yet he continued with a softer voice. "She loved the natural springs at the Lost Lake. She must have spent every weekend there when she was pregnant with you, floating for hours. Her hair became stiff with minerals because she went so often. Even when you were born, she loved to take you there. You were a hellion as a young child. A squalling, pink-faced terror and the only thing that stopped you from bursting our eardrums were those springs. You'd happily float in your mother's embrace for hours, just like you had when she was pregnant."

Tallis's eyes were glassy, but he snapped, "Sweet story, but what does that have to do with anything?"

"When you were five, the Gaer took the Lost Lake and the springs. It had been such a balm to your mother, it lessened her pain in the water. But after the Gaer infected it, she worsened, and there was no longer an outlet from the pain. The Heads said it would recede, but they were wrong of course. There was no way to fight the Gaer, so they let it take the last place your mother found solace."

I gulped, a knot forming in my throat. She had been a strong boost, apparently, though I hadn't met her. She died when he was only six. The remaining two members of his fathers triad had scattered around Melbak, too grief stricken to stay together. But I knew intimately the hole she'd left in his life, a shadow and ache that didn't abate. He felt the absence of her all these years later. Albion looked out the window. A distant view of the dark, rippling Gaer on the Lost Lake was visible.

"I've looked at that lake for more than a decade, watched as the Gaer took more of it, took the woods and crept closer still, even up to my office. We build pillars that can repel it. We go higher and more cloistered in our safe areas and turn a blind eye as Melbak bleeds black. The Heads don't care, they don't see the connection with the dwindling boosts and the rise of Gaer. I've read every text I can get my hands on, and the oldest ones talk about the connection boosts had to the wellbeing of Melbak. But without them the Gaer has grown wild and willful. Do you think it will stop at the Lake? Do you think it will be courteous to us? Let us have a slice of land to live happily upon?"

"What does this have to do with anything, Dad?" Tallis asked, his voice soft and sulky. He was being deliberately obtuse. Albion's tail swished through the air, filling the silence with a whistle of reproach.

"It has everything to do with it, my son. I will not sit here and let the Gaer take over, hoping more boosts present so that Melbak can return to its former glory. I can't even visit the tree that was planted for your mother, as that whole grove is contaminated. The Heads are happy to do nothing, they are not the ones affected.

They control the funds and can build higher and higher. What about those who cannot?

"I have been traveling to different planes for years, desperately searching for a match to the profile of boost blood. In all the planes I visited, even of all the humans I tested, Cami is the only one who was a close match. She matches over ninety-nine percent of the profile. The next closest I ever got were the Draken, and they were only twelve percent. You know the stories of the Plague, the role humans supposedly had in it all. The Heads won't allow the trial to go forward without proof that humans can be reliable boosts. They want to know if the risk is worth the reward. I understand you feel blindsided, but this is bigger than you or me. It's about the future of Melbak."

"Why me? I don't want–" Tallis said.

"Stop being a spoiled little brat!" Albion exploded. "This human could be the key! She could solve it all for us and you are still thinking about yourself."

"I'm in love!" Tallis shouted, his hands flashing red. Albion threw his head back and laughed. It was a guttural explosion, his eyes filling with tears.

"What you feel for Cove isn't love. It's a sad little boy pinning his hopes on a pretty face. Love is sacrifice, pain, tearing yourself apart for the better of someone else. I am doing this for you because I love you and I loved your mother too much to have her memory swallowed up as this world implodes. You will accept Cami as your boost and when the Heads see how successful it is, I can find more like her. You will do this Tallis," his face turned dark "don't make me force a binding agreement on you."

I sucked in a breath as Tallis swore. "You can't do that!"

"You don't know what I'm capable of, what I'll do to ensure this succeeds. I'm being kind enough to give you time to nurse your wounds, but make no mistake, my son, you will do your duty, one way or another."

Albion's chest rose and fell rapidly, and his eyes were bright with barely restrained wrath. His tail swiped behind him like it wanted to wrap around Tallis's neck. Tallis's tail was curled around the chair leg, like an anchor, but I knew better than the equate his stillness with acceptance.

"Make peace with it, Tallis. Your boost will be a human. I won't speak to you about it again. Do you understand?"

Tallis nodded curtly, his face dark and tense. Albion glanced at me. "Are you going to defy me too, Fenar?" he asked, his voice like butter, but I heard the threat laced between the words. I shook my head, not trusting my voice wouldn't betray me.

"I made a binding agreement with Cami that she will come to no physical harm here." He flicked his eyes between the both of us and his eyebrows raised. "I trust I don't have to worry about that happening?"

"No, sir," we both replied, Tallis's voice grittier than mine. He was barely holding onto his temper right now.

"Dismissed, then. I expect to hear about a successful boost soon."

Albion's tail slashed through the air, cracking like a whip, and I jumped out of the chair, hurrying towards the door. Tallis followed, his steps heavier than mine. He frowned the entire way out of his dad's building, pausing only as we hit the path towards home. A small grin cut its way across his face, like the slow slice of a blade. I shivered at the malice that leaked through it as he looked at me, his eyes darker than I'd ever seen them.

"He said no physical harm, right?" he said, his voice eerily low.

"Yeh? What are you thinking right now?"

"He said nothing about mental or emotional pain. I may not physically hurt the human, but I can still terrorize her." He smiled again. I shivered.

"Wait, Tallis, what the *shek* does that mean?" He turned and walked away from me.

"It means I have plans to make and supplies to get ," he threw back casually, disappearing around the corner as my stomach churned with foreboding. What was he going to do now, and did I want to stop him?

Cami

My LIFE WAS COMPLETELY upended, but at least the food in Melbak was a treat. After the two nasty points of the triad had scampered off—slammed the door, no less—Wellyn gave me a tour.

They did not design the kitchen for cooking. It seemed that was an archaic practice that didn't exist anymore. Instead, all their food came from a slot built into the wall, a voice-activated machine that, once given instructions, would close and reopen with the food laying in it. I'd asked for pancakes from Dilly's, a café around the corner from my house. I didn't think it would work, but it seems the technology knew no bounds, producing a stack of perfectly fluffy pancakes with caramelized bananas and mascarpone on the side.

"This is amazing," I said, my words muffled by the pancakes stuffing my cheeks full like a chipmunk. Wellyn looked at the meal with a cocked head and leaned forward to smell it.

"It is sweet?" he asked, puzzled.

"Try some if you like."

He was quick to pick up a fork and shovel some into his mouth. I enjoyed how his eyes widened, his face effused with wonder. Before I could offer him more, he'd already taken two more mouthfuls. I glared a little at that. I will share food, within reason. Not chocolate though, nobody can touch my chocolate. He looked sheepish as he quickly swallowed.

"That is incredible! It is like a dessert but hardy enough for a morning meal." He ordered himself one, sliding half of his onto my plate. I protested, but he shook his head. "Payment for taking more than offered earlier. And for introducing me to my new favorite dish."

"What do you normally eat for your morning meal?" I used his word for breakfast.

"Not sweet food. Usually a mixture of grains and milk or eggs." I wondered what animal the milk and eggs came from but decided not to think too much on it. I didn't need to know they drank rat milk or something equally horrifying.

I wanted a coffee, but it seemed Wellyn wanted to show me more of the apartment. He walked back to the hallway and into his room. Off the side there was a small door I hadn't noticed before. He opened it and motioned for me to enter. It was a space that only allowed for two people at the most, the walls a smooth and stark white.

"This is the cleaning room. If you'd like to undress in a moment, it will cleanse you." He pointed to a button on the side. "Just press this when you're ready and it will activate."

I stared around in dismay. I had been craving a shower since I got up, the musk of my nervousness thick on my skin. There was something relaxing about standing under the pelting water, letting it wash away dark thoughts. I'd taken to having long showers since Dad's accident. It was a way for me to let go for a moment. I could break down under the stream of water and no one could see my tears. I could pretend it was just water.

Wellyn mistook my look and hurried to add, "It's not as big as some cleaning rooms, but it's very efficient. You'll feel refreshed, I promise."

"It's not that, it's just... there's no water? I'm kind of used to bathing with water," I explained, and his face took on a strange look. "I guess I should get used to doing things differently," I said more to myself as he seemed to come back to himself.

"You like water?" he asked. I raised my eyebrow at him. Weird question.

"Uh, yeah, but it's fine. I'll just give this a go." He huffed an embarrassed laugh when he realized I was waiting for him to go. He hurried out of the room, sliding the door closed. The door was made of a crystal material similar to frosted glass. I could see his dark outline and relaxed, knowing he couldn't fully see me.

I shrugged out of the shirt I'd stolen from Wellyn and slid my underwear down my thighs, folding and setting them on a shelf. New clothes would have to be a priority. I pressed the button and waited as it listed options: full clean, hands only or custom clean. I figured I'd try full clean and see how that went. A whirr hummed in my ears and as beam of icy blue light passed slowly over my body. The cold prickling sensation against my pussy made me gasp. I hadn't considered that. It was a weird sensation, but Wellyn was right, it sure was efficient. My hair felt glossy and stripped of all pollutants, doused in a light floral fragrance.

"Is everything alright, Cami?" Wellyn called through the door, and I cleared my throat, uncomfortable that he was still there.

"All fine, just wasn't expecting it to feel that way."

"I've left a pile of my clothes on the bed. You're more than welcome to wear them. I'll see about getting you something to wear while I'm out organizing furniture later."

I waited until I heard his bedroom door close and quickly got dressed. He'd left out another soft t-shirt and a pair of light, linen-type pants. They were comfortable but I wanted my own clothes.

Confused after yesterday's dramatic arrival, I'd left my bag at Albion's office. There was a packet of photos tucked in the bottom. I didn't need my clothes, but I refused to give up the pictures.

I caught sight of myself in the mirror in Wellyn's room and had to do a double take. Damn. I looked good. My skin was clear, no bags under my eyes, and even the blemish I had on my chin was gone. I looked like someone had photoshopped me. *Another plus for Melbak*, I thought as I padded out to the lounge area. Wellyn turned and gave me a wide grin. He'd dressed while I'd cleaned and appeared ready to go.

"I'll be back in a few hours," he promised. "Explore all you like, but I'd stay out of Tallis's and Fenar's rooms, if possible."

"I hate to be a pain, but I brought a bag with me that I left at Albion's office yesterday. Is there any way you could get it for me?"

He nodded so hard his curls shook on his head. Damn, it was adorable.

"Of course!" he promised and left with a lingering look at me. I made myself a coffee, or rather, ordered one, and sat on the window seat, tucking one cushion under my legs and holding onto another for a while. I could see the Gaer moving from here and it disturbed me how it drew my eyes. No matter where they shifted to, they always came back to the pulsing darkness. I wondered what would happen if I were to touch it. Nobody had explained, but I assumed it was dangerous.

A flock of those flying rats flew past the windows, little pink tails streaming out behind them, and that was enough to make me abandon my post. I walked down the hallway instead, opening the door to a different bedroom. I stood in the doorway and peered around, not wanting to enter and set off an alarm I couldn't see. Junk filled the space just like the spare room. Piles of clothes like mountains on the floor, the bed barely visible under masses of cushions and velvety blankets. There was a musky scent of wet fur, so I closed the door quickly, fearing that whoever's room this was had one of those flying rats as a pet. I shuddered at the thought.

I opened the last door and looked about, indulging my snoopy self. This bedroom was more put together but it felt cold and clinical. There was a desk by a window with sparse collection of objects, a metal bangle, ornate box and a hunk of what looked like seaglass. There was an abundance of gray and white, like it had leached color from the room. Hospital chic. There was the slight smell of ash, but I couldn't see a tray for smoking. I wondered idly if they did that here.

I returned to the spare room and started hauling out boxes and junk into the living area. If I was going to have a room set up here, then I would need it cleared. I was halfway done when I heard someone entering the apartment.

"Hello? Tallis, are you in?" It was a feminine voice. I walked out, wiping the sweat off my brow with my sleeve.

"Can I help you?" I asked, startling the gorgeous girl in front of me. She was tiny with a straight silver bob brushed neatly behind her pointy ears. Her delicate features made her seem elflike, a bit like Wellyn. She had a sweet button nose and sea-foam eyes. Her forehead had two nubs protruding from it—mini horns. Even those looked cute. Her eyes widened comically large as she spun around and saw me.

"Oh! Oh, who are you?" she asked, her hand coming to flutter at her chest. She wore a silver sheath, her feet encased in matching slippers.

"I'm Cami. Who are you?" I said, not wanting to say too much after what Tallis had warned me this morning. She came closer, frowning as she took in the clothes I was wearing, obviously not mine by their ill fit.

"I'm Cove," she said. "You're a human? Why are you in the boy's apartment?"

Cami

Now it was my turn for my eyes to widen. Oh shit. This was the one Tallis had mentioned, the girl he'd wanted as his boost. I couldn't blame him, she was stunning. But she didn't have the right blood, Albion had said. I took a deep breath; I hoped she wouldn't lose it like Tallis had.

"Yes, I am a human. Tallis's dad brought me here yesterday."

"A human," she breathed, looking apprehensive. "Tallis didn't tell me that. Is that why he stayed in my room last night?" Her face creased with even more confusion.

Inexplicably, I felt a pang of hurt at that comment. He had spent the night with this girl. I smothered it immediately. He wasn't mine, no matter that his dad wanted him to suck my blood down like his favorite cocktail. I shrugged and shifted on my toes uncomfortably. I didn't want to say anything about being his proposed boost, not if he hadn't even told his girl I'd moved in.

"You're cleaning out the boost room?" she asked, peering past me to see the pile of junk I'd been laying on the side of the wall. I ran a hand down the side of my neck and grimaced. Wellyn could have helped me navigate this awkwardness.

"I'm making space for furniture," I said slowly, choosing the vaguest way of explaining in hopes she might give up questioning me. I was sure Legion could be territorial and I didn't want to get in between a girl and her man, but Cove walked past me, stepping into the room and doing a little spin.

"Do you know what a boost is?"

Oh, I know, I wanted to say, but I think my cheeks did that for me. They got hotter the longer she stared at me. Her eyes churned like a wave hitting the shore and I didn't know what to say to placate her.

"His dad brought you here yesterday? A human? How is that possible? Humans were banned from Melbak hundreds of years ago." She stepped closer to me, her diminutive stance not especially threatening, but I also didn't know if she had flaming hands like Tallis or some other ridiculous power.

Her expression was strangely open, like a book flicking through pages. Doubt, hurt, anger, jealousy. They all flittered across her face while I stood staring at her, scared to move in case I jarred her into more aggressive actions. I preferred my body parts together. But then I remembered the binding agreement Albion made: no physical harm can come to me here. I let myself sigh a little in relief, discretely, so I didn't rub it in the face of this girl who appeared to be having a breakdown. She stared at me with shimmering eyes and

I wished I could wrap my arms around her. She looked so wounded and lost right now.

"You're their boost? Tallis has a boost, a human boost," she whispered, but she didn't need me to agree. She already knew. I wasn't about to confirm it because I wasn't entirely sure myself and I didn't want to incur the wrath of her boyfriend.

I heard the front door open and I backed away, hoping Wellyn could talk Cove off her ledge. I looked with bright eyes to see Tallis walk through the door. He had a few bags around his wrist and he gave me a twisted smile when he spotted me waiting on the edge of the lounge room.

"Ah, boost, I've just been out collecting supplies. My hands are tied about you being here, but don't think I won't make you pay for it," he said cheerily, swinging the bags up and onto the couch. His gaze narrowed in on the window seat and the mussed cushions, his lip curling in displeasure.

"Tallis?" Cove called his name, watery and soft, and I watched as he instantly transformed. Stiffening as he cocked his head toward my bedroom, his eyes filled with warmth and panic, a dizzying mix.

"What did you do?" he hissed as he raced past me into the boost room—not mine, if he had any say. I parked my butt on the couch and listened as he obviously consoled her. His voice was soothing, pleading, low and melodic like a poem. Hers rose sharp just once, a scratch down a board until silence. It dragged on for such a long time that I felt inordinately uncomfortable. It was not a moment I wanted to be in any way privy to and I wish I had slid past and hid in Wellyn's room, especially when

Cove came out, dashing her hands across her cheeks. Tallis followed her, his face promising terrible things when he looked my way.

I stiffened as Cove came towards me, hesitating before she reaching out and dragging two fingers down the side of my face. A startled laugh warbled out of her when I flinched. It was tentative and weak, but it sounded like a wind chime, regardless.

"Can I just apologize and introduce myself? I'm Cove, a good friend of the boys. It startled me to find out they had a boost. I imagine you know little. From what Tallis has said, you were unaware of what you were getting yourself into. It's a great honor to be a boost, one I always hoped I might have. I imagined we'd all be in the same position, without the luck of a boost. It's no excuse and I hope you can forgive me for my outburst."

She drew her hand back gingerly, wiping it surreptitiously on her sheath and tucking it behind her as she turned those earnest eyes on me.

"Don't apologize to human scum."

"You don't need to apologize." Tallis and I spoke at the same time, and I glared at him. Human scum aside, we both knew she didn't need to apologize. Even though she'd just wiped off her hand to divest it of my supposed germs. Cove looked over her shoulder darkly at Tallis and he cleared his throat, breaking her gaze.

"I'm Cami," I said. "Don't apologize, I have no designs on Tallis and I'm sure he will not use me as a boost, anyway."

Cove lit up, her head cocked in confusion. "What do you mean Tallis won't?" she asked, turning to look back at him. "You must, Tallis. The benefits to you will be unimaginable. How could you turn that away?"

Tallis looked uncomfortable, avoiding her eyes and pressing his lips together in protest.

"Well, I'm a human and I think he, uh, thought it might upset you. Fenar said relationships can occur outside of triads, though, and I certainly won't be upset if you continue dating."

Cove let out a peel of laughter and Tallis froze, confusion written all over his face. She choked back her laughter as he stayed quiet. Dangerously, deathly quiet. He was barely holding himself together. I looked down and saw his fists were slightly red, clenched tight to his side.

"Tallis and I have never dated. I love him as a brother," Cove clarified, shooting Tallis a bemused look, apparently oblivious to how he was shaking with rage. It wasn't clear from his viper-still body, but one glance at his eyes showed his instability. The fire was there, dark flames begging to flay me alive. I took a step backward, swearing I could feel a wave of invisible heat hit me from his gaze alone. *He can't hurt me, he can't harm me*, I kept repeating to myself as Cove turned.

"Tallis?" she questioned, wandering towards him. He looked at her, reluctantly removing his scorching gaze. "The rumors about humans are from hundreds of years ago. We have the technology to ensure they can't spread disease like during the Culling. This opportunity is a blessing. Why wouldn't you take advantage of it? She's human, but she has the scent of a boost, a strong one."

He snarled, apparently losing the ability to form words. Cove ran her hand down his bicep, looking concerned as he visibly shook.

The door opened, and I almost fell apart when I saw it was Wellyn. I skirted around Tallis and Cove and darted towards him. He gave me a wide, open smile when he saw me, and I wanted to keep rushing and slam into his body. I wanted to feel arms around me right now, to coax away the sheen of fear and anxiety that was burned into me. Tallis couldn't hurt me, but damn if he didn't frighten me. What would happen if he put those fiery hands on me, I wonder?

"Hello Cove. You have met our boost, Cami?" he said, and something about him calling me his boost soothed my bruised insides. It felt like a claiming. I stood as close as possible to him without throwing myself into his arms. I could feel the familiar coolness seeping off his body, calming the sweat that had beaded all over mine.

Cove glided over, her silver sheath whispering in the awkward tension of the room. She gathered Wellyn up in a tight hug, squeezing her arms around his middle and pressing her face into his chest. I stiffened at the tender hold she had on him. Weird.

"I'm so happy for you, Wellyn. You must be so pleased for your creature," she said brightly, stepping back and putting her hands on her hips. Wellyn shot me a nervous look before clearing his throat.

"It's a miracle," he replied quickly. "But what brings you to visit us?"

Cove smiled, "I came to invite you to a soiree Ambrose is throwing tomorrow night. You must come, Cami, Ambrose is a masterful host."

Tallis growled from across the room, looking more thunderous by the second.

"Does Ambrose know you invited us?" Wellyn asked and Cove shook her head.

"He said for me to invite whoever I like. He must know I would insist on having my best friends attend."

"Likely he wanted you to bring Sesab. He's still determined to recruit her for Head Aydro after she spurned him last week."

Cove scoffed, warmth flooding her face. "He'll be waiting a long time. Sesab isn't interested in working with Ambrose during the Vinko. She is determined to be chosen for Head Avanti's team. Say you will come?" She clapped her hands together, looking at Tallis like a child begging for a treat. I watched as he faltered under her pleading gaze, this hard, angry man who had done nothing but glare and snap at me like a wild dog. For her, he softened, but still only shook his head.

"We have things to discuss," he paused for a moment, "as a triad."

Cove bit her lip, her throat working as she swallowed deeply. Her relationship with him confused me, but I would not get in the middle of that.

"I understand. It's a wonderful time for your triad. If you change your mind, message me on my reader." She gave Tallis a chaste kiss on the cheek and followed it up with one for Wellyn before nodding my way.

"I hope we can be friends in the future, Cami. If you have questions, you can always talk to me."

I nodded, my head spinning at her generosity. After the way the triad had spoken about me being human, I expected to be met with derision, but she had been nice enough.

The door clicked behind her and chaos broke loose. Wellyn pulled me into him, ducking behind the kitchen island. I felt a blast of heat and a roar that made my eardrums scream.

Tallis had lost it.

I could see the lick of flames reach the ceiling. Wellyn tucked my head under his chin, his lips coming to rest on the shell of my ear.

"You're safe. Let him burn himself out."

"He's lost control?" I replied, my voice shaky. "Albion made an agreement thing to protect me."

Wellyn's arms tightened around me. "That was clever of him. Tallis wouldn't truly harm you. He just has a temper. He has flame powers, but his mood can influence them and right now he is furious."

I didn't believe I was safe for a second, but I didn't refute Wellyn. I couldn't describe the level of hatred I'd seen in Tallis's eyes. It was an unfathomable depth, one that I didn't deserve.

"I'm fine," Tallis gasped, and Wellyn's tight arms loosened around me. He rose and ordered a glass of water, taking it to Tallis with practiced movements like he'd done this a thousand times before. The air was thick with the acrid smell of ash, but there were no scorch marks anywhere to be seen. Tallis was on all fours but moved to push himself back on his heels, sweat pouring down his face as he accepted the glass from Wellyn with shaking hands.

"Flame proof," Wellyn murmured as he came to stand beside me again. His fingers grazed my elbow and he looked at me searchingly. Maybe he expected me to run from the room screaming. "I promise it won't all seem so crazy soon."

I didn't reply, my head a pingppong of the past and present. My thoughts briefly skirted towards my family, but I didn't dare let them linger. I couldn't think of them yet. Even the merest thought brought sharp, hot pricks behind my eyes.

My photos! I needed to make sure they were safe.

"Did you bring my bag by any chance?" I whispered to Wellyn, and he gave me another of those unguarded smiles, positively cherubic. He pointed to the door where my battered bag lay. It looked so innocuous, but I tore my eyes away from it in case Tallis got any ideas about rifling through before I could hide my photos.

"Thank you," I said softly as Tallis groaned and got to his feet.

"Get away from me, human. If I see your face for one more second, I am going to go up in flames again," Tallis growled at me, his voice scratchy like gravel. He looked pointedly past me, over my shoulder, his chin tipped up as he sucked down deep breaths. I didn't wait to give him a chance to prove it. Getting out of that room sounded perfect. I snatched up my bag and went into Wellyn's room, closing the door behind me. I held my bag to my chest like it was a lifeline and leaned against the hard surface. What in the world had I got myself into.

Tallis

THE HUMAN FLED, THE whites of her eyes stark in their sockets. My body trembled, an aftereffect of losing control of my flames. Wellyn reached a hand forward, his face tight with disapproval, but he kept his mouth shut, thankfully. I took his offer and pulled myself up with a groan, stumbling to the window seat and falling into it. I let out a grunt, my muscles tense under my skin. My jaw ticked when I saw the cushions were out of order, and I hurriedly arranged them the way they were supposed to be. I ignored the thought of the human rubbing her grubby hands over them, polluting them with whatever diseases humans were sure to carry.

"Want to talk about it?" Wellyn asked, perching on the couch with his body turned towards me. I squeezed my eyes shut and threw my arm up to cover them, hissing at the movement, hating how weak I felt. I hadn't lost control like that in years.

"No," I grumbled, knowing I sounded like a child but too weak to care in that moment. He hummed and I could hear the words forming on his tongue. He wanted to probe, but I didn't know if I had the stomach for it. The flames had burst out, but they had scorched me on the inside first. Cove's comments lit the match.

I love him as a brother, she'd said.

The words Fenar had thrown back in my face this morning came back to me. *She says she loves everyone.* It was true. Cove was a spark, always bright and shining. I was the shadow, she was the light. It was what kept me gravitating back to her, waiting and wanting. She balanced my darkness. A sad little boy pinning his hopes on a pretty face.

I let the voices clamor in my mind for a moment before I felt the fires rising again. I grappled with them, clawing at their edges before stuffing them back deep inside me. My heart was aching, overflowing with bruising hurt. I shifted my arm and cracked an eye to see Wellyn watching me patiently. He'd thrown his leg over his knee and offered an encouraging smile.

A wave of rage crashed over me at the sight. That he was so fine, so unaffected by all of this. He looked settled, happy and content. I had seen how he had vibrated this morning, barely controlling his creature. If that was the case, then getting rid of the human would be harder than I thought. I hoped to force her out, to break her so she would run. I had been making plans all morning, thinking of ways I could mess with her head and scare her. Perhaps if she saw Wellyn's creature she would be so frightened she would go to my dad for a different triad.

But as I looked at Wellyn, I knew I couldn't do it; he had been waiting for years for the right person. His creature wouldn't handle rejection well, and Wellyn...he was too tender. I couldn't do it to him, not as a friend and brother. I wouldn't involve the others, but I would do everything in my power to break the human.

Cove might have felt for me as a brother, but she could have changed her mind in the future. Now there was no chance of that. When I held her in my arms earlier, it had felt strange. My arms engulfed her and my heart raced at the closeness, but not in the way I expected. It had made me feel sick, especially when she spoke. Cove wasn't upset about not being *our* boost. No, she was upset about not being any triad's boost. She wanted that honor with a different triad. She didn't even imagine herself as being part of this family. She was upset knowing that her closest friends were experiencing something she would never get the chance to have, jealous for our "good fortune." When I'd tried to talk to her, to tell her how I felt, she'd cut me off, not even caring that our boost was a human. She was more curious than anything.

I sat up slowly, a sharp pain pulsing at the base of my skull. "You don't think I'd be successful in getting rid of her?" I said, waving to the pile of boxes.

Wellyn didn't blink. He just shrugged. "Hopeful thinking and planning, more like. I know you're tied up about Cove, but I won't lie and say that a boost isn't what I've always dreamed of. We are one of the last triads I would think to be given the honor."

His violet eyes glowed and I flinched at his direct stare. Knowing his creature was lurking close to the surface for the first time in years was sobering.

"You do what makes you happy, Tallis, but don't ruin this for me. I don't care if she's a human. I want her blood. My creature needs it, demands it. It's been more active in this last day than in years. I think with her blood I might coax it out."

He looked so refreshed, his skin was glowing and his curls were a vibrant red. It was the best I'd seen look him in a long time. His creature had withdrawn some years ago, refusing to come out or even communicate with Wellyn. I didn't have a creature, not like Fenar and Wellyn, but I knew how vital a healthy relationship between a Legion and their creature was. I steeled my resolve. There would be other boosts; Cove might still present. What was one more year in the scheme of things?

"She will follow my rules as head of this triad. You might want her as a boost, but Fenar and I do not."

"I never said that," Fenar said as he sauntered into the room, his bright yellow eyebrows arched. The unnatural color would likely be different in the next month. He was always changing it to some eye-catching shade.

"You want a human for a boost?" I said, scrunching up my nose.

Fenar shrugged, molding himself into the couch, his long legs dangling over the side. His arms came up and rested behind his head.

"The human part is distasteful, if the rumors are to be believed. But the boost? I can swallow that, surely. No pun intended." He smirked and I felt an urge to smack him. He sniffed the air, eyes narrowing as he looked at me.

"You have a blowout?" he probed, and I crossed my arms, not ready to answer, but Wellyn jumped in before I could even think what to say.

"Cove popped in while we were out and met Cami," he said, and I shot him a dark look. His eyes widened, like he didn't understand my ire. Fenar watched me with his face pinched.

"Ouch. How'd that go, big guy?" he teased, the undercurrent of concern still present.

"Shut it," I growled, glad that I'd burnt out most of my fire for the meantime or his prying voice may have made me explode again.

"How'd the sweet human handle that?" he asked Wellyn, looking back into the hallway where I was sure the nosy human was listening to every word.

"She was a little frightened, but she didn't cry or even scream."

The pride in his voice rankled me. I snorted. He had such a low bar for this puny human. Wellyn stiffened, but he didn't comment. *That's right, buddy, I am the leader of this triad.*

"So, you want to run the boost show?" Fenar drawled, his eyebrow cocked as he looked at me. "Will that help you get over the fact that we're stuck with her?"

He'd been there when my dad had verbally slapped me this morning. He heard how desperate my dad was about this, that he would do anything to make sure this scheme was successful. Wellyn made a little noise in the back of his throat. I expected him to stay silent, but he surprised me by piping up, his voice steady.

"Within reason, I won't agree to her being hurt. She doesn't want to be here anymore than you want her here."

"We can't hurt her. Albion made a binding agreement," Fenar said, his eyes closing lazily, Wellyn clicked his tongue, annoyed.

"I know that, but you can still cause pain, even if it's not physical."

A chill washed over me, and I quickly schooled my face into a blank slate. Of course, tender-hearted Wellyn would be quick to think of every aspect of his little boost. Fenar looked at me, waiting for me to refute the claim. I thought he'd be on my side after this morning, but I needed to be careful now.

"Think of our younger selves, forced to prove ourselves worthy to be called Legion. We had to complete trials to be considered adults. I'll accept her as a boost when she proves herself. We should make her show she's worthy of supporting this triad." Seeing no immediate objections from the two of them, I continued, "I want to test her, tease her and find out if she's breakable. If she's too easy to snap, she won't make a good boost," I explained, thinking it sounded reasonable to me.

Legion grew up fighting, tricking and testing each other. It was a society of cutthroats. Underneath every soft-hearted Legion like Wellyn and Cove was still a spine of steel. As teenagers, we all went through the grueling trials to prove we were worthy Legion. It was different for everyone, but no less harrowing, requiring intelligence, strength and grit to pass. Successful Legion were sorted into triads and given opportunities to be recruited by one of the nine founding families.

"She'll have to get used to being tested if she's a boost," Fenar said slowly, nodding at the logic in my argument.

I crowed on the inside but kept my face carefully blank because Wellyn looked uneasy still.

"We grew up that way. She needs to hold her own," I pressed, barely containing myself.

"Within reason, Tallis," he warned, and I nodded like I had considered his plea and was agreeing. The human wouldn't know what hit her. She'd go crying to my dad within the week to find another triad.

Cami

I CRAWLED INTO WELLYN's bed after taking out my photos and stashing them underneath the clothes in one of his drawers.I couldn't look at them yet, the memories of my family were still too raw.

I had been foolish once. I'd thought I was invincible, and it had cost others a hefty price and changed our lives forever. Huddled under the covers, I'd tried to block out the sound of sobbing and the overpowering stench of alcohol.

I was still suspended in that nightmare when a hand shook my shoulder gently. I launched out of bed, my heart pelting against my chest. "Dad!" I cried out, my eyes bleary from sleep. Red curls filled my vision as alluring violet eyes widened with worry.

"It's only Wellyn. You fell asleep." He massaged my shoulder as I peered around the room. My thundering heart calmed at his cool touch.

"Oh, I must have been dreaming," I said evasively. He hummed a little under his breath. I could tell he wanted to ask more, but looked towards the bedroom door, slightly ajar.

"We wanted to have a meeting, to discuss some things," he said finally. As I moved, the covers fell to my waist. Wellyn gulped, his head whipping to the door, and I looked down in confusion. I was only wearing my bra. I'd gotten too hot at one point and flung off the shirt he'd given me. He darted towards the door after I yanked the sheets up with a yelp.

"I'll give you a second," he said hastily before exiting like his ass was on fire. I felt disorientated from the sleep, not rested, somehow still stuck in the limbo between nightmare and reality. Even though it felt like this new reality was a nightmare. I dressed quickly and sidled out to the lounge area.

Tallis sat on the window seat, his jaw working as he watched me like a specimen under a microscope. My skin prickled under his perusal. Wellyn patted the seat beside him and Fenar chuckled softly under his breath from where he lounged on the opposite couch. I shot him a sharp look, his eyes flaring with more amusement.

"Sit down, human, we have to set some rules in place," Tallis began, his voice arching as he stared down his proud nose at me. Wellyn scooted closer to me, his thigh pressing slightly against mine.

"I have clarified that this is going ahead, despite my wishes to the contrary." I wondered how effective the binding agreement would be when flames engulfed me. "But you will remain here upon conditions. You are a human, not used to the ways of Legion, and I won't accept you as a boost until you prove you are worthy."

I sank into the soft material of the couch and raised my eyebrows at him. "I thought my blood made me worthy." I saw the snarl that he quickly extinguished. Wellyn cleared his throat at my side and I looked at him. His face was open and bright. It was so refreshing to look at him instead of Tallis's constant rage.

"Legion and humans are similar in some ways. We have most of the same characteristics, but Legion have powers. Some of us even have different creatures we can change into. You saw a bit of Tallis's power close up before. They teach us to be resilient and worthy of a boost. We must complete trials as young adults, three in total, to test our physical, emotional and mental strength." He stuttered a little before continuing, "You have a boost's blood, according to Albion, but you haven't passed tests according to a Legion's standards."

"I'm not worthy of you," I scoffed. "Is that what you're trying to say?"

Wellyn ducked his head, obviously not wanting to say it out loud.

"You're soft as butter, baby, that's fact," Fenar drawled, kicking his legs out and interlacing his fingers over his stomach. He shrugged when I looked at him. "If you were Legion, you'd be able to support us and we'd be happy to have you. This is all new to you. We don't expect you to understand what a momentous decision this is."

A flash of irritation tightened in my throat, unsure of what response they wanted from me.

"I think you overestimate how invested I am in how this whole," I waved my hands in the air, "farce plays out. Feed like the second-rate vampires you are or don't feed, I don't care. It's no skin off my nose, *baby*." I sneered at Fenar, who snapped his head back, a bark of laughter escaping him.

"You'll do as you're told." Tallis's icy voice interrupted our stare down, and I turned to him, rolling my eyes.

"Yes, master," I said in a simpering voice. "Or do you prefer sir? Bossman?"

Wellyn stifled a grin under his hand as Tallis leaned forward, his fingers digging into his knees as he looked at me.

"If you don't please me, if you fail any of the rules I set, then I will dock whatever Albion is paying."

"Because I'd really choose to be transported to another world so I can be treated terribly by a spoiled little brat, for money," I derided and enjoyed the reaction that Tallis gave me. He launched out of his seat, stalking towards me with his finger outstretched.

"How dare you," he hissed, his legs hitting my knees as he loomed over me. Terrible rage twisted his face, like he wanted to tear me into a million pieces. "I could destroy you, ruin your pointless, insignificant life in seconds,"

I couldn't help the low laugh that bubbled up and out. It came from the part of me that welcomed death, that had thought about meeting it ever since that night. I had contemplated death on more occasions than I could count. The only thing stopping me was my family, who still needed me even though I didn't understand how they could stand the sight of me. Tallis took a step back, bewilderment washing away the rage as he cocked his head in confusion. It lasted only a moment before he straightened, a slow and sinister smile curling his shapely lips.

"I see," he said, almost gleefully. His hands snuck into his pockets as he rocked back on his heels. "Who does the money go to? Not a boyfriend?" he observed my face. "Your parents?" I flinched and cursed myself for being so easily led as Tallis nodded, not missing the slight movement.

"You will follow my rules, or I will ensure your family receives nothing."

It was my turn to launch forward, Wellyn grabbing my arm to stop me. I twisted like an animal, much to Tallis's merriment. His smile grew and morphed into the smuggest expression I'd ever seen.

"I don't answer to you," I said through gritted teeth.

He shrugged. "I'm a spoiled little brat, remember? Stamping my feet to get what I want. And I always get what I want. So, you'll play my games, human, or your family will pay the price. Whose bidding do you think my family will do?"

I looked at Wellyn, whose eyes widened in sympathy as his fingers squeezed my arm in a gesture of solidarity. But he didn't speak up. He remained silent as Tallis stood over me, gloating. I looked at Fenar and he shrugged. His gaze drifted towards Tallis, lips pursed like he didn't agree either, but no protestations came forth.

I slumped back in the lounge, shaking Wellyn's fingers off my arm with a noise of disgust. I saw his wounded look but I didn't care. He wasn't my friend. If it came down to me or Tallis, Tallis would win. Wellyn would be happy to let the megalomaniac do whatever he wanted with me. I couldn't jeopardize the money meant for my family. Even if Tallis was lying about his reach, I couldn't chance them being left defenseless.

"What do you want?" I said, fight bleeding out of me. His teeth flashed white as he leveled a winning smile my way.

"That wasn't so hard, was it?" he praised, and I ducked as he leaned in to pat my head.

"I'm not a pet," I growled as he pulled his hand back, tucking it behind his back.

"Yes, you're right, a pet would be infinitely more useful and wanted."

My cheeks flooded red at his insult. I wanted to punch him, just once, enough to split his lip and knock that awful, smug look off his face. I didn't care that I'd likely break my fist on his rock-hard face. It would be worth it.

"You will wear, eat and do as I command," he continued, mightily pleased with himself. "If you cannot follow those simple instructions, your family will receive nothing."

Tallis smiled like he'd won a prize. "Or you can always go back to my dad with your tail between your legs and see if some other desperate triad will deign to take you."

I frowned. "There is no other triad. Your dad made it pretty clear that the Legion Heads would only approve the trial for you three."

"Then you had better hope you can prove yourself worthy. Looks like we are the only option your family has right now."

"You're an asshole," I spat out, but he didn't seem bothered by my outburst. It seemed to please him. He leaned over me, caging me into the back of the lounge with his arms on either side of my head. I leaned as far back as the material allowed to avoid being close to him. I could feel the puff of his hot breath on my cheek.

"That's right, human, get it all out now while you can," he taunted quietly, his voice sounding rough as if coated in smoke. My eyes fluttered closed as he paused there for a moment before pushing off, his mocking laugh echoing about the otherwise silent room. Wellyn whispered something to me, but I didn't hear. I was retreating in my head, my thoughts a whirlwind.

He wanted to break me, to get me to cry off to his dad, because he was being forced to have me. Tallis was about to realize there was nothing I wouldn't do to ensure my family remained cared for.

Cami

I AWOKE IN A bed that I didn't recognize. The sheets felt odd against my skin, constrictive and rough. I knew it wasn't the fault of the sheets or the bed, and the room was fine enough. It was the fact that I was feeling betrayed. Wellyn had spent most of yesterday clearing out the mess and setting it up for me, but there was only a bed and a side table at this point. The walls were a pale eggshell blue, close to the color of my childhood bedroom. I had a cleaning room, which I'd used last night before crashing.

I'd expected to sleep deeply, having walked around yesterday in a cloud of disorientated thoughts. Tallis and Fenar had left immediately after the meeting, the former with a sneer and the latter with a frown. It looked incongruous on Fenar's face. He always had a sardonic grin at the ready, I was coming to learn, and a sarcastic quip to fire at me. Wellyn had flitted about me like a moth drawn to a flame. His pinched expressions had grated on me, the woeful looks he tossed my way when

I rebuffed his efforts at conversation. I wasn't interested in being friends with someone who wouldn't even stand up for me.

Although, what did I expect? He'd been kind, but perhaps that was his intention. I kicked myself for latching onto the sparse care with disgusting ease. They were not humans; they were Legion, and that was something I didn't understand yet.

When I had finally ducked under my covers, I'd fallen into a tormented sleep. Not from my usual set of nightmares, but from a darkness that stalked me through a forest. It snatched at my heels and begged me to free him. His words were fierce whispers that devolved into the howls and snarls of a monster. I seemed to stay trapped all night, running from the shadow until I woke, drenched in sweat and feeling even more exhausted. I was desperate for some coffee. I pulled myself from the bed, trudged the kitchen and tried to order one. A red light flashed.

Denied.

A flat voice spoke from the machine. I tried again, enunciating differently. Still, it came back denied. I mourned for a moment that Melbak didn't have coffee but figured round two of pancakes could assuage the ache for caffeine. I asked for pancakes from Dilly's, picturing the decadent, golden slices.

Denied.

I gasped and tried again, getting the same response.

"Broken piece of shit," I growled under my breath.

"It's not broken," came a voice from over my shoulder and I startled forward, catching my hip on the edge of the bench. A curse cut from me as I clamped my hand to my throbbing hip. I whipped my head around to see Tallis standing on the opposite side of the bench.

"I have programmed it to allow only certain foods for you."

"Why am I not surprised?" I glared at him, my mood sinking down lower every second that passed. I wanted a coffee. Tallis shrugged and winked. It should have been teasing, but on him it was cutting. My head was throbbing, aching behind my eyes, and I gritted my teeth a little. If I would not get coffee, I had better get used to withdrawals.

"I have chosen your meals with optimal nutrition in mind. You order them like this." The way he spoke was so condescending, but I watched as he shouldered past me and spoke to the machine.

"Morning meal for human," he demanded and a plate of gelatinous sludge appeared. He slid it toward me, a look of utter glee lighting up his face. It was indecent how handsome he was; he was smiling malevolently at me right now and yet was still one of the most gorgeous people I had ever seen. A faint odor wafted from the plate, reminiscent of boiled eggs.

"I have a name, you know," I said, determined not to show how grossed out I was. I picked up the fork he slid over to me, contemplating which area of this disgusting slop would taste better. If any.

"Yes, your name is human," he replied, mildly. He leaned his elbows on the bench and leaned over to prop his head in his hands. "Go on, try it. It's called seffe, a staple for young Legion being tested."

I hooked my fork around the sludge. It didn't deserve a name when it looked so inedible. I lifted it to my mouth, hesitating for a moment as Tallis's eyes lit with challenge. I shoveled it in. It reminded me of my Aunty Dianne's leftover casserole. There was no way of knowing what was in it and was best eaten drenched in sauce. What I would give to have some type of condiment to tip over this, but I didn't think that extended to my 'diet.' Sauce wouldn't have fixed the texture anyway, so slimy it slid over my tongue, finding every taste bud and filling my mouth with its horrid taste.

"Good?" Tallis taunted in his smoky voice.

"Tastes like ass," I said, keeping my face blank as I shoveled in another mouthful. "But I imagine you already know that." Aunty Dianne had gone through a phase of serving up her famous casserole at every family event and I'd become a pro at swallowing quickly to get the least amount of taste in my mouth. This was no different. I swallowed each mouthful like a pill, chucking it down with the point of my tongue. With each bite I took, Tallis seemed to draw inward. His eyebrows bunched, his shoulders tightened. He prowled closer, leaning forward, and watching my face like I was a specimen he was trying to dissect.

"Are you going to eat?" I asked, nonchalantly as I could manage with the foul substance rolling around my cheeks. I fought the urge to shiver and give him any sign that this petty little play was bothering me.

"Why does it reek in here?" Fenar asked, his nose screwed up as he walked into the kitchen. He was shirtless, and I paused, my fork suspended in the air as I took him in. He was arrogant for a reason, it seemed. His chest was golden and sculpted, a dusky smattering of hair trailing down to his low-slung pants. His shockingly bright hair wasn't natural, if the dark trail was anything to go by. The seffe plopped off my fork and onto the plate, drawing a smirk from Fenar. He looked at my plate and shuddered.

"Really Tallis? Seffe?" He crossed his arms over his chest, not that I was looking. I was too busy trying to swallow the last few bits of my disgusting breakfast. Tallis shrugged, a twisted smile taking up space on his face.

"It's a staple for testing—" Fenar impatiently waved away the spiel Tallis had begun spouting off. He made his way over to the food machine and ordered a plate of what looked like eggs and toast, though the eggs were pale pink.

"Maybe a decade ago, before the Heads deemed it damaging to morale." He waved his cutlery towards Tallis. "Just be honest and say you want to make her miserable."

I pushed the plate away, empty of every morsel. I felt a surge of glee as Tallis's smile soured and Fenar let out a short bark of laughter.

"You could barely finish a bowl of the stuff without your eyes watering, if my memory serves." Tallis's hands bunched into fists at his side. He shot the laughing man a glare.

"Shut it, Fenar," he growled and jerked his head to the hallway. "Time for you to get dressed, human."

I slid off the chair and followed Tallis, wondering what clothes he was going to dress me in. From what I'd gleaned from the triad and Cove, Legion preferred simple sheaths, robes and flowing material. I hadn't seen

Tallis in anything but black or blue since I met him. A bit on the nose for his personality as a straight up villain.

"The cleaning room first," Tallis said when we entered my room. "You stink of sweat and I need to ensure it cleanses you of any lingering germs." He wrinkled his nose as if I was the foulest thing he'd ever smelled.

Shrugging, I went into the small room, shed my clothes and allowed the strange sensation to wash over me. I was getting used to it, but I still missed the feeling of water from a shower. Tucking the pang of longing into a box with the rest of the pining thoughts I had, I labeled it "too late and suck it up, buttercup." I lingered in the small room longer than I needed too, until I heard an impatient huff from outside. Not wanting to walk out there naked, I poked my head through the door and held out my hand, shielding my body. Tallis scoffed and handed me a black bundle.

"You can relax, your body holds no appeal to me, human." He sneered at the word human, and I rolled my eyes as I went back into the cleaning room. The unadulterated hatred he was showing me was almost tedious. However, I was too wrung out to let it hurt me. My nerves were tangled ends under my skin and they'd been wrenched on hard enough over the last day, so much so that I felt numb.

I sorted through the clothes, a loose black sheath and a billowing long-sleeved robe with a wispy belt that cinched in the middle. I looked like a shapeless shadow. There was no underwear, though, and I rubbed my legs uneasily under the soft material. Without that tiny scrap of material, I felt strangely exposed. I came out of the cleaning room expecting that Tallis would be gone, but he stood in the middle of the bedroom with something cradled in his hand.

"That fits you well," he said, even though the material was swamping me. I guess that was his point. "Spin around," he ordered, his tone daring me to argue. I dutifully presented him with my back and squeaked when I felt material cover half of my face, Tallis's fingers working at the back of my head as he laced it. I winced as some of my hair caught in the knotted clasp.

"A mask?" Whirling on him, my hands immediately flew to the back of my head. Tallis waggled his finger at me.

"Ah ah ah!" His dark eyes raked over me in obvious pleasure. "You'll keep that on if you want to keep to my rules. You know what will happen if you don't."

My fingers spasmed on the strap at the back of my head, but I pulled them away, letting them slowly lower to my side. The sick prick gave me a toothy smile and clapped his hands.

"So obedient! You're infinitely more palatable when you're muzzled."

I narrowed my eyes in a glare, brushing past him to go to the kitchen. Wellyn had woken in the time I was getting ready and had a plate of pancakes in front of him. Fenar leaned over him, darting forward to snatch little pieces.

"Quit it!" Wellyn wailed, leaning over his plate and trying to wave Fenar off. "These are mine."

"What are they? They're so sweet." His eyes closed with pleasure as he savored the flavor on his tongue. I was full from that seffe, but looked longingly at the pancakes anyway, my stomach satisfied but my soul needing that maple-soaked, fluffy clouds. Wellyn gasped in surprise when he saw me, his fork clattering to the ground. He shot off his seat and rounded the bench, his gaze flying over my shoulder.

"What the *shek* is this, Tallis?"

"Why, this is her uniform, of course," he said casually, unruffled by Wellyn's reaction.

"Bit extreme, no?" Fenar said, his jaw tight. His eyes flicked away from me as if the sight made him uncomfortable. Wellyn dithered in front of me, wringing his hands and looking at Tallis with a tortured expression.

"My rules, remember?" Tallis said in such a tranquil voice I wanted to scream, but I couldn't even speak. I didn't want to admit it, but the sensation of the mask was suffocating. The short, warm puffs of my breath were unnatural. I wouldn't give Tallis the satisfaction of ripping it off, not when he was looking at me so smugly.

"Tallis," Wellyn said, "those masks are punishment for unruly children, to put one on her is—" I felt a tratorious pang of betrayal as his voice, which started off stern, ended wavering. He would not stand up for me. Tallis was the obvious leader of this triad and Wellyn seemed too timid to want to get in between anyone. I sighed, rounding over to the window seat and sinking into it. I wouldn't stand there like a fool when I couldn't say anything.

"It's distasteful," Fenar said coldly, surprising me with his open dislike of the mask. "Black is so predictable. You couldn't pick something with flare?" My heart sank. I guess I wasn't getting out of this contraption soon.

"It is sufficient," Tallis said like he was describing the weather. I took a deep breath, turning my attention to the window instead. Grey clouds filled the sky, heavy and slow, moving like they were carrying a storm. I could see the darkened trees, the veins of Gaer like a deadly web over their trunks. I wondered what the landscape looked like before the tar-like substance had taken it over.

"We'll be going to Ambrose's tonight. While we are out of the apartment, do not remove the mask. I will know," Tallis called to me, his footsteps echoing out as he made his way to the exit.

"Come on, you're due to start in the Vault soon, right?" Fenar coaxed Wellyn, who hissed something under his breath. Fenar let out a beleaguered sigh and, after tapping his foot a few times, left as well.

I wondered how I had found myself in a place that looked and felt so much like hell. The skin around my mouth was moist, a sensation that made me want to shudder. I felt Wellyn creeping closer, but kept my eyes trained stubbornly on the window. He cleared his throat.

"I know this doesn't seem fair, Cami. If I could stop Tallis, I would, but it's better to indulge him. I can tell you're strong. This won't be forever. We have all had tests like this before. I know you will prevail. You have the backbone of a Legion."

He shuffled next to me, obviously hoping for a response, but I wasn't in a giving mood for cowards. He only wanted to be my friend when Tallis wasn't around. It was emotional whiplash I didn't have time for. I could only rely on myself, and to even entertain anyone else was a recipe for pain. We hung in this moment fraught with tension, no sounds and no movement. Frozen by our thoughts.

He might have thought I had the spine of a Legion, but I believed I was stronger than any of them as a human. I had gone through too much to crumple now. I would wear this horrid mask and the robes. I'd eat the disgusting food and endure whatever petty things Tallis did to me. They didn't realize I was a mass of broken shards on the inside, nothing they could do to me could be worse than what I did to myself.

I don't know how long I sat staring at that bleak sky, but it was long enough that Wellyn gave up and left. My neck was stiff and my body protested when I finally stood and stretched. I hadn't gotten used to the mask, and I didn't think I would, but I couldn't chance taking it off. Not if what Tallis said was true and that he had cameras or some other way of monitoring me in the room. My fingers itched with a growing urge, I always leaned towards drawing when I felt I needed to process. An idea sparked in my mind and a slow smile spread over my face behind the mask. I started my search for what I needed.

Wellyn

I PULLED MY READER from my pocket and swiped through to the apartment feed for the hundredth time this morning. Cami hadn't moved from the last time I had looked less than five minutes ago. She was a dark smudge sitting cross-legged on the couch, her head bent over a piece of paper. She was writing something, it seemed. Occasionally, she'd look up, tapping where her lips should be with a pen.

I shuddered at the sight of the mask. When she had walked out of her room this morning, I wanted to rip it off. I don't even know where Tallis had found one. They were for disobedient young Legion during their youth and only for extreme cases, children who needed severe disciplipine. It was a symbol of unworthiness, of shame. Even now it was a rare custom. Cami wouldn't understand the double-edged reason Tallis had made her wear it. She thought he did it because it was uncomfortable but any legion that looked at her would know what an insult it was to her as an adult. It marked her as being less controlled than a child, in need of harsh discipline.

I looked down the dark corridor I had snuck into, the tall shelving blocking me from the view of Madam Reason, who would have given me a wanring for lax work. Again. She'd already spotted me once with her narrowed gaze, her graying hair loosening in its tight bun, as she shook her head with disapproval. But I couldn't concentrate on my work today.

I wanted to leave early, but I'd already used up my weekly allotted time yesterday. Madam Reason may have allowed Seb Decker to leave, but she didn't favor me like she did him. He was from a noble family line, Hoppe, and had powers she could appreciate. No doubt he'd leave his apprenticeship and move on to bigger places. The Divine Vault, perhaps. He had options whereas I was a ward of the Heads with a creature no one had a use for except as a source of ridicule.

I rubbed a hand against my aching chest where the bond between my creature was held. It had responded yesterday for the first time in years. At the sight of Cami, he liefted from his fegue state inside me, causing my body to shiver in response. He had risen closer to the surface than I could remember, enough to convey his approval, his hunger and desire for the human.

She'd mentioned wanting to bathe in water and I had to fight the raging hard-on that sprung in my pants. I goggled at her like a fool while she had waited for me to leave. But all I could imagine was being naked with her, water sliding over our bodies and pressing them together, slick and shining. Even now I had to bite my fist to stop the groan that wanted to escape.

After allowing myself one more long look at Cami on the couch, I tucked my reader back into my pocket. I wasn't supposed to access it while working, but I couldn't help but flaunt the rules today. I would bear Madam Reason's ire so I could see Cami, even if only for a few moments.

My stomach turned with guilt as I pushed the now empty cart back to for more books. She hadn't replied to me when I tried to speak to her this morning, and I didn't blame her. No doubt she expected me to leap to her defense, to admonish Tallis and have him remove the mask. If she was my boost alone, I would have never allowed the treatment he was insisting on. But this was a compromise. Tallis would only have escalated if I had stepped in. He would have found something far worse to torment her with. He would get bored soon enough.

I knew she wasn't going to give him what he wanted. Tallis wanted her weeping, begging for mercy, but he wasn't looking closely enough at her. She had a steel determination deep inside her that would match any Legion. Fenar said she had eaten a whole bowl of seffe this morning without flinching, something Tallis had once failed to do in training. Fenar and I were used to the stuff. Food was not always a given as wards of the Heads. We were lucky to be fed at all and didn't have the luxury of being able to afford an ordering machine, and so had endured many bowls of the foul food. It was barely edible. I thought someone had purposely designed it to be as disgusting as possible. It was nutrient dense, but food ought to taste delicious as well. Like the pancakes Cami had shared. I perked up at the memory. Perhaps I could order her those for tomorrow, a way to show I was there for her even if she'd felt unhappy with me.

"Master Leave. It does not take ten minutes to empty a cart if one is applying themselves to the best of their ability." Madam Reason sniffed, her golden spectacles slipping down her nose like they disapproved of me as well.

Master Leave. I shuddered. No one called me that but her. It was the surname given to all those who couldn't claim a family name, one that had been used to mock me when I was younger after my family had abandoned me.

I returned the cart to its slot on the wall, ensuring the sides didn't touch as was required. I kept my head low and nodded in response to Madam Reason. She didn't want a reply. She only wanted to berate me. I had learned that lesson quickly when I had first started working in the Lower Vault two years ago. I should be annotating like Seb was currently, his dark hair low to the table as he used a glass to examine the edge of a piece of document. We had started working here simultaneously, but I was still an assistant while they had promoted him to Level One Archiver. My creature roiled under my skin, startling me so that I kicked my toe on the cart as I passed it. I smothered a curse, cutting Madam a quick look. She had seen, of course. She wouldn't let an opportunity to discipline me pass. I couldn't tell the reason she disliked me so much, whether it was my birth status or my inferior power. Either way, she gloried in making an example of me.

"Master Leave," Madam Reason's imperious voice sliced in the air, nasal and unwelcome as always. "Do you require time to re-read the manual on proper treatment of Vault property? It seems you have become lax in protocol and efficiency."

I shook my head, clenching my teeth to hold in the barrage of words I wished I could say to her pompous face. I had written the manual for all the new staff at the Vault, not that they gave me credit for it. Madam Reason had conveniently forgotten, and obviously had never read the revised version herself because I'd slipped in a clear description of her under the "To Be Avoided At All Costs" section in the etiquette chapter.

My hand itched to take out my reader again to look at Cami's dark curls instead of another pile of books that would have replacements as soon as I took them. But I hefted them against my chest anyway. The sooner I finished, the sooner I would be at home and with my boost again. Seb Decker may come from an academically renown noble family, but he would likely never have a boost. I let the warmth of that knowledge sink through my body and soothe my irritable creature. Here I was under the boot of Madam Reason, likely to never escape with my poor status. But I had a boost. I had a boost and no one could take that away from me.

I'd let Tallis play his little games and work his rage out about losing the future he had planned with Cove. I wouldn't let anything dampen my excitement at being handed an opportunity I never thought I would get.

Fenar

A FIST SLAMMED INTO my face that sent me sprawling on the hard training arena floor. I groaned into the ground, a puff of dust obscuring my vision. The round toe of a boot nudged into my stomach, and I rolled over, staring up at Trainer June with narrowed eyes. I threw my arm under my head and reclined like I was relaxing on the ground. My nose smarted from the hit and if I didn't have the healing power to fix it up before tonight's soiree, I might have been a little more peeved.

"What the *shek* is going on with you today, Fenar?" she said, holding out a hand to hoist me up onto my feet. Dueling pairs filled the circular training area, though none of them spared us a glance. Training for the quadrennial Vinko had started a few days ago. I should have been throwing myself into this training, single-minded about the idea of victory. My goal was to be chosen for Head Aydro's team this year, they were one of the only houses who didn't focus on blood purity. They were also the only team with the resources to beat Head Lamott's team, which I was determined to make happen. If I had a choice, I would wipe that whole house to bits. This was going to be our first Vinko. The family was callous, corrupt and everything that was wrong in Melbak. The hurt that Rayfe Lamott spread was personal and we had vowed to avenge our triad brother on his behalf. Tallis was on the far side, his hands swinging like a windmill as he prepared to launch a fireball into a target. June stepped into my line of vision, her hands on her hips. She was not the type of legion to let a question go unanswered and I knew she would not let me get away with anything, regardless of our past. She was a unique woman, lean and lithe, a true warrior. She had served Head Aydro until she lost her hand in the last Vinko. A glove covered the metal replacement now. She always hid it when sparring, not enjoying the curious looks from upstarts who hadn't learned the loss of her hand did not hold her back. She had become more formidable, her injury pushing her to become one of the fittest trainers in the arena. Most of the others were on the other side of washed up, with paunches and faces that dragged with the melancholy of disappearing youth.

I brushed off the orange dust from my front, not missing the way her eyes followed my hand. I shrugged and stared at the sky instead. The cloud cover had only thickened as the day went on, now as dark as my mood. She knew I'd been off all day. This wasn't the first time I'd found myself thrown to the ground. June wrapped her hand around my arm when she could see I was about to stalk away. I tensed, and she cut me a wry smile.

"You seem like you could use a workout of a different kind," she said under her breath, her eyebrows rising in a silent offer. It was tempting. June liked to assert herself the same way in bed as on the training grounds. She wasn't above using her muscles to dominate, not my usual style, but I'd enjoyed the lack of strings and the absolute physicality of our times together. I didn't know what was holding me back, but the idea of casually *sheking* someone right now didn't sit right with me.

My wolf rumbled inside me and rolled its eyes. I knew why he wanted to be celibate. He wanted the boost. A human. My stomach flipped; it was a strange twist that I didn't see coming. She was quite gorgeous in her own way, with thick dark curls and a snarky little mouth. I'd been furious when I saw what Tallis dressed her in this morning. A child's mask. But I didn't intervene. He needed to get his frustration out somehow, and there were worse ways he could have hurt Cami.

"Not today," I replied, feeling awkward when I saw her quickly covered hurt. We'd been nothing but casual. I hadn't promised to anything to her, so it was strange to see the reaction.

"Then get in position," she said, all professionalism again. I sighed and widened my legs, ready to get pummeled once more.

———⋈———

With training finally finished, I used one of the cleaning rooms at the arena to tidy up. My finger traced the line of my nose, pushing some of my healing power into the swelling that marred it. I had a decent scrape on my cheek, so I minimized that as well. My body ached fiercely. I was ready for a few drinks to forget about this day. Tallis clapped me on the shoulder and grinned at me in the mirror.

"There won't be a chance of being recruited to Aydro's team if you perform as poorly as you did today," he teased, and I punched him in the shoulder with a growl.

"We can't all be flame fighting extraordinaires." I said, feeling disorientated by my poor performance.

"Ready for Ambrose's?" Tallis asked.

I eyed him and scoffed. "Not as much as you, evidently."

His smile widened, his curls falling forward over his dark eyes.

"She didn't take her mask off all day today; she must be starved," he said as we walked to the portal.

"You tricked her?" I had thought little about his instructions to her, but of course she would have had to remove the mask to eat. Tallis lifted a shoulder.

"She's cleverer than I thought," he admitted. "I thought her appetite would drive her to remove it."

"Can she order anything except seffe?" I asked, and Tallis chuckled under his breath.

"She can also have fluco and conozon."

I wrinkled my nose, squeezing into the portal with a group of others. The familiar feeling of my skin suctioning to my body settled over me as we shuffled towards the back, our apartment being one of the lower areas with our status. We had to wait for the other occupants to be transported before reaching our floor.

"Tallis, I wouldn't offer that shit to my worst enemy."

The smile he gave me was malevolent, and I shuddered a little at how deep he was leaning into this idea of "testing" Cami. He wanted the girl to fail or quit. He wanted her to run crying back to his dad, hoping he wouldn't have to deal with the repercussions or the blame. Albion had been clear. Tallis had to get on board, but he would do everything he could to push the boundaries of those rules, the threat of a binding agreement enough to make him toe the line.

"She managed well this morning," he said begrudgingly as the portal shuddered, sending those inside wobbling on their feet. I'd only caught the end of her first foray with the notorious morning meal Legion ate while going through trials. It was made deliberately disgusting to weed out the weak-minded and the spoiled from the ranks. It had impressed me to see her shovel it in without even grimacing.

I paused at our door, hearing no noises inside except a tiny, muffled snore. As I made my way inside I saw the little human had made a comfy nest of the couch. A blanket dragged from my collection was half on the floor. She was curled in a little ball with her hands tucked under her. She would have looked sweet and innocent if not for the garish mask covering half her face.

Tallis rolled his eyes and went straight to his room, stomping past her, annoyed at the thwarted chance to spar with his shiny new toy. I strolled a little closer, driven by a burning curiosity. The scent of salt was thick as I leaned over her. There was a slip of paper tucked under her arm. I gently maneuvered it out from under her, drawing a furrowed brow from her but no other sign of wakefulness. I flipped the page over and quickly smothered my laughter. She'd had a fine day, it seemed, translating her frustration with Tallis into a truly hilarious comic.

Regulations and Policies of Bossman.

She'd titled it, and underneath there was a picture of a toddler with his head thrown back in the throes of a tantrum. Burning orange fists, shot upwards in outrage. He had a small, straight mustache which seemed strange, considering Tallis had no facial hair. A smaller version of Tallis's tail dragging limply on the ground.

"Follow my rules or else I'll cry!" she'd written in a speech bubble. I pressed the sheet to my chest and sucked in a deep breath to temper the guffaw that desperately wanted to escape. This was perfect, too good to pass up.

I folded the sheet and tucked it in my back pocket. I offered the human a fond smile, not that she noticed in her comfortable slumber. This would liven up Ambrose's later tonight. Tallis would blow the roof off. Hopefully, he wouldn't blow up the entire room, although it would mean Ambrose would have to redecorate. That would be a boon for us all.

I whistled as I walked to my bedroom to get ready.

Cami

I woke from my impromptu nap groggy, wondering if I was sleeping so much now to make up for the lack of sleep I had gotten on Earth. This was the most time I'd spent not working. It was strange, like my body was using this time to recuperate.

The mask had cut into my face at an angle that made my cheeks tingle as blood raced back into them. I poked my head up, swiping my hair out of my face, and listened for a moment. There was movement from someone in the apartment, which was unfortunate. I got to my feet, intent on sneaking into my room and holing up there, but my stomach growled in protest. It wanted more food no matter how I tried to tell it the only food on offer was inedible and that starving was preferable to eating that slop again.

I remembered the comic I'd drawn and pulled up the blanket to look for it. There seemed to be an inordinate amount of soft furnishings in this masculine dominated space. The comic had helped me deal with some of the rage I'd been feeling that morning. There was something so calming about drawing Tallis as a mini dictator, and a few more ideas for longer comics had crossed my mind while I drew before I'd fallen into a nap.

But I couldn't find the drawing. I ripped away the cushions to see if it had become jammed underneath. The pencils I'd found in Wellyn's room were on the side table, but there was no comic. I got on all fours and peered under the lounge to find nothing but a pile of dust that made me wrinkle my nose.

"No need to fall to your knees in my presence, human," the tyrant spoke. The inspiration for my comic strode into the room with a shit-eating grin on his face. Tallis couldn't do or say anything to make me jeopardize the deal I'd made for my family's benefit, but that didn't mean I couldn't glare at him, which I did with relish.

I stood up and dusted off the black potato sack robe he'd picked out for me. I don't know if he thought it would embarrass me, but it was comfortable, like wearing a nightie all day. The material could have breathed better, but it was loose. I felt a bit like a rich widow swanning about a resort...if they had transported the widow to a hellish wasteland and forced to share their blood in a magical binding agreement. Tallis had changed his outfit into a tunic style with linen pants underneath. It was a similar silver to the sheath Cove wore yesterday. He flicked a dissatisfied look at the wrinkled robes I was wearing while he strapped a red band around his upper arm.

"We are going to a soiree tonight. It will be your introduction as our boost. Avail yourself of the cleaning room and try to do something with the"—he waved his hand impatiently at my hair—"situation on your head."

I pointed to the mask, an eyebrow raised.

He raised his hands and clapped them slowly. "You may remove your mask," he said, magnanimous, like he'd given me a gift. His dark eyes danced as I gave him a mocking bow and swept past him to my room. A low chuckle followed me. He was impossible. I untied the mask and tossed it on my bed with a sigh. It felt like such a pitiful freedom, but the fresh air felt so good in my lungs.

"I was hoping we could talk," came a voice from the corner. I shrieked and turned, my hand at my heart. Wellyn was crouched in the corner, his violet eyes wide with shock.

"What are you doing in here?" I spat out. "Why are you hiding in the corner like a creep?" My face felt so gross and I was dying to clean away the griminess the constant hot, recycled breath had ingrained into my skin. Wellyn jumped to his feet and shuffled nervously.

"I didn't want to sit on your bed," he said, as if that explained anything.

"Tallis, our gracious overlord, has given me permission to clean, so say what you want and get out." I hoped he would freeze from the chill in my voice. He ate pancakes in front of me this morning and didn't say a word when Tallis muzzled me like a dog. I owed him nothing. But he looked so crestfallen at the obvious distrust in my voice, his shoulders falling a little and his sweet mouth moving like he was choosing his words like precious jewels.

"I know you're angry with me." He looked up, waiting for confirmation which I didn't give him. I only crossed my arms and raised my eyebrows.

"You don't understand my reasons, and that is fair. Despite what you think, I am someone you can rely on. I am someone who will do right by you."

"Just not when your friend wants to dress me up like a petty revenge doll and spoon feed me the most disgusting meal on the planet. Your planet and mine!" I couldn't help my outburst. My stomach took that moment to growl, asserting how it felt about the one pitiful meal it'd been slung today. Wellyn nodded sagely.

"I want to make up for that, actually." He pointed to the side of my bed. A plate of pancakes. I couldn't believe I hadn't noticed it. I rushed over, letting out a squeal and falling on the meal like the animal Tallis thought me to be. It was cold and the pancakes had soaked up most of the maple syrup, but my tongue zinged at the contact. I closed my eyes and moaned. Sugar, blessed sugar! Wellyn came a little closer, carefully, like he didn't want to spook me.

"I'm sorry it's cold. I ordered it when I got home and brought it in here while you were still asleep on the couch. That way Tallis couldn't say I was ordering it for you. There are viewers in the main area only."

Well, that confirmed my thoughts about whether they could watch me. I knew that dark-eyed freak had been watching and hoping I would take the mask off while he was out. It made the uncomfortable, gross feeling worth it to get that small win. I quickly chewed the large mouthful I'd taken, swallowing hard to the get rid of the lump in my throat.

"You want to apologize?" I asked, thinking I could use this to my benefit. It didn't mean the gorgeous redhead was off the hook, but I could at least get some secret perks if he was willing.

Wellyn nodded vigorously. "I didn't want to test you, but Tallis is right. It will legitimize you in Legion eyes. It doesn't mean that I don't feel horrible about it."

"Pancakes from Dilly's and a cappuccino or a coffee," I replied, and his forehead creased until he understood what I was saying.

"Caw-fee?" he clarified, and I nodded like a bobble head doll.

"You want my forgiveness, buddy?" I said, shoveling in more pancake. "It comes through caffeine."

He gave a curt nod, and I jerked my head to the door.

"I need to get ready before the sadist comes looking for me," I said, putting the plate aside. I had finished the meal obscenely quickly, but I didn't let myself feel embarrassed about it. Wellyn slipped through the door saying nothing, for which I was grateful.

It took only a short time for me to get ready, although slipping on the mask with its material still damp and cool hammering home how unejoyable this night is going to be. There was a red armband wrapped around my bicep. Butterflies fluttered in my stomach. The first time I would leave this apartment was to go into a room full of Legion. wondered if they'd be more like Wellyn, kind and sweet, or Tallis, fiery and calculating. Perhaps they would be curious and mature like Cove. She would be there tonight, and I could admit that I wanted to see more of the boys' interactions with her, the one Tallis had desired as a boost.

The journey through the portal exacerbated my nerves, a whirling blue slip in the wall that made my skin seem to shrivel around my muscles when I'd stepped through it. The journey only lasted a moment, but it made my stomach dip and skin ache when I exited. My thoughts whirled in my mind as Tallis led the way down a cluttered hall. The floor was strewn with ornate rugs trimmed with tassels, and the walls were packed with frames depicting battle scenes and portraits of men with handlebar mustaches and horns. The spaces in between had a busy green wallpaper that I couldn't stare at too long without feeling nauseasated. There were armchairs scattered along the way, delicately carved and adorned with plump cushions. It was so different from the triad's corridor and apartment, which seemed more clinical with its silver accents and sparse furniture. The coziest spot was the window seat, and that was unofficially Tallis's favorite place to brood. This, however, looked like it had been thrown together by an eccentric aunty who was a secret millionaire.

Fenar and Wellyn pressed me between them. There was not quite enough space for me to walk comfortably, but I appreciated the sense of security at least one of them gave me. Fenar hadn't looked at me once since we'd started walking, playing with his hair instead. There was one section that wouldn't sit right, and it was irritating him how disobedient it was being. He kept licking his hand and fussing with it, trying to get it to stay down. It reminded me of my brothers and the cowlick they both had at the crown of their head. I squashed down the memory. I couldn't think of my brothers when I was about to enter a dangerous situation. I packaged it up and pushed it into a box deep in the back of my mind. I couldn't be hurt physically, that was a comfort at least.

We stopped at an ornate set of doors that swung open of their own volition. There was a platter filled with glasses hovering on either side of the entry filled with a light blue liquid that bubbled like champagne. Fenar snatched two, immediately pouring one down his throat and tossing the glass to the side. I flinched, anticipating the shatter. Instead, the glass transformed into a wispy butterfly, its wings tapering into thin trails that danced through the air until it dissolved into nothing. I was glad I was wearing a mask because otherwise my gaping mouth would have been hanging open.

Fenar mistook the noise of wonder I made and said with a sneer, "Gaudy right? Ambrose can't help being ostentatious."

The room was gigantic, the crazy aunt vibe continuing into every available space with a haphazard crush of art, trinkets and shelves crammed with books. My fingers itched with a sudden urge to rifle through drawers. I just knew there'd be a diamond the size of my fist tucked under a pile of papers, forgotten. Ambrose was a hoarder, for sure. I spied a few items that looked suspiciously human-like. The room was spacious, with sweeping ceilings that led towards an glass ceiling. There was a spiraling staircase that led to a rooftop patio.

The crowd stilled when we entered, their curious gazes burning holes through my dark robes. Whispers started up like a wildfire, furious and fast as more Legion realized there was something different about the newest guests.

"Kerys triad!" called a haughty voice, and dapper gentleman with the thickest, lushest handlebar mustache I'd ever seen wound his way through the crowd. I noted the curling horns first, like a ram's, nestled in his brunette locks. But despite that, he looked clean cut, a thick turned-up collar ringing his neck. He strode toward us with the innate grace of someone born into luxury. His hands swept up like he was encouraging Tallis to embrace him, and I noted the red armband on his ash colored coat.

"Ambrose, this is a lovely soiree," Tallis replied, not offering a hand to the host. Ambrose only gave an amused laugh, letting his hands drop to slap the side of his trousers.

"I hear congratulations are in order. Or not? Interesting attire for a boost, human aside." Ambrose peered around Tallis, his hazel eyes drifting down my form and up again. He sniffed a little, his mustache ruffling like a cat shifting in its sleep.

"A work in progress," Tallis said smoothly.

"Don't let Nakasha get her claws into her, she's displeased to not be the only boost in the room."

A shiver ran down my spine. Who was Nakasha and did she have actual claws? Not a fear I thought I'd have to seriously contemplate. I remained silent. Of course, the mask was useful in covering my abysmal poker face.

"She is the only true boost, she knows that," Tallis placated, his voice smoky. I rolled my eyes at the insult of my lesser human blood. He clapped his hand on Ambrose's shoulder and made to move past him, but Ambrose shifted subtlety to block him. Ambrose was a good head taller, a fact that must have irritated Tallis as his tail swished once before settling again.

"Come and find me later, I'll give you some tips on how to manage the transition," he purred. Tallis stiffened. I didn't quite understand what was happening except that Tallis obviously didn't appreciate the mildly condescending offer and was bristling at the power Ambrose was showing. Fenar pushed Tallis to the side and engulfed Ambrose in a rough embrace, his hand clapping him on the back loudly. He shot a look at Tallis, who huffed and strode past into the crowd.

"How are you, Rosie?" Fenar asked. Ambrose's neck colored at the nickname.

"Don't call me that," he snapped before remembering himself and putting on a brighter expression. The crowd ahead of us was slowly losing interest, the chatter starting up again. I could tell I was still a topic of conversation with how often eyes seemed to dart back to me. I shuffled a little closer to Wellyn, dangling my hand down to brush against his fingers. The guilt he was feeling was a useful shield. I didn't know what polite company was like in Melbak, but with the abundance of claws and fangs, I wasn't taking any chances. He tucked my hand into the crook of his elbow, giving it a little squeeze. He leaned to whisper in my ear, his breath tickling the shell.

"There is no need to be nervous. Everyone will be curious, but they won't overstep. You belong to us. These red arm bands denote your status as a boost."

I didn't like the sound of belonging to anyone but myself. But I also didn't want to alienate him enough to leave me alone right now. Especially when Tallis had effectively muzzled me.

Ambrose caught the movement and gave a sly smile and wink to Wellyn.

"Clever man, you need all the boost you can get with your little creature!"

Wellyn breathed sharply through his nose, his jaw tight, but he didn't reply. Fenar threw his arm over Ambrose's shoulder and drew him away into the crowd. I raised an eyebrow at Wellyn, but he just shook his head.

"Don't ask," he muttered, walking forward instead. The crowd parted for us, the whispers following like my own personal soundtrack.

A human boost? It's absurd.

The Kerys triad doesn't deserve a boost.

Will their status change with the boost?

I wouldn't mind a taste from a human. The rumors about disease are just fear mongering.

I wanted to cover my ears; the snippets burrowed into my brain like worms. Wellyn's shoulders were stiff as we maneuvered around people. Tallis appeared in front of us, glowering. His hand snapped out, curling around my other arm.

"She's not your date, Wellyn, she's here to be tested," he admonished, his fingers pinching the sensitive skin under my arm. He didn't wait for Wellyn to reply, dragging me through the crowd. I looked back and glimpsed his face, looking downcast.

"This way, pet," he said, pointing to a wooden bench affixed against a shelf. It was too high to get into without a leg up, something Tallis took into his own hands. He hoisted me up and set me on the uncomfortable seat. My feet dangled above the ground and I realized belatedly I was stuck here unless he helped me down. His hands strangled my waist.

"You're going to be my good girl tonight, aren't you? Do as you're told and stay," he teased, a smirk twisting his lovely lips into something nasty. I rolled my eyes, tempted to kick out at his sharp nose and show him what kind of girl I was. I closed my eyes and took a deep breath. My family, I chanted.

At an insistent poke on my upper thigh, I opened my eyes to see a large man scrutinizing me. His eyes were snake-like, and they narrowed as I squealed, the sound muffled by the mask.

"A human," the Legion said, leaning close enough that I could smell his spicy cologne. He reached up and groped my upper arm. "Puny muscular structure."

I pulled my arm from his assessing grip and his bizarre eyes flared with surprise as his lips pulled into a grim line.

"Well, I never. I can see why Tallis has you dressed like a child in a mask, you clearly need discipline."

His haughty voice made me roll my eyes again, and he made a noise in the back of his throat like I had mortally offended him. He stalked off and someone else came to replace him. It was a stately looking man, with deer like antlers.

"Oh my" he breathed, as he shuffled closer "A human, I never thought I'd see the day" he stuck out a hand. "My name is Kevin, I would like the shake your hand in the human way of greeting" I leaned down and shook his hand, trying to interpret his peculiar excitement at seeing me. It was the opposite of all the interactions I'd had so far. Kevin didn't leave me hanging for long.

"I am somewhat of an aficionado of human culture, in fact I have my own collection of human objects" he stared up at me with his antlers quivering "I even changed my name, Kevin, from one of my favorite earth movies. I have a vast collection of human items, perhaps I can ask your advice about—" he was cut off by a clearing throat and turned with a flush on his cheeks. There was a beautiful woman, her head reaching my knees in this prime seat. Her tanned skin gleamed in the light of the candles mounted next to me. Like a glacier, she was smooth, all sharp edges and cold. She iced Kevin with a cold look.

"I knew I would find you over here" she hissed under her breath "I asked you to put aside your proclivities for *one night*!" She leaned close to Kevin "You are going to walk away, right now and we will discuss this later". Kevin started to interject, to explain himself I thought, but Nakasha held up a finger. Kevin shot me a quick look of apology before slinking away into the crowd. Nakasha reached a hand up and I stiffened at the sight of her claws, sharp, long and painted gray. She pressed them into my thigh, so deep that I winced, and a husky laugh escaped her.

"Look at me, human," she ordered, and I met her eyes with apprehension. I wriggled in the seat, moving my hand to dislodge her tight grip on my skin. "You are not to entertain Kevin, he belongs to me. Sit still, like the good girl Tallis is training you to be." She dug in deeper. I swallowed the whine of pain that wanted to come out.

"You are as featureless as they described. It's horrifying," she sneered, twisting her claws. She was going to draw blood. "You know they won't ever accept you, right?"

This had to be the other boost. She was encased in a form-fitting red sheath, daring enough to show a sweep of lush cleavage. She looked glamorous, but snooty, like Ambrose. They matched, if she was who I thought she was.

"Nothing to say?" she taunted, digging her claws in further before yanking them out. I hissed and glared at her, pointing to my mask and shrugging. She put her hands on her hips and pursed her lips. A gentleman came up behind her and pressed his lips to the crook of her neck. She melted against him, her claws dragging down the arm he encircled around her waist.

"Don't waste your time on the featureless freak, Nakasha." I ignored the sharp pain in my leg and focused on them. I was right. This was Ambrose's boost and another of her triad's members. She cooed at the man.

"Oh Pyke, I'm just reminding the human of her place." He sniffed the air, his eyes landing on my thigh.

"Did you have to make her bleed?" he said, resigned. "It's such a mood killer, my love."

I hovered my hand over my thigh where she'd clawed me and lay my fingers gently on the skin. There was no pain. This must be the binding agreement coming into effect. So, I could still be hurt, but it would heal quickly. I didn't really like the idea and certainly wouldn't be sharing it with Tallis. Who knows what painful torture he could come up with?

"Sorry, darling." Nakasha pouted. Without sparing me a glance, he sighed and ushered her away. Someone else who wanted to poke, prod and question me quickly replaced her.

"It's no fun to torment a human when they can't run or shout for help." Twins with twisting brown horns protruding from their hair were sulking in front of me. They'd been whispering all the horrible things they wanted to do to me, one of which involved stripping my skin off in lashes. One tilted her head, examining me with intensity.

"Let's go see if we can convince Tallis," she said, and they clapped with glee. Fenar materialized behind them, throwing his arms around their shoulders.

"Now, now, my devious twins," he chided, giving me a cursory look-over. "I'm sure we can find something more fun to do than scare the human." His voice was low and suggestive. He winked at one and waggled his eyebrows, and they smiled, linking their arms with his in agreement. I felt a strange pang in my chest and rubbed it absentmindedly as he walked away. Those Legion had been scary; I wouldn't want to meet them in a dark alley. They'd probably cut my liver out and eat it. As the crowd got slowly more inebriated, I could see that being a fun piece of entertainment for them.

Another woman stormed up to me, her face already scrunched in anger. She was clutching a glass of that bubbly blue liquid.

"You don't understand what your presence here will do," she hissed at me, her shoulders quaking with rage. Dark hair slung over her shoulder in a severe braid. She could use it as a noose if she wanted to.

I had dealt with variations of this same thread hroughout the night. Legion really didn't approve of humans. We were something like a novelty or a pet, certainly not on the same level as Legion. Most seemed squeamish about even touching me, thinking I carried some unspeakable disease. Linking my hands, I let them sit in my lap. With my mask on, there was no chance of arguing back, and I found it was more enjoyable to ignore the angry ones.

I had my eyes trained on my lap when a shock of liquid hit my face. Blinking rapidly, I felt the liquid soak into my robes. I looked down at the furious Legion, her fingers strangling her empty glass.

"Boosts deserve to die out, just like the cursed Legion planned." She spat at me, literally spat, the glob landing on the hem of my robes.

"That's enough, Ziggie," a voice called. I turned to see Cove racing from the group of gawking onlookers. She pushed the woman's shoulder and sent her stumbling.

"You wouldn't understand, Cove, you want to be a boost," she sneered.

"Who let you in? Go spread your bad omens somewhere else." Ziggie shot her a dark glare before stomping away. Cove looked up at me, wincing at the bedraggled mess I made. I smelled sweet, but the drink had molded the top of my robes to my body. It was heavy and sticky against my skin.

"What is going on here?" she asked, her pixie-like face perplexed. Her crimped silver hair and electric-blue eyeshadow looked like a look a five-year-old might insist on, but on Cove it was fashionable. I pointed to the mask and she clicked her tongue, holding up a finger and stalking away. It wasn't long before she was back, Tallis's arm in her grip as she dragged him towards me. I stiffened as his dark hellfire eyes met mine.

"Explain this to me, Tallis." She huffed at him, speaking in a low tone so that others couldn't hear her. He rubbed the back of his neck and sighed.

"I'm testing her like she was any other Legion."

"She's human! Why would you put her through something the poor thing does not know and probably couldn't handle, anyway?"

I felt a bit miffed at that. I'd handled many annoying and insulting things tonight without losing my temper or even attempting to take the mask off.

"I won't accept a boost that can't stand respected amongst Legion."

"You won't allow her to garner any respect if you mask her like a naughty child. Did she say something that insulted someone?" Cove crossed her arms.

"She says insulting things all the time," he replied, his lips twitching. Cove shook her head like he wasn't listening to her. Which he wasn't.

"Human or not, she's a boost. That is precious. Ambrose would never do this to Nakasha."

That was the right avenue to take. Tallis reeled as if slapped. Obviously, Ambrose was a sore point, and Tallis certainly didn't like being compared and found lacking. He bent his head to Cove and snarled at her.

"Ambrose is a spoiled, pompous prig."

'He is,' Cove agreed, "yet he treats Nakasha as a queen. They bless her with everything and receive her bounty for it. Don't you want to reach your full potential? I don't understand why you would spurn this opportunity!"

Her eyes turned misty as she looked up at me briefly. Tallis pulled her closer, trying to hold her in his arms, but she yanked away, coming closer to me and shaking her head.

"If you were my boost, you'd be my queen. That's what I always imagined," he cajoled, almost sweetly, leaning over her shoulder. She whirled around to face him again.

"If I were your boost? Tallis, even if I were a boost, it wouldn't be your triad I chose."

The color drained from his face and he grunted like she'd punched him.

"What?" he whispered.

Cove looked uncomfortable, her fingers coming up to pinch her nose. "I thought I was clear to you the other day, the way I've always been clear to you," she said, her voice small and imploring. It was clear to me that she didn't want to say it, but obviously not to Tallis as he looked hopeful again.

"Because you were waiting to present. I'm the obvious choice. We've been best friends since we were children."

Cove gave a strangled sigh. I removed my mask, deftly undoing the knots, about to interject when she spoke again.

"Tallis, you are my best friend and I love you as a brother. That's it."

"You could come to love me," Tallis said, still looking utterly dumbfounded.

"No, Tallis," Cove explained softly, her small fingers kneading into his arm. "I honestly thought I'd been obvious. You, Fenar and Wellyn are the brothers I never had."

"I'm in love with you," he blurted out, like the words were vomit. I shifted uncomfortably in my seat, not wanting to be witness to this private moment. It was a repeat of when I first met her. Tallis seemed to realize that as he looked up at me and froze, his tail knocking off a book from behind him as it waved erratically. Cove rushed to comfort him, patting his arm again.

"It's ok, I shielded around us," she said, and he relaxed a little, shooting me another narrow-eyed look. I realized what she meant. No one else could hear what we were saying. A point of frustration, judging from the longing looks a few Legion were shooting at us as they tried to inch closer.

"You love the idea of me, Tallis, the idea of us fitting together neatly like a puzzle. But love is mess, passion and fire. You've always been afraid of your fire, so you think you love me, because its easy, comfortable. But you will have to get burnt to feel actual love. I don't want to be comfortable. I want to be consumed, utterly engulfed with emotion."

Tallis stayed silent, his jaw clenching as he faced the bookcase while Cove continued to run her hand down his arm. He jerked her off.

"Don't. I need you not to touch me right now."

"I understand. Can I take your boost to refresh herself? You can't mean for her to sit here the entire night."

Tallis cast her a look that said he clearly did mean for me to sit there all night. He looked away from Cove, like he couldn't stand the sight of her, glaring at me instead, his eyes drifting down to the soaked part of my robes. I felt strangely exposed; the material clung to my chest and revealed every curve.

"You removed your mask," he said, emotionless. "I will discipline you for that."

Cove protested, shaking her head, her silver hair a riot.

"Tallis, don't be this person. It's cruel and unnecessary. Please." Her wide eyes must have worked because he nodded briefly. "Can you lift her down? I'll take care of her from there."

He wrapped his hands around my waist and hoisted me down from the seat. My legs tingled from disuse and I placed a hand on him to stabilize myself. I gasped as I felt a shock of energy through my fingers. He pushed me away from him, shock etched on his brow, and Cove wrapped her arm around me.

"Come with me, Cami let's sort this mess out." She cut a quick path through the mingling crowd, guiding me down a quiet hallway and opening a door at the end. She nodded her head.

"There is a cleaning room in there. It should give the option to remove the stain and freshen up." She looked down the hallway, seeing onlookers approaching. "I'll keep the curious away."

I nodded my thanks, not sure how to articulate it as I was still feeling muted from my time with the mask. Slipping into the room, I felt along the wall until I entered another smaller chamber. The lights came on immediately and I could see I was in a huge cleaning room. It was the size of my bedroom at the apartment. Beautiful matte stone ran the length of the floors and walls. There was a slumped red lump in the corner and it shifted as the lights came on and Nakasha's head popped up.

"What are you doing in here?" she sneered, the effect lessened by the rivulets of makeup running down her face. Her eyes were bloodshot and her face lacked color. Red welts flared on her arms and chest. She was a mess.

"Do you need help?" I asked. Even if she'd been nasty to me, she was obviously in pain. Nakasha struggled to sit up, her arms shaking until she lay down again.

"You're in my cleaning room. Why?" The haughtiness rapidly drained from her voice.

I motioned to my wet robes. "One of your guests threw a drink on me. Cove brought me here and said I could freshen up."

Nakasha groaned, her forehead furrowing in pain. She waved a limp hand.

"The second option. Hurry and get out."

I turned and stood in the middle, letting the light pass over me. The tingle was lighter than usual. The feeling of the liquid being leached out of my robes made me shiver.

"Who threw the drink?" Nakasha asked. I chewed on my lip, trying to remember her name.

"Ziggie, I think?"

Nakasha snorted and shook her head. "That lunatic? She hates me too. Of course she would sneak in and create trouble. She is just jealous. She wants to be a boost. Who wouldn't want to be a boost?"

"She sounded like a barrel of laughs," I said wryly.

"She always tries to accost me whenever she sees me, don't take it personally," she groaned.

It felt mean, but I preferred sick Nakasha. She was much nicer than the version I met before. It was like they weren't even the same person. This Nakasha looked minutes away from passing out, however.

"Let me help you," I offered hesitantly, expecting her to rebuff me. She looked at me through narrowed slits, her head drooping as if giving up.

"I came in here and found I didn't have the energy to get back."

I helped her sit up and slid my arm around her back, grunting as her full weight threatened to topple me over. I shuffled her out of the cleaning room and moved forward into the darkened space to where Nakasha pointed. Her bedroom was palatial. In the dark I could make out an enormous bed, enough to fit four people at least. I propped her on the edge and helped her lay her head down. I reached down and swung her legs into the bed. She hissed as my hands wrapped around her calves.

"Sorry," I said quickly, pulling the covers over her. She laughed, empty and quiet.

"Enjoy your time now, you'll be like this soon enough." Nakasha pulled the surrounding covers, only her head still visible.

"What do you mean?" She was what I was, what Albion hoped me to be.

"You're a boost. A human one, but I can smell the power of your blood." Her voice tapered off and her lip curled. "They don't want others to know, the Heads, but boosts get sick after they join with their triad. It starts off small—headaches and fatigue. Now I'm getting welts and I vomit at the most inopportune moments."

"This will happen to me?" I frowned. Nobody had mentioned anything like this.

"The pressure of sustaining Melbak. There aren't enough boosts and we who exist pay the price. The Heads have tried to find a cure for decades. There is nothing that can be done. They are trying to make a synthetic boost, but that has failed so far. Perhaps your human blood will be the key." Her voice was faint yet still derisive.

I hummed and tapped my fingers on my legs, not sure what to say. My stomach felt like it was being strangled. Nakasha reached out and wrapped her hand around my wrist.

"Tell Ambrose I have retired? He'll know that I'm feeling unwell." She dropped her hand to the bed, looking forlorn now that her sickness had stripped her of bravado.

I nodded and rose, choking on the sense of foreboding in the air in my lungs. Cove was alone, thankfully, as I left the room. She looked at me with a critical eye, reaching out to finger the robes, now like new.

"These are horrible. Tallis chose them, I'm guessing."

I nodded and she grimaced with a heavy sigh. Her blue eye shadow glimmered in the low light.

"I don't understand why he is doing this," she spoke low, more to herself than to me. Sharing my opinion wouldn't help, so I kept quiet. I wasn't getting in the middle of this. Hopefully, I could keep my head down and I wouldn't end up sick like Nakasha. I spotted Ambrose and tugged on Cove's arm.

"I need to speak with Ambrose," I whispered to her, and her eyes narrowed in confusion. She didn't complain though, just took the lead, weaving through the crowd and tapping on his shoulder.

"Ambrose," she said, clearing her throat. He turned with a genial smile at the ready. It didn't falter when he saw me. I could tell he was a natural charmer, well-practiced at these events. He flashed me a smile and tilted his head.

"What can I do for you, Cove?" he said, ushering us out from the crush. I tried to ignore the stares and whispers that followed, not loud enough for me to discern what they were saying, but a constant stream that nattered in my ear.

"Go ahead," Cove said, looking at me expectantly. Ambrose let out a surprised cough.

"You want to speak to me, little human?" He crossed his arms, and I felt uncomfortable under his perusal. He'd shed the coat and was wearing a white button-down shirt with the cuffs rolled up. I stepped up to him, close enough that my robes brushed the tops of his shiny loafers. He raised an eyebrow, a faint wrinkle in his nose as I stood on my tiptoes and muttered to him.

"Nakasha asked me to tell you she's retired."

Only because I was looking did I see the tightness of his jaw and the way he stiffened and then slumped. He didn't question my words, just nodded, losing some of the sheen he had been projecting since we'd arrived.

"I see. I appreciate you telling me," he said sincerely, and his chest rose with a deep breath. Cove, who was looking between us as if there was a missing puzzle piece, met my eye as I nodded.

"I will do the same," I said, still quiet, but for her benefit as well. Ambrose dipped his head.

"You may visit Nakasha again," he offered, and I gave him a tight-lipped smile. It wasn't high on my list of things to do, considering I wasn't sure which version of Nakasha I might get. Cove linked her arm with mine and drew me away.

"You are lucky to get an invitation. She's notoriously fussy. I heard she confronted you earlier. You must have impressed her somehow."

I didn't reply, knowing the only reason she would invite me back was solidarity. I was a boost, just like her. If what she said was true, then I would be like her soon enough. Sapped of strength and hiding in a bedroom. I shuddered at the thought. There had to be a reason for it. Perhaps I could do some research and try to find out why.

I heard muffled laughter as we walked past a group. Someone was wiping tears from their eyes. They were clutching a piece of paper and showing it to their friends. It set off a louder flurry of laughter, which startled Cove, and she gave them a curious look.

"Shall I get us a drink?" she offered, looking about for one of the floating platters. I blanched. Absolutely not.

"Nothing for me," I said aloud, shivering at the thought of being drunk in a room full of Legion. I couldn't stomach the idea of being in the same position that had landed me here. No, drinking was not for me. It had destroyed my life once. Never again.

"I am going to go now," I said, clutching at the mask in my hand. I didn't want to put it back on and play Tallis's pet again.

"Are you allowed to leave?"

I bristled at the innocent tone she used and shrugged, shaking off the sudden desire to look around to make sure I wasn't being watched. I wasn't a toddler or a possession and Tallis hadn't specifically said I couldn't leave on my own. A cheeky smile took over my face before I could stop it.

"You'll keep my secret, won't you?"

Cove chuckled and pointed down a winding hallway.

"That's the exit. I trust you can find your way back to the apartment?"

I winked, butterflies filling my stomach at the thought of freedom and at Tallis's face when he realized I wasn't coming back to be a masked punching bag anymore. She bit off a laugh and shooed me away. I needed no more encouragement. I all but fled for the exit, keeping my head down and suppressing the urge to skip.

Wellyn

AMBROSE'S WAS TEDIOUS. I didn't want to be there and it must have showed in my face, as even those who knew me seemed to avoid me. Tallis and Fenar were swamped by sycophants and gossipers who wanted to congratulate them on having a boost and find out how it occurred. Nobody cornered, asked or sought my favor, not that it surprised me. I often kept to the outskirts of these things, not wanting to catch any glimpses of my blood brothers. They were on good terms with Ambrose, and even though they wouldn't recognize me, given I'd been erased from existence in their eyes, it was too hard to see them. A reminder of how lacking I was. They were tall, muscular and accomplished. They could use the noble name of our family, unlike me, the outcast.

Tallis was from the Legion family Kerys, one of the founding families. He was more at home amongst Ambrose's kind than he would admit. His childhood prepared him to deal with those who smiled while they slashed the tendons of your knees, making you falter at their feet.

Fenar was a ward of the Heads, like me, but he was worth something. His wolf was a fearsome creature and his enhanced senses helped him become a warrior with a frightening reputation. It certainly helped that he was handsome and a notorious flirt. Women adored his humor and were happy to fall into bed with him. I had spotted him with the Casp twins earlier and he seemed well on his way to another wild night.

I gritted my teeth and avoided the room that Tallis had set Cami up in. It was part of his testing and I couldn't intervene on her behalf, not that I didn't try. He'd just sniffed, those dark eyes rolling with irritation.

"We discussed this! My rules stand. I want her humiliated, teased and taunted. Let's see how she can handle herself in a room of Legion before you swoop in and protect her."

I swallowed my protestations, hoping Cami could hold herself together for the night. I knew if I went in there I wouldn't be able to hold myself back. My creature was moving restlessly under my skin, wanting to be close to her. Tallis set himself up in the corner where I was sure she couldn't see him. I watched him watch her, his dark eyes dancing with amusement and sick pleasure at seeing her at the mercy of our fellow Legion.

My fingers itched to snatch up a drink for the numbing warmth that would spread through my body, but I learned a long time ago that being drunk always ended up worse for me. I was a part of the Kerys triad, but the other Legion did not accept me. Even if they knew my true bloodline, stories of my creature had filtered down to everyone in this room and many had taunted me with the fact at some point. Ambrose never missed an opportunity to lance me with a dig. I didn't trust them not to do it again, and I would not put myself in a position to make it easier for others to be cruel. Tallis had passed his tests, like all Legion, in a manufactured arena, but Melbak had tested me in darker ways. Mine had come in the shadows, split lips and sneers. As a child, I'd learned to read a room and knew when to make myself scarce, lest I was attacked. Cami was like me. We were outcasts.

So, I moped in the corner until I couldn't take it anymore. I saw Tallis talking with Fenar and I stomped over.

"Where is Cami?" I asked, perturbed that none of us had our eyes on her. Tallis clapped his hand on my shoulder.

"Relax, you're so wound up over her. She's with Cove, if you must know. She had to freshen up."

He frowned briefly at the mention of Cove and I wondered if their meeting had been a good one.

"Cove?" Fenar's head snapped away from the crowd as he plugged into the conversation again. "She's not with Cami. She's been talking to that group over there for the last half hour."

I followed his line of sight. She was holding a slip of paper, her hand clutching her mouth as she laughed. I walked over to her, surprised when I felt Tallis slide up beside me.

"Cove, where is Cami?" I asked, trying to quieten the flurry of fear building inside me. Cami was fine. She couldn't come to any harm here, but still I had thoughts of her locked in a dark space, her useless human limbs unable to fight back and free herself. My creature surged inside me, agitated. Cove clutched the paper to her chest, her eyes flickering to Tallis with barely concealed mirth.

"Oh, oh Bossman." She choked on a laugh while her companions covered their mouths. "I don't know where she is," she admitted, her shoulder popping casually. Tallis narrowed his eyes at her, snatching the paper from her hand. His eyes widened comically as he looked at whatever was there. He scrunched it up and threw it on the ground, his hands turning orange.

"Who did this?" he demanded, sending Cove and her friends into peals of laughter.

I spun on my heel, hurrying to the room where Tallis had perched Cami to be tormented. The spot where she had been all night was empty. I couldn't breathe for a second, my hand gripping the doorjamb as a wave of dizziness crashed over me. My heart thumped in my chest, hard enough that my ears pulsed from the force.

"Where is she?" It was Fenar, he looked worried, which surprised me. I couldn't stop my mind from cycling through worst-case scenarios. I certainly couldn't speak. Would someone have taken her? Fenar answered my unspoken question.

"No one would touch her, even if she is a human." His lips pressed together, losing all their color as Tallis stormed up to us.

"The human?" he bit out, looking like he wanted to set her on fire, not to help locate her for her safety.

"Check the cleaning rooms?" Fenar hedged, and at Tallis's nod, he slipped through the crowd. He moved quicker than I would expect to hunt down a human he didn't truly care for. My creature was roiling inside me. Each turn made me feel like I was going to vomit.

"Could she have left?" I said, my voice cracking. I couldn't look at Tallis, my eyes glued to the space she had inhabited. People seemed to give it a wide berth as if she was still there.

"She can't get into the apartment without one of us." Tallis's voice was uneasy and to his credit, he looked mildly contrite.

I turned on my heel, my eyes searching for a flash of black, a mask, a curvy brunette with a spine of steel. I couldn't see her, but somehow, I knew.

She was gone.

Shadow

A PRICK OF LIGHT cut through the darkness.

A beacon that I had no choice but to follow.

I had been sleeping for a long time, lost to all-consuming black. I could feel it containing me still, within me, unescapable.

Hope surged, an emotion I wasn't familiar with. It cut through me like a spark to thick, dry kindling.

The light was calling to me. I urged forward.

Cami

MY FEET DANGLED OUTSIDE in the space where the holographic staircase would appear if the button was pressed. I had left the party successfully, feeling a rush of giddiness as I'd hurried down the corridor and into the portal. I'd remembered the sequence Tallis had swiped in the air and even made it back to the apartment, but I couldn't get the door open. It required one of the triad's hands. I sat on the floor for a while before indignation had pushed me to my feet. I wasn't going back to that party, to drag myself there and lower my eyes and beg for help like Tallis would likely make me do.

Instead, I found my way outside. It was the first time since I'd come here and the scent in the air had been a slap to the face. It reminded me of camping. Nostalgia swallowed me up so suddenly that tears pricked my eyes. Dad had taken me camping when I was a kid, just the two of us. We slept in a tent, toasted marshmallows and swam in one of the local rivers. He had taken his fishing rod out and I spent the time watching his line

for movement, reading books and drawing comics. He'd
strung up a hammock for me once, but I had wanted to
be close to him, the spice of his aftershave and sweat,
the scent was safety to me. All things that sounded so
insignificant, gross even. Who would covet sweat? But
it took me back to a time when I was small, easily
encompassed in my dad's arms. When he was the sun
and my every look tracked his movements, desperate for
the rays on my skin.

Things got too busy when the boys were born,
especially with Percy's cerebral palsy. My parents
seemed to work more and more, depleted in energy. I'd
been bratty as I tipped over the cusp into adulthood. It
had taken its toll on my dad, especially. He bugged me
to go on another camping trip. I didn't want to, couldn't
think of anything worse than being in his company
without phone service. I had turned him down that day
when everything changed. When fate had shown me the
importance of family and given me a debt that I would
never be able to pay.

All of that weighed on me as I leaned my head on the
pillar. I stared out at the dark and listened to the strange
sounds, drowsing a little. I wiped the grogginess from
my face with my palm. There was a slight breeze which
shifted strands of hair off my face in a gentle caress. My
feet tingled, the sensation lost from the time I had spent
sitting.

I looked down and yelped, yanking my feet up,
scrambling back from the ledge on all fours. I peered
over the ledge, seeing the undulating spread of Gaer and
the tendril that had been reaching up, about to touch my
foot.

"What in the world?" My fingers shook as I inspected my boot to make sure there was nothing on it. I had another look, it was still there, the one tendril reaching up, quivering in the air. I froze. I could feel the despair pouring off of it in waves. Desperation hit me in equal parts.

It felt? Albion had said it was sentient, but what was it? The tendril coaxed me, waving to me as if trying to get me to come closer. I scooted forward to get a closer look at the strange substance. It looked like the night sky made into liquid, the stars like glitter shining in pure black. It lifted higher, a tentative stretch that made my eyebrows furrow. What was it doing, trying not to spook me?

"Can you speak to me, understand me?" I asked it, feeling stupid. I wrapped my hands around myself, checking that I was close enough that it couldn't lunge at me.

The tendril moved up and down, resembling a nod, which made me shiver. It could understand me? I scooted a little closer, cocking my head, and it bounced with excitement.

"Will you hurt me?" It shook its pointed end vigorously. "What do you want?"

It seemed to point at me.

"You want me?" I said, mystified. I laughed despite myself. "You'd be the only one."

My fingers wrapped around the ledge without thinking, only to adjust my seating. But the tendril didn't hesitate. It lunged forward, wrapping around my fingers. A searing pain coursed through the skin it touched. I cried out as I watched the Gaer seep into my skin. I saw white for a few seconds until the hold it had on me snapped clean and I stumbled back on my ass. I didn't wait, scuttling back to hit the wall, my breath panting as I held my hand to my chest. The door to the building slid open, and it took me a second to realize it was my triad who had come racing out. Wellyn looked about wildly, sliding on his knees before me and yanking me into his arms.

"Cami, what is it? We heard you scream." His hands danced over me obsessively, checking for injury and reassuring himself I was safe. Fenar peered over the edge.

"Don't! It's Gaer," I cried, and he stumbled back. Tallis steadied him, lifting onto his toes to see the Gaer over the ground.

"Did it touch you?" Tallis said, looming over me, his face pale as he glanced between the ledge and me. My throat seemed to swell as I fought for the words. I was still cradling my hand. I looked down at the unmarred skin as if it the black had never covered it just moments before. There were no marks. Even the pain had subsided, leaving nothing but a warm and comforting tingle. I don't know why, but I shook my head, the lie feeling like a blanket to shield me from the shock of what I just experienced.

I needed a second to breathe and the three of them were crowding me. Wellyn with his hands softly caressing, Fenar looking at the ledge with a bristle and his sharp fangs poking through his teeth, and Tallis with his arms crossed, tension radiating off him.

"What would happen i-if it did?" I asked, trying and failing to keep the stutter out of my voice. Fenar took off his coat and slung it around my shoulders. The adrenaline crash was hitting me and my teeth were chattering like crazy. Tallis's eyes promised murder as he answered my question.

"You'd be dead. It turns skin black immediately and death follows soon after."

"Can you stand?" Wellyn whispers in my ear as I looked at my fingers with confusion. They weren't black. They felt good, warm and tingling. Maybe I had imagined it. I nodded, and he helped me to my feet, Fenar coming up behind me to badger my arms into his jacket. He squeezed them once, like he had to check I was alright as well.

The journey back to the apartment was tense and quiet. I had hoped to fall into bed, but Tallis put that idea to flames as he exploded and whirled on me as soon as the door was closed. He backed me up against the kitchen bench, pressing me into the sharp edge and caging me in with his hands.

"What were you thinking, leaving Ambrose's? Going outside? You could have been hurt!"

I was stunned silent, the proximity of his rage stealing any words I could have said.

"You are the most foolish human to exist!" He ranted, not done with shouting at me yet, apparently. "I should wring your neck! You clearly don't value it."

I grimaced in disgust as bit of spittle flew from his mouth and hit my chin. Wellyn and Fenar stood in the back again, letting him scream and shout at me as usual. I put my hands flat on Tallis's chest, grunting at the static that jolted down my fingers at the contact. His eyes widened, and he trailed off as I used everything in me to shove him away.

"Get out of my face," I warned, pointing a finger at him when I saw him start towards me again.

"That's enough, Tallis," Fenar said, stepping in between us and positioning my body so he shielded me from the fuming Legion. Wellyn slid in next to him, forming a barrier.

"She disobeyed, she must accept punishment!" He raged, standing his ground. My eyes kept drawing to my fingers, the pins and needles still racing up and down. I wanted my mom. I wanted a reprieve in her arms, the safety of being cared and provided for. I wanted someone to switch this nightmare off and take me back to Earth where I was a wreck, but at least I knew what was going on. Ever since I'd arrived here, my brain had been overloaded. I hadn't caught up, just sunk deeper into overwhelm. I couldn't let them see that though, especially not Tallis, who hadn't let up his glare. His hands crossed over his chest. I expected Fenar to relent, but he shook his head.

"Not tonight. You've punished her enough with that mask. She's endured humiliation and taunts according to your wishes. She needs rest. You can continue your futile games tomorrow," he admonished Tallis, who seemed stunned into silence.

Wellyn vibrated in front of me, his skin shivering like he was freezing. He fished his hand back, groping for me and latching on to my wrist. He seemed to have a wordless conversation with Tallis, who didn't seem capable of responding. Wellyn broke off the intense eye contact and turned to me. His hand slid to my lower back as he turned me and marched me towards my bedroom.

"Did you see that—his creature?" I heard Fenar whisper in awe.

Wellyn and Fenar standing up for me was shocking, but the redhead's reaction was more surprising. Wellyn had looked to Tallis for guidance since I'd met him, content to let him be the voice of the triad. I wondered if it cost him to speak up, to push out of what was his obvious default setting of silent obedience. He seemed so different from the other two, but I couldn't deny the warmth that spread through me at his fierce protection. I had been so close to cracking, my nerves jangled from the draining night and then the Gaer. The memory of the pain didn't marry with the delicious heat that seemed to course through me now. I couldn't think, my thoughts disjointed and many. They piled in on each other, crowding my mind.

Wellyn pushed my shoulders, urging me to sit on the edge of my bed. He was kneeling in front of me, busily undoing my laces. His fingers wrapped around my ankle gently as he pulled my boots off, goosebumps erupting at the coolness of his touch. It felt like an anchor and I craved it. In my frazzled state, I leaned my forehead forward until it rested on his shoulder. The coolness engulfed me and I let out a sigh, my lungs burning from holding my breath. Wellyn inched forward. I felt his fingers press on the bed as he adjusted my weight.

"Cami?" he asked, my name loaded with questions and worry.

"Thank you," I said softly, slightly muffled in the space. "I couldn't—"

"Don't thank me, we never should have agreed to his terms." His words were sharp but I knew they weren't directed at me. I felt the prick of them anyway, the regret. "You should rest, you had a scare with the Gaer, and Tallis's tests had to have been horrible."

He eased me down, tugging lightly on the robes.

"Do you want me to take this off?" he asked, and I shook my head, already half asleep. I was running on adrenaline and I had hit my wall. I heard a creak and shuffle as Wellyn settled himself on the floor, obviously intending to watch over me as I slept.

Cami

I ROSE FROM MY bed, my forehead drenched with sweat. The scent of salt made me wrinkle my nose and my tongue felt like a drying slug caught in the blistering sun. Not a good look. I made to swing off the bed before I realized my sheets were different, the white replaced by black silk. It pooled around my naked waist.

My naked waist?

As I realized I was completely nude in the bed, my hands flew to my chest. My eyes darted around the room, blinking against the pervasive darkness, knowing I looked like a startled animal. My skin prickled at the sensation of being watched. I couldn't see past the bed and there were no noises, but I knew I was not in the apartment. I don't know how I knew it. There was a pressing on my body, like the air here was heavier and tangible.

A hiss came from the corner and a light flared to life. I squealed, yanking the sheets up over my body.

There was a shadow sprawled in a seat. A giant, muscular shadow.

"You have a beautiful body, precious one," it spoke, the heat in the low, masculine voice making me shiver. I clutched the sheets about my neck, my mind racing for a clue to what could have brought me here.

"Who are you? Where am I?" I said, my teeth clenching together so quickly my tongue narrowly escaped being chomped on.

The shadow chuckled. "You have the scent of a boost. Does the cruelty of this curse never cease?" he said, speaking more to himself and not answering my question.

"I'm not your boost," I retorted, annoyance overriding the fear I knew should course through me right now, finding myself in a strange bed with not a scrap of clothing on.

"Fear not. I would never hurt you,"

"Where am I?" I asked again, squinting my eye to make out his face. It was like he was made of shadow; his form was there, but the details were missing. I could see he was tall and broad, the lines of his face smooth onyx. I could see a smile, but it looked like bleeding water colors.

"You are only dreaming, precious. My name is Eykc, and you're here as a harsh twist of fate, it seems."

Leaning forward, my grip on the sheets still tight. I was dreaming, that made sense, but there was something familiar about this place and I couldn't put my finger on it.

"I guess we are doing this, then. What's a strange nighttime journey when I've been uprooted from Earth?

My name is Cami. I'm normally clothed when I meet new people, and not in their beds."

He chuckled again under his breath, his head shaking slowly. "I should have known," he said, voice guttural and tortured. "Of course, you, as a boost, are the key to ending all of this."

I flopped back in bed, shifting on to my side so that I could keep Eyke in my sight.

"There is a triad who I am a boost for already. Sorry to disappoint you." I propped my head on my hand. The chair creaked under his weight as he kicked his long, thick legs out.

"A triad? Is that how they solved our absence? A boost needs a fourth. They cursed themselves when they trapped us in this state." His voice was so deep it sounded like gravel.

"What curse are you talking about?" I sat up, catching the sheet as it went to slide down and reveal more of me than I wanted.

"How are the boosts? I imagine they suffer, as you would have had I not found you. I will need to receive your boost for it to truly work."

I thought of Nakasha and the welts spreading over her skin. How she had curled in the bed, her limbs looking frail even after she'd pierced my skin with deadly claws earlier. I felt my eyelids droop, my head slipping from my hand.

"Melbak is withering, isn't it? It needs all twelve founding families to function. If I'm in here, then it means we failed. They cursed us."

Eyke's voice flowed over me, and I realized what made this place seem so familiar. My whole body was tingling like when the Gaer touched me.

Eyke

My fist slammed against the hard confines of my cell. There was no give, which I found out the first ten times I did it. Cami, the boost, had disappeared and with her the calm that had spread over my racing heart. Now she was gone.

My heart was hammering away in my chest, the thump of my pulse in my ear. It roared like a waterfall as I swiped my arm down on the small table, sending it hurtling into the wall. The crash muffled, this strange space muting any loud noises. I couldn't stop myself now. I tore the silk sheets from the bed and crushed them into a bundle and let them hit the wall as well. How much time had passed since I had failed and was sent to a maddening slumber?

I had no memories, just impressions and a hunger that drove me searching, instinctively knowing the only way to end this cruel curse was by taking a boost. The one thing I swore I would never do. The idea of it would have disturbed me, were I still the Legion I once was. But

Cami's sharp scent still lingered in the air, turning me wild like a beast. I gripped the base of the bed, sending it up and grunting as it turned on its side. In the space of a moment, everything I once stood for had melted around me.

My chest heaved as I looked at the mess in the room. The absence of a door, sparse furniture that I had designed for someone else, yet I was here instead, betrayed and trapped for such a long time that Melbak was suffering from our absence. Unless the others had managed to escape. I had wanted the prejudice to stop. I had wanted to prove the strength of our families. Instead, they had won.

So why was there a human boost here again? Were the Heads truly that desperate that they would turn to the very thing they punished us for? Was the past about to repeat itself?

I leaned against the wall, my chest aching with pressure that I swore would crack my ribcage open. That had been what I was trying to stop, the unfair balance after the sanctions they placed on us. A soft hiccup pressed its way past my lips when I thought of House Kindale and its sub-houses, Lea and Canoste. Legion who had become imprisoned because of past association with humans. Now I had to go down the same path, to take the boost that had appeared to me. She was what I'd mindlessly been searching for while in the Gaer form. I'd found her, I'd hunted her, and I'd claimed her.

My stomach still roiled at the idea of triads. They'd truly struck us from our rightful place. But could I be the fourth when it went against everything I fought against?

I sunk to my knees, bringing the black sheets to my nose and letting Cami's scent of surround me. My heart slowed to a languid thump and I squeezed my eyes closed. This room could not contain me forever. Gripping the bed frame, I heaved it so all four legs were back on the ground. I lifted the table and set it on the hard ground, slowly righting the room. I was still alive. I was still sane. Everything else could wait.

Cami

THE NEXT TIME I woke, I was in my actual bed and I could tell I was still dressed. That was a bonus. I supposed Eyke had been telling the truth, that I'd been dreaming. But why had my skin tingled like my fingers had after the Gaer seeped into my skin? He'd mentioned a curse, the same thing that Ziggie had said to me.

Wellyn was in the corner of the room, his back jammed up against the wall and one arm tucked under his armpit. His mouth was open as he snored softly, his russet curls a mess, falling half over his face. I cleared my throat and he jerked awake, his head slamming back into the wall. He winced and his hand came up to rub at the spot.

"You slept here all night?" I asked him, and he nodded, looking sheepish.

"It was impossible to leave. I was worried about you after last night," he said, his teeth clenching as if he waited for me to argue with him. A burst of warmth spread through my chest instead. He'd given me space but watched over me. He'd stepped up to Tallis, finally. I smiled. He startled, his eyes widening in shock.

"Thanks, Wellyn, it was a shit night. I actually appreciate you looking out for me."

He scrambled to his feet, a wide smile cracking his own face, his cheeks pink. "Why don't you go to the cleaning room? I'll order you pancakes."

I needed to get clean, having slept in my robes last night. What I really wanted was a bath. I needed a good soak with bubbles. Lots of bubbles. Wellyn must have seen something in my face as he hurried to add.

"With cappuccino, I remember."

"Do you have pools here? I am craving a soak in water. I'm so used to being able to have a bath all the time."

Wellyn stumbled, leaning against the wall, his eyes open wide again. Okay, I guess water really is a rarity here. He swallowed deeply, his Adam's apple bobbing.

"There used to be the Lost Lake, but the Gaer has infected it. The springs would have been perfect. They are hot springs, but Gaer often infects them as well. It's no longer safe for Legion."

At the thought of a hot spring, I groaned. "I would give anything for a dip in warm water right now," I confessed, and Wellyn chewed on his lower lip.

"Perhaps I could take you there? The Gaer might have spared it today. I am only working until midafternoon. You could accompany me to my work, I'm sure, and I could take you there afterwards."

I pulled my bag out and rifled through it, pulling out a pair of casual denim shorts and a loose, dark tee shirt.

"Where do you work?" I hadn't given it much thought where they all went during the day.

"I work at the Vault. I'm an assistant there."

An idea popped into my head. Perhaps I could investigate what Ziggie had talked about last night, what my dream had obviously taken inspiration from and created in its vivid confines.

"Do they have history books? I feel like I should familiarize myself with Legion, boosts and everything. Considering I am your boost."

Wellyn flushed darker and shuffled his feet. I could see he was vibrating again.

"Absolutely, I can set you up with everything you need!" A touch of glee seeped into his voice. I had to grin.

I held up my clothes. "I'm going to get changed," I said and Wellyn nodded, darting for the door as if he was glad he had an excuse to leave.

I refused to wear the robes or the mask, although I don't know where it even ended up after last night. I was going to wear my own clothes. Tallis could jump off a bridge.

It turned out to be a non-issue. He only gave me cold once-over when I walked out, leaving within seconds without even uttering one word. It was almost strange to see Tallis and not fight with him. Fenar was missing as well, it seemed. When Wellyn slid a plate of pancakes in front of me with a steaming coffee, I groaned, leaning over to take a whiff. I had missed coffee so much.

"Pancakes for my pancake," he said shyly, his lip turning up in a lopsided smile.

"Pancake?" I laughed, and he shrugged.

"You're sweet, aren't you?" he teased, and I shook my head as I dug in. Was he flirting with me? I couldn't deal with his adorable self.

"I don't know about that, but I'll let it slide for now."

The Vault was a cross between a library and an archive. It had the musty scent of books that had congregated in one space for too long. Only a short walk from the apartment, it was a nondescript building also on stilts that opened into high ceilings and rows and rows of books. I walked into the circular center and looked up, taking in the mass of shelves. There was a staircases that led to what looked like numerous storeys and I could see cubicles tucked in the eaves.

"Master Leave. This is a place of work, not a social area. Your friend can only access books if she has the paperwork." A nasal voice came from above me and I looked up to see flaring nostrils, narrowed eyes and hair snatched back so tightly that the eyebrows were raised in a permanent question. An older lady with ears drooping like an elephant was regarding me like I was a speck of dirt.

"Madam Reason, this is my boost, Cami," Wellyn said, pride effused in his expression as he glanced over at me. My stomach jumped at the warmth in his voice, the ease of his claim on me. Like he really wanted me to be his boost and wasn't ashamed that I was a human at all. Madam Reason dropped the paper she'd been holding and gaped, her gaze running between the two of us.

"A boost? You have a boost? Oh, but she's human," she stuttered, a mixture of disgust and shock flooding her face.

"You scored the human boost?" Another, deeper voice came from the staircase, and I looked towards the man wandering down the steps. "I heard they had given a triad one. I didn't realize they were scraping the barrel for volunteers." He had jet black hair shorn close to his head. He tucked his hands in his pockets, but I could see golden scales running up his exposed forearms. He flashed me a handsome smile and bent his head in a small bow. Wellyn stiffened beside me, and I didn't miss how he skirted closer.

"Seb Decker. It's a pleasure," he said to me, flashing me another smile. The scales didn't cover his whole body, but his skin had an unnatural sheen, like the sun had burnished him with its rays.

"Hi," I said, taking my cue from the rigid tension in Wellyn's body. He didn't like this guy. They weren't friendly, despite what Seb's tone and mannerisms suggested. Seb looked me over with unfiltered interest, a hunger showing as he boldly walked around me. He stopped and clapped a hand on Wellyn's shoulder, harder than necessary.

"How has your creature changed from the boost?" he asked casually, and Wellyn shrugged his grip off his shoulder. I'd heard this mentioned before. I knew Fenar had a creature, a wolf, but Wellyn had mentioned nothing to me of his.

"Cami will do research while I work today. I trust that as a boost she'll have the access she needs."

He spoke to Madam Reason and nudged me forward with his hand on my lower back. She didn't reply, her fingers scrabbling at the paper she'd dropped, a red dot stamped on each of her cheeks. I wondered why it

seemed such a surprise that Wellyn had a boost. I knew
boosts were rare, but it seemed the reactions came from
Wellyn having one rather than me being a human.

"What are you interested in, Cami?" Seb tried to
squeeze up next to me on the narrow staircase as we
walked to the upper level. I looked at the shelves and
chewed on my lip.

"History of boosts? I want to learn about the past, as I
am obviously not from Melbak." I said, reluctantly.

"I will get you what you need," Wellyn said, his voice
low.

Seb chuckled amiably, "You can't do that Wellyn,
you're just an assistant." He said it with a slight sneer, like
I should know Wellyn's position. "I am the Level One
Archiver. It's my responsibility to serve the needs for any
visitors to the Vault." His scales flashed in the light that
streamed through the windows. Wellyn vibrated behind
me. Seb flashed a satisfied smile at him. He had won
some silent battle when Wellyn deflated a little. Turning
to me, his fingers skated down my arm.

"Seb will take care of you while I work. If you need
anything, he can get it for you," he said through gritted
teeth, shooting Seb an unreadable look before marching
down the stairs. Seb sighed and motioned for me to go
into a nearby cubicle. I slid into the padded seat and
looked at him.

"Wellyn and I started at the Vault together you know,"
Seb said leaning on the desk, flashing me those shiny,
white teeth again. "Such a shame that he hasn't managed
a promotion like I have."

"You sound real cut up about it," I drawled, raising
my eyebrow. He rocked back on his heels, assessing me

again. I didn't like the weight of his gaze and the ease in which he indulged himself, like he was entitled to it. To me.

"I'd like those books now, if you don't mind," I said, tapping the table with impatience. The agreeable air Seb was putting on faltered as a dark look flashed over his face.

"Of course," he said tightly, disappearing into the shelves.

The stack on my table grew so much that it shielded me from the rest of the Vault. Ensconced in my book fort, I flipped through thick tomes whose spines cracked as I opened them. Seb had given me a scanner that interpreted the language written in the books, but it was tedious to use it. Asking it to translate the words to English seemed to make the scanner implode and information took forever to access.

Frustration bubbled in my veins. I'd learned nothing new about boosts in all of my reading. There didn't seem to be relevant information up until two hundred years ago. I had read a lot about the founding families, which niggled in my brain until I remembered what Eyke had said last night. He'd mentioned twelve founding families, but there were only listings in the books of nine. They chose the Legion Heads from the founding families via a competition that occurred every four years called the Vinko. I could find no mention of cursed Legion or boost sickness, but I also didn't want to ask Seb if he knew anything. Something told me he would use the information to leverage what he wanted.

Seb returned to pester me every so often, placing another book he'd thought might interest me. He tried to engage me in conversation, probing for answers about whether I had boosted Wellyn yet, and it seemed to agitate him I wouldn't give him a straightforward answer. The mask he projected slipped each time. He tried to charm me, his leer ever-present as his fingers grazed against mine every chance he got.

"Any triad would be lucky to have you, despite your human nature. I don't believe the stories about humans causing the Culling you know." I tried not to roll my eyes. I just loved how Legion considered it a compliment to want me despite being a human.

I slammed the book shut and shifted it to the side with a sigh. "More than half of my triad would disagree. Apparently being human is a big turnoff in Melbak."

I couldn't help the comment that snuck out, and I regretted it immediately when Seb took it as an invitation to stay. He leaned his hip against the table, effectively boxing me in.

"You could have your choice of triads. You don't need to stay with the Kerys one, you know." He inched closer, his handsome face dropping to whisper, "You have given none of them a boost yet. Until then, you could move on to one who would treat you like royalty."

"I don't have a choice," I corrected him, thinking on what Albion had said. The Heads didn't want to chance a human boost before I proved I would give the same benefits as a Legion. Seb's lips twisted in a smirk.

"They'd like you to think that, but Tallis is a fool and Fenar and Wellyn are unworthy. Their blood is almost worthless in Melbak. Why should they get a boost when there are triads with more deserving lineage?"

I leaned away, not liking the manic way he was looking at me. His fingers shot out, circling my shoulder and digging in. He pressed into me, his face close as he sniffed behind my ear. I froze, any noise I could have made silenced, shocked by the tight grip he had on me.

"You might be human, but you smell stronger than any other boost I've scented. They should have taken your blood the second they had a chance. Right now, you're a precious commodity and I—"

"Get. Your. Hand. Off. My. Boost." Wellyn's voice was coarse gravel and pure fury. Seb took a second to release me, and backed away immediately with a shrug.

"Relax, Wellyn. Cami and I were just talking." I sucked in a deep breath, my own fingers massaging the ache Seb's rough grip had left.

"Don't talk to my boost. *Shek* off and leave her alone. Now!" Wellyn ordered. He kneeled and folded me into his arms. I relaxed into the cool shell of his embrace, tucking my head into his neck. It felt so natural to find comfort in him like this. I heard Seb snort and stomp away.

"Did he hurt you?" he whispered, his fingers running through my dark hair. I shook my head, not wanting to speak. "I've finished up now. Shall we see about a dip in a spring?"

He wouldn't stop touching me, his fingers shaking as he threaded them together with mine. Not even when Madam Reason gave him—and by default, me—major stink eye did he stop. He all but dragged me past a glowering Seb, who opened his mouth to say something as we passed but reconsidered it when he saw the set of Wellyn's jaw.

We wandered to the edge of the blackened forest and he triggered a path that rose out of the ground, columns wrapped in the Gaer-resistant material. I accepted his hand as he hoisted me up, and we walked tentatively down the path. I watched the Gaer roil underneath us, wondering if it would extend like it had last night. But it didn't seem to even move, only sluggishly shifting like it was exhausted.

Interpreting my thoughts, Wellyn said, "It is more active at night." He looked at me. "Will you tell me what Seb said?"

"You don't like him?" I asked, knowing it already but curious to hear tender-hearted Wellyn say it.

He scowled. "He only cares about status. Unfortunately, Legion agree with him. My parents abandoned me as a child. According to everyone else, my bloodline is unworthy. Legion used to be divided, there was no peace until nine founding families brought us together and made a binding agreement for peace. If you don't belong to one of those families, they consider you lesser. I am only in my position at the Vault because Tallis is in my triad. He's the only one of us who can claim a respectable bloodline. Kerys was one of the founding families. Even then, they won't promote me no matter how hard I work. I'll always be worthless, because my bloodline is nothing and my crea—" he cut off, looking furiously into the tree line.

I wanted him to finish his thought, but he brightened and pointed ahead. "It looks like the way is clear." He grinned and the tension in his features wiped away, leaving it boyish and beautiful, his freckles stark against his pale skin. His ruddy curls begged to be spun around my finger.

I looked ahead to a white domed building, the surrounding ground covered in fallen debris but no Gaer. My heart skipped as Wellyn grabbed my hand, yanking me towards the entrance. We slipped inside and I deflated a little. It was beautiful, the ceiling opening in an inner circle, letting the sun shine down on where the spring would undoubtably be, had it not been teeming with tendrils of Gaer. Cathedral-type windows lined the side of the walls and the back opened to a spectacular view of a Gaer-blackened lake. The spring itself was black, glittering and sludgy. Wellyn's face fell, and I sighed, patting him on the back.

"It's okay, maybe another time," I said, masking the disappointment I felt. He shook his head and looked down at the ground.

"I got my hopes up for a moment. I'm sorry to fail you again." He meandered over to the carved stone bench in the wall and sank into it, staring at the Gaer woefully.

"You didn't fail me," I said, wanting to smooth the pain from his expression.

"Seb is right, you know. You could have your pick of triads. There are only a handful of boosts that presented this year and still so many triads left wanting. Legion are desperate for boosts. I never even entertained the thought that I would have one."

"Do you want me to pick a different triad? Albion made it sound like yours was the only choice I had. I can't afford to have him stop payments to my family. Especially with Tallis's threats."

Wellyn shot me a look. "Of course I don't want you to. I am honored to have you as my boost. If you choose to share your blood with me, that is. No matter what you decide, I will make sure your family gets what was promised. You must miss them."

My chest ached at the thought of my family, and I massaged it softly. Wellyn scooted closer, his leg pressing against mine.

"They are everything to me," I admitted. "I-I made a mistake, a huge one, and my family paid the price. Fixing the past is impossible, but I can do this. I can make sure they want for nothing."

"What happened?" Wellyn asked, his fingers closing around mine. I looked at the spring infected with Gaer and swallowed hard. I hadn't spoken to anyone about that night. The blistering fight I'd had with Ma, and the grounding which had sent me into a rage because I was an adult and could do what I wanted. Dad had asked me to go camping with him again and I'd told him I would rather choke on a chicken bone. I'd slammed the door to the bedroom so hard it had woken Percy and he had been crying.

"I wanted an escape. Everything felt too heavy. I was an only child for a long time, until I was thirteen years old. When my twin brothers were born, Percy and Aaron, it was like a bomb had exploded my life as I knew it. I loved them, but Percy had challenges. He has a disorder that means he needs lots of care," I told Wellyn, swallowing thickly. "I felt burned out and my parents were always too busy for me, it seemed. I snuck out of my house and went to a party. I didn't know these people very well and my friends bailed after an hour. But I stayed and made poor decisions."

My memories of that night were fragmented. Shards of shattered glass that sliced when I remembered, invisible cuts that bled inside me. Hazy memories of drinking, a plastic cup filled to the brim with dark brown liquor. It tasted foul until it didn't taste like anything. The room was spinning, the muffled speakers and the dark bedroom. Grabbing a hand and leading him somewhere. Strange lips against mine and my body, spreading my legs and rolling away after. His face a blur, but the lingering smell of cologne, my skin drenched in it. I'd thrown up in the toilet, missing it a little, leaving a chunky brown mess on white tiles. Hands curled under my arms, pushing me out the door. Raised voices. Fury at the mess I'd made. Then the way my fingers seemed like they weren't attached to my body when I tried to use them. The echo of a phone ringing in my ear and dad's disembodied, fatigued voice when he picked up, finally.

Thinking about it made me want to be sick. I should have known better.

"I asked my dad to help me, to come and get me because I couldn't walk, let alone drive."

Wellyn listened while I sifted through the murk of that night, my eyes unseeing as I filled them with memories. How dad sighed, how he'd bit his tongue from chastising me and promised he'd be there soon. The pathetic fumbling as I tried to nudge my drunk, addled mind to send him my location. How I'd fallen asleep on the porch of a stranger's house, shivering in the cool night. I'd woken in the early morning, my skin stinking of spirits and my mouth like a desert. My first thought had been anger. It incensed me that my dad hadn't come to get me, his only daughter. I'd ordered a rideshare and gone home, stumbling in the door with streaky makeup and vomit-stained clothing, the inside of my legs sticky with a strangers cum. I stood there clenching my thighs together in utter shame as my aunty opened the door, looking ruined.

"A car hit my dad on his way to get me, so bad that he broke his back, lost the use of his legs. As if that wasn't bad enough, he got an infection while he was in the hospital and has been struggling ever since. My ma spends all her time at the hospital. My two brothers live with my aunty. Without Dad's income, they had to sell the house I grew up in. They needed money for Dad's hospital bills, for my brother's carer and to take the pressure off."

I couldn't meet Wellyn's eyes, knowing I would see the judgement I felt every time I delved into that box of jagged memories. My eyes filled with tears.

"I ruined everything because I had a tantrum, thinking my life was so hard. I drank so much I made choices I never would otherwise. I'm here because it was the only way for me to make it right. On Earth I was working as much as I could, but it still wasn't enough. With this money, my family can be together again. So, it doesn't matter, you see? As long as they get the money, I don't care what happens to me. I deserve it." I felt the stab in my heart, the hatred I felt towards myself sharpened into a weapon I could wound myself with. Wellyn's thumb was stroking mine and I could feel the slight tremor of his body. My hand jerked in his hold, bile rising in my throat. I was nothing, a disgusting waste of space. I deserved every bad thing that happened to me.

"Don't," Wellyn whispered, his fingers coming under my chin and turning it tentatively to meet his eyes. They were the strangest color, violet and shining like they were back lit. I hadn't seen them so luminous before. "I can see how much that hurt you to share. You think I'll hate you? Is that it? You couldn't be further from the truth. You made a mistake, but you gave up everything to make it right. Do you know how brave you are? I knew you were strong. I could tell nothing Tallis could do would break you. Many Legion have failed the tests you have survived, and even battered and hating yourself, you are powerful."

His eyes searched mine, soft and wide as I tried and failed to stop tears from coasting down my cheeks. My chin wobbled in his grip. He didn't think I was disgusting. I didn't fill him with hatred. Redemption was something I couldn't fathom, so used to thinking of myself as tainted. I ruined my dad's life. I almost ruined my family. And yet, Wellyn looked at me with awe, like he understood my pain and didn't judge me at all.

He leaned in and brushed his lips against mine gently. I gasped at the soft sensation, the sweetness of the kiss. So much more than I ever deserved. He wouldn't let go of my chin. I tried to jerk away, but he shook his head.

"You are not that person who made a mistake. You are a boost now. My boost, if you'll have me. Let me be yours. I'll spend the rest of time proving how brave and powerful you truly are. You can't spend the rest of your life hating yourself for the choices you can't change. You left your family, sacrificed yourself to ensure they had what they needed to be together and secure."

I hesitated.

"Seb mentioned that until one of you takes my blood, I am still 'available.'"

Wellyn's face darkened. "He said that? He wants you for his triad?" His hands dropped to my shoulders, squeezing them like he needed to touch me.

"Something like that. That I'm a precious commodity," I clarified, and he cursed, eyes flashing with that bright light again.

"Would you?" he asked. "Please be my boost? Forget Tallis and Fenar, could you be mine?"

Cami

My heart battered against my ribcage as I absorbed his words. He looked so tense, almost ravenous in his desire. There was something about being close to him that soothed me, unlike Seb, who had distressed me like bugs crawled under my skin. If Wellyn was my boost, I was safe. I wouldn't be a pawn that someone else could use, a commodity to be traded and coveted.

"How do we..." I faltered, "I don't know how to do it." Wellyn lowered his head onto my hands. He seemed to be stunned, his mouth gaping like a fish out of water. When he rose again, he was buzzing. I could feel the vibration.

He looked positively radiant. "Cami, thank you for this gift."

He held my hands reverently in his shaking grasp, then reached into his pocket and pulled out a small blade. He flicked it open and pressed the tip to my wrist. I squeaked at the prick of blood pooled up from the small nick. He lifted my wrist to his mouth, kissing it tenderly before licking slight wound. It sent a shiver through my body. Obviously, something was twisted and wrong in my brain if the sight of someone sucking up my blood turned me on. He groaned, his eyes rolling back before he fell on my wrist, sucking on the skin and laving his tongue over the wound.

I looked down to see his hard length pressed against his pants. At least I wasn't the only one affected by this boost. Every time he swiped his tongue over my skin, it set off a million arrows that flew straight to my core. My clit was throbbing when he finally released my wrist. The wound was unnoticeable except for the flushed skin where Wellyn had sucked as if his life depended on it. He fell to his knees in front of me, pressing his forehead to my thighs.

"Thank you, thank you." He mumbled garbled compliments, like how my blood tasted like sunlight, how I was the most perfect boost to have ever lived, how much he wanted me. I flushed a little at the last comment. I could see the evidence that he might want me physically still straining in his pants.

Movement from the corner of my eye made me gasp. The Gaer in the spring was disappearing, folding up into itself. The spring water left behind was a clear and beautiful turquoise. I could see the bottom of the white spring and where the water flowed in from outside. Wellyn jumped up, shielding me with his body.

"What is happening?" he said, his voice slightly slurred and mystified. I watched in amazement as every drop of Gaer sucked in on itself until the spring was clear. Still messy from disuse, but not a dark spot to be seen. Wellyn turned and looked at me in awe.

"It's a miracle. I've seen nothing like it," he spoke in a hushed tone.

I tugged him to sit next to me again. "What caused that?"

Wellyn stroked his hand down the side of my face. "If I had to guess, I'd say it was you. Your boost gives power back to Melbak as well as me, perhaps making it strong enough to drive out the Gaer. We'll have to ask Albion."

I was tingling all over and the slight vibration from Wellyn made my mind drift. There was something undeniable about being pressed this close to him. Even after everything that had just happened, his body still gave off a chill. I ran my fingers down his arm, enjoying the way it made him shudder.

"Why are you so cold all the time?" I asked, and he ducked his head immediately. "You don't have to tell me," I added, seeing how my question had shaken him.

"I-I want to," he said hastily, licking his lips. He sucked in a wet breath and looked at me from underneath rusty eyelashes. "I want to so much."

I wanted to run my fingers down his jawline, but seeing he needed some space, I sat back, putting some distance between us.

"You know, Legion are powerful in different ways. Some look different to what you know, with horns and tails, and some have creatures which you have heard about, no doubt. Fenar has a wolf creature. It's powerful. Legion value strength over everything."

He gulped and looked up at me. I could see the vulnerability there.

"You have a creature," I said, and he nodded, his freckles looking like paint splatter on a white sheet of paper. He was so drained of color.

"He's different. I've met no one with a creature like mine. Melbak isn't the best place for him, with water being so rare now."

"He needs water to survive?" I guessed, itching to know so I could crawl into him and soothe the fear etched on every one of his features. I was straining towards him, needing to be close to him. He looked like he was going to be sick.

"Yes," he said softly, swallowing audibly as he seemed to struggle with the words. "I used to get ridiculed as a child if I ever let him out. There were wolves, bears, griffins and even ratids, but my creature was so different from those land-based animals. Eventually he drew away from me, refusing to come out anymore, and even stopped communicating with me. He drew so deep into my mind that our connection was almost separated."

I reached for him, gripping his knee, hoping to be his anchor as I saw the pain swirling in his vision.

"Oh Wellyn, I'm so sorry for you and your creature."

His hand skirted over mine, like he couldn't believe I'd want to touch him.

"Until I met you, Cami," he whispered, eyes bright and locked on me. "My creature rose to the surface for the first time in years. He has wanted to meet you since that first morning when you walked out wearing my shirt." His lip quirked in a tiny smirk.

I smiled. "He wants to meet me? Do you want me to meet him?"

Wellyn looked like he might faint, his lips as pale as his skin, his cool hand clammy over mine.

"W-would you? Would you want to see my creature?" I could smell the reek of fear between his words. It scared him that perhaps I was going to reject his creature, ridicule it like others had so many times before. I leaned forward and pressed a small kiss to his cheek. Settling back on my haunches, I motioned to the warm springs, clear now of Gaer.

"It would be my honor. And he has a perfect place to come out now. As long as the warmth doesn't bother him," I said seriously.

Wellyn choked out a noise as he shook his head. "I need to strip." He hesitated. I nodded, taking off my shoes. As Wellyn stripped down, I dipped my legs in the water. I took in the lean line of his body as he ripped his shirt over his head. He was hairless except for a dusting of red curls that led down to his... half-hard cock. Wellyn dropped his pants with a chuckle as I caught my breath. He was a decent size, proud and thick, jutting from a nest of red hair. I looked away as he walked down the marble steps into the spring. He hissed as the water submerged him to his neck.

"Ready?" he asked, nervous again as he chewed his lip, waiting for my response.

"I can't wait," I promised, leaning forward to watch as his creature emerged. There was a flash of white light.

In Wellyn's place was a giant octopus.

He coasted through the water, his many tentacles languid. He poked his head up and I could see the creature's eyes were the same stunning violet as Wellyn's, but brighter like a torch shan through from inside him. He looked at me almost hesitantly, so I dipped my hand in the water, inviting him closer.

"Hello gorgeous creature," I said, admiring how big he was. He was the size of a Great Dane, his tentacles reaching out even further. Two of them wrapped around my ankles, tugging gently.

"Don't pull me in the water while I have my clothes on," I admonished. "I'd love to swim with you another time, though."

That seemed to placate the creature as he stopped pulling. Instead, his tentacles wound up my legs slowly, almost sensually. I shivered at the sensation. The coolness of Wellyn's skin made sense now, a chill emanating from the slight pull of his suckers as they ran over my calves and up my thighs. A warmth flooded between my legs and I sucked in a surprised breath. The creature watched me intensely.

Suddenly, there was another flash of white. I shielded my eyes. A startled squeak escaped me, which was quickly smothered by a pair of lips on mine. Instead of tentacles there were now two hard hands, fingers digging into my thighs. Wellyn pressed into the space between my legs as if starved for the feel of my skin on his. Half out of the water, his lips attacked mine, his head slanting and pushing deeper as he swallowed every gasp I made, sucking in the breaths that I took like he could only subsist on the oxygen that I had in my body. His hands circled my ribs, holding me still in his grip. I moaned a little at the feel his cock pressed up against my core. I ground against him and his head swung back, a sigh falling from his red, swollen lips. His eyes swirled with intensity as his chest heaved.

"Thank you," he whispered, leaning forward to press a kiss to my throat. "Pancake, you're a gift."

"Wellyn," I breathed as his fingers skimmed the seams of my shorts. I was aching fiercely, the heat between my thighs demanding to be touched.

"My creature wants me to take you, to make you mine." His whispers sent shivers through my body and I arched into his cool chest. Even in the warmth of the springs, he was still shockingly cold. I wanted to feel him pressed up against my whole body.

"Yes," I panted, chasing his lips. "I want that."

He fell on me again, my body bowing under his slick weight and my clothes soaking from the water running off his skin. His nimble fingers slipped under my shirt to palm my breasts in a heady, frantic way. When his fingers passed over my nipples, I jolted.

He growled. "That sound is going to be the death of me." He pushed my shirt up so it bunched around my neck. His lips clamped onto one of my nipples and he sucked, his tongue swirling over the sensitive skin.

"Fuck!" I called out, my legs wrapping around his waist and pulling him closer. It was like he'd sucked on an ice cube. The inside of his mouth was cool like his skin and the sensation sent my skin into a riot of goosebumps. He nipped the swell of my flesh with his teeth and I wanted it harder, wanted it to bruise.

Something primal rose in me, and when I caught his eye, I saw it reflected in his face as well. His eyebrow raised in a question as his teeth grazed over my skin. I sucked in a little breath and nodded frantically. My body was close to exploding. He struck like an adder, his teeth scoring my skin in an instant. With the flare of pain I cried out, but it quickly reduced to a whimper with the sweet press of his tongue as he laved the mark. The knowledge that he was tasting my blood again sent a flush spreading through my body and made my toes curl.

"I need you," I said breathlessly, rubbing against him without shame. He sucked on his mark one more time, leaning back to look at the blue-black imprint of his teeth on the side of my breast. I pulled my shirt off, lobbing it over my head and tossing it to the side.

"I've wanted nothing more," he whispered, his fingers stroking down the side of my hips now, reverently. My fingers shook as I reached for the button on my shorts, popping it open quickly. "You want me? My creature? Us?" he asked, dragging my shorts down achingly slow. I keened as those fingers massage my calves, too far away from my pulsing center.

"I need you," I said again. It sounded like begging. And I was. I'd never been this turned on in my life. If he didn't fuck me soon, I might combust. I shivered all over, wriggling closer to him, trying to get the friction I desperately needed. His violet eyes looked darker than I'd ever seen as he hooked his fingers around my underwear and pulled it to the side. The material cut into my sensitive skin before ripping away. I was naked in front of him, splayed out on the marble. He pushed back, sinking in the water until his face is level with my pussy.

"I have to taste you first," he murmured, his icy breath puffing onto my dripping lips. I almost shrieked when he swiped his tongue between my folds, gathering up the cream that he'd created with his touch and kisses.

"*Shek*, you taste like flying." He dove back in again, his tongue dipping into me and swirling around my clit. "I never want to come down." It was obscene how slowly he licked, like he wanted to swallow me whole. I needed more. As I clenched around nothing, I couldn't help but whine.

"I know, I know," he crooned, sliding two fingers inside me and curving them back. My eyes rolled into my head and I fell to my elbows, head lolling back as he pumped his fingers in and out. I could feel it building. My breath came in brief spurts as he focused on my clit again. That cool tongue, everything I never knew I needed. My thighs trembled around his head.

"I'm coming," I gasped as I exploded. My back arched and my fingers scratched on the marble, desperate for something to grab onto as I floated back into my body. Wellyn smiled against the skin of my inner thigh as he pressed a sweet kiss there. His expression was smug when he looked up, filled with a heat I knew I returned.

"Wellyn, that was amazing," I said after finding ability to speak again. He planted his hands on the side of the spring and pressed up, his toned body rising out of the water. I was speechless again as I eyed his cock. It looked painfully hard, slick with water. He kneeled on the edge, leaning down to press my thighs apart. He settled in between the space, careful to avoid my clit while it was still so sensitive.

"I need to tell you something," he said, his voice low. His chin glistened from my juices. He leaned over me, his hard body pressing mine into the cool marble. I wrapped my legs around him.

"You want to talk right now?" I smiled cheekily, and he nipped the hollow of my throat.

"This is important," he chastised, and I gave him a nod to let him know I was listening, a feat when my whole body was a mess of nerve endings all firing with raw need. He looked nervous for a moment, sucking in a deep breath as he ducked his head, seeming to steal himself for a moment. I tensed. This had been a beautiful moment and it hit me that it could be a game, another one of Tallis's cruelties. I tried to wriggle back, but Wellyn pressed down on me, his face flooding with panic.

"No, no, please just—" he choked on his words. "This is hard to get out."

I stilled, feeling unbelievably vulnerable underneath him. He looked at me, his gaze cataloguing each detail of my body.

"I want to be inside you, I want this with you." He gulped. "It's always been important for me to do this with someone who accepts me fully, who accepts my creature. No one has been as supportive as you are. He's only ever experienced ridicule and judgement, except from Tallis and Fenar."

I ran my hands down his bracketed arms and shook my head.

"Wellyn, your creature is stunning, just like you," I said. He offered me a small shy smile, pressing a sweet lingering kiss to the corner of my mouth.

"I have never done this before." His words fell out in an exhale, and his freckles flared on his face as his skin flushed. I froze, my mouth dropping open momentarily before I slammed it shut again. Did he say what I thought he said? Was he a virgin?

"Wellyn, you've never..." I trailed off, and he winced slightly, nodding in confirmation.

"Never," he rasped. I could feel how brittle this moment was. One wrong move and this sweet man would shatter in my hands. Excruciatingly slowly, I tightened my legs around his waist. I drew his hardness close to me, rocking against him sensuously. I was dripping wet and the shock of his cool cock against my swollen clit made me moan.

"You want me to be your first?" I asked, angling my hips so the head of his cock slipped between my folds. His head came down to rest in the nook of my neck and shoulder and he nodded into the flushed skin.

"You don't mind?" Wellyn asked, his eyes fluttering closed and his face tightening like he was in pain.

"I'm honored. But not here. Not like this. If this is important to your creature, then I want to do right," I said in a low voice. A tortured moan stuttered from his lips and his eyes snapped open to behold me like I was precious gold. His fingers tangled in my dampened hair and he collapsed on me for a moment. His tongue swiped into my mouth, messily and hungrily.

"Doesn't mean we can't have fun in the meantime," I urged him, my voice taut with need. The feeling of him against me was incredible, but I needed the friction, the glide and frenzy of our bodies meeting. He dropped his head to the nook of my neck again, gasping out incoherent words as he moved. They were reverent prayers, praise and curses that he pressed into my skin as his cock moved in between my soaked folds against my clit.

"This won't last long. I'm sorry," he said breathlessly. I only smiled, pulling him down to kiss me again. His hand snuck in between us, circling my clit desperately like he needed me to feel what he was feeling. I could feel another orgasm building, my groans becoming a sinful chorus with his.

"Can you please, baby, come, come, come," he chanted. He tossed his head back and scrunched forehead his as he thrust harder. He chased his pleasure, hard and fast, no longer thinking clearly but only wanting that release for both of us.

"Yes!" I screamed as his fingers tossed me over the edge, the glide of his cool cock against my clit making me shake. Wellyn choked on a groan, his hips bruising against mine as he tumbled after me into bliss. His cum flooded the front of my pussy, the only warm part of him. His cock jerked as it streamed out of him, covering me, claiming me. He collapsed on top of me, his weight suffocating in the best way. I threaded my fingers through his hair and pulled his face up to kiss him deeply. It was languid this time, both of us melting into each other.

We kissed for a long time until my body ached from his weight and shivered from the cold. He pulled back, gently untangling himself from me. Embarrassment heated my face at the feeling of his cum trickling down my legs. But the way he rocked back on his knees, his eyes drawn to the apex of my thighs like a hawk, settled any of my nerves. His fingers pressed into the tops of my thighs and he bit his bottom lip.

"That is the hottest sight I've ever seen," he admitted, obviously enjoying the view of my pussy utterly ruined with his cum. Heat flared in his eyes as he took in the sight of me naked and sprawled in front of him. "I can't wait to make you mine." The heat in the promise was searing as he stood and held out a hand to me. He pulled me to standing and passed me the discarded clothes we'd tossed around.

"I promise we will make it a moment to remember, make it worth it for you," I said as I washed Wellyn's release off my skin and pulled on my damp shorts. It wasn't exactly comfortable; the material rubbed against my tender flesh with no underwear. That ripped scrap was a naughty memento to have. Wellyn lifted one of my hands to his lips and pressed a kiss to my wrist. His eyes scorched as he looked up at me.

"I want to feel you against me already," he admitted. I laughed softly, my cheeks flushing with heat.

"What about Fenar and Tallis?" I asked. I didn't want to utter their names but knew that as soon as we left this place, it would be inevitable. Wellyn sighed deeply, his eyes looking at the springs, so beautiful now they were free of Gaer.

"I'll do whatever you want, Cami," he said sincerely. "As soon as I saw you, I wanted you. I consider myself blessed to have you as my boost."

"I don't want them to know yet. Honestly, I'm afraid of what Tallis will do when he finds out."

I didn't want the teasing and taunting the other two would start up as soon as they realized. I wanted the memory of this day to stay untainted for as long as possible. It had cracked something open inside of me, sharing something that had been festering inside me, polluting my insides. Wellyn hadn't judged and had given me the most precious gift in return. He'd shared his secret. He'd taken a chance on me to show his creature and been brave enough to trust I wouldn't hurt him.

All this from a boost. It crossed my mind that I'd only known him a few days. It felt like years. I was inside him now, tethered to him deep within his very being.

The memory of his tongue collecting my blood sent a jolt of heat through me. "How does it feel?" I pointed to my wrist, getting so caught up in the moment I didn't think about the fact that Wellyn was the first of the triad to take my blood. He cracked a huge smile.

"I feel a little different already. My creature is vibrant and strong in me, but that could be due to the orgasm," he said. I laughed, whacking him with my arm. I looked out into the darkening sky, knowing our brief interlude was ending. As if on cue, my stomach growled.

"I wish we could stay here but I am starving." I sighed and his face fell, though he was quick to hide it. Acting on instinct, I threw my arms around his middle, rubbing my face in his chest.

"We're good, right?" I asked, hating how transparent I sounded. But I was safe with Wellyn. After what we'd just shared, I didn't doubt it. He'd looked after me since I came to Melbak. I wanted to trust him.

"I've got you," he promised, and I let him hold me a moment longer.

Fenar

A SHARP WHISTLE CUT through the cacophony of the training ground. Weapons clattered to the ground as the four Legion Heads appear on the viewing platform. My fists clenched at my side as I felt the cool gaze of Head Lamott sweep over me. I could tell from the distance that there was no flare of recognition. Even if Wellyn was here, I doubt he would react. He was a machine, focused on growing the power of Lamott and the two sub-houses, Filay and Hoppe. The thin gold circlet of a Legion Head flattened the copper curls of his hair. I wanted my wolf to tear it off his head. It was a travesty that he could hold a position of power after what he did to my brother. He murmured something to his son Ronen, who stepped forward and pointed to a group of top tier fighters. Tallis snorted next to me, and I cut him a quick look.

"Figures. Brute strength is all Lamott cares about," he sneered under his breath. The fighters Head Lamott was discussing preened under the obvious favor being shown to them.

"Let them. They use every muscle except the one in their thick skulls. We must focus on being chosen for Head Aydro's team," I said under my breath. Head Aydro was searching the training ground with Ambrose, who was advising his mother with a finger twirling his mustache.

My chest squeezed a little at the thought of not being chosen for the Vinko. I would prefer to fight for Tallis's sub-house Kerys, or the other sub-house Trellys, but there was no point. They didn't have the resources and it was better to pool with a stronger allied house to ensure success.

I didn't miss the loaded looks Head Avanti and Head Lamott shared and Tallis hummed under his breath. "That's concerning. They are normally much better at hiding their alliance."

There were four Legion Heads. With only three Head families, the fourth Head was chosen from a sub-house. Head Avanti won the last Vinko, so the fourth Head was chosen from his sub-house, Custray. Head Custray leaned over the railing, her dark eyes missing nothing. She had a sharp tongue but a considering mind, not that it mattered. Head Avanti held the genuine power, and she deferred to him, no matter that the gold circlet glinting in the light gave her power.

Ambrose motioned to Tallis and me, and my brother gritted his teeth at being summoned like a peasant.

"Play nice, Tallis, we can't do a thing if we don't get chosen. And that's far likelier to happen if you scorch Head Aydro's precious heir."

I looked at him, rolling my eyes at his thunderous face. He'd been in a horrible mood all day. I knew how deep his resentment of Ambrose went, his former best friend. Still, he had to put his animosity aside for the bigger picture. Aydro needed to win. We were outnumbered by rival houses who were all gunning to squash us.

"See mother, you recall Tallis Kerys and his triad mate, Fenar." He coughed to cover the awkwardness of my lack of prestigious bloodline. It didn't matter. I knew I was more fit than half of the people in the training ground and my creature, combined with my healing power, made me an extreme asset.

I nodded my head respectfully, letting my wolf come out and snarl through its row of sharp teeth. I knew what they wanted, and it wasn't to make small talk with the likes of me, a no-name ward of the Heads. Head Aydro nodded with approval, lacing her thin fingers over her stomach. My wolf padded forward on four legs, knowing we were fierce to behold.

"Kerys is lucky to have you, Tallis. I hope we can count on your strength during the Vinko? Will all your triad fight?" Her soft voice carried as she addressed Tallis, and I noticed the stiffened shoulders of Head Lamott as he obviously listened in.

"It is possible," he said vaguely, and I grinned at the idea of making Head Lamott regret his actions towards my absent triad brother. "We have the human boost, as you know. By the Vinko we should see the benefits of the power they bring."

I pressed my wolf against his leg, surprised to hear him talk about the boost in any positive way. He pushed me away.

"We are at your disposal, should you need us," he demurred, letting his eyes drop in a show of respect. He could play the gentleman so well.

Ambrose clapped his hand on Tallis's shoulder. "Of course, of course, we need you both." He looked to his mother. "Aydro has chosen you to fight the Vinko. Do you accept?"

Pleasure spread through my body, my chest filling with anticipation. I met Tallis's piercing stare and my wolf yipped. We would avenge Wellyn and Tallis would bring glory to his family line. Perhaps, if I fought well enough, they would give me an honorary family title.

"We accept, gladly," Tallis said, fisting the soft fur of my wolf's scruff.

I focused on the rod-straight back of the man I utterly despised, Head Lamott. We were one step closer to destroying him. When Head Aydro won the Vinko, we would finally have the pendulum of power swing our way. I didn't care for the politics of the founding families, but I cared about my brothers, and this man had scored Wellyn to his soul and left scars too deep to heal. For that, he had to pay. I was more than happy to help finish him.

Cami

THE SKY HAD DARKENED considerably by the time we made our way through the path to the apartment. It had been difficult not to reach for Wellyn's hand on our return. I was buzzing in the most amazing way. I had shared my darkest secret and Wellyn hadn't judged me; he had made me feel better about the guilt I had been carrying for so long. There was no mark on my wrist, but the skin felt sensitive and each brush against my side sent a shiver through my body. I couldn't stop thinking about Wellyn's body against mine, how desperate he had been, how it had felt to have him slip in between my legs like he belonged there. His declaration, trusting me with his own secrets.

Was this because of the boost? I'd never wanted someone more, never felt so turned on in my life, begging and panting for him. It was like a flip had switched and now all I could think about was how to get more. I chanced a look at him and caught his heated gaze. I guess I wasn't the only one feeling that way.

"Could you do something for me?" I asked.

He smirked. "I can do a lot of things. Whatever and wherever you want." I loved the lick of lust that threaded through his words, flushing with ideas.

"Yes, that please, but also can I give you something to keep? I don't trust Tallis not to destroy them and they are super precious."

Wellyn dropped the smile and nodded with a serious face. "Of course, you can rely on me. I will keep it safe. You can trust in me."

I floated at the sincerity in his voice. His hand brushed against mine and I snatched it up. He pulled me to him and pressed me up against the wall outside the apartment. His lips crashed into mine, hungrily taking and devouring me like we hadn't touched each other in an age. He swallowed my moan, releasing me to rest his head on the crook of my neck.

"I can't stop thinking about earlier. I can't wait for you to be mine in all ways," he admitted in a whisper. He bumped his nose with mine.

"You're not the only one."

"This has been the best day of my life," he declared, his arms wrapping around me in a hard embrace. My heart clenched at his words. He was killing me with his sweetness. I disentangled myself and looked at the door to the apartment like it was my nemesis.

"How bad is it going to be?" I asked, and Wellyn's face fell. He tried to pull me into his arms again, but I held up a hand with a sigh.

"We'd better get used to not touching each other."

He gave me a pained look that lasted for a second before he said, "Tallis will be a complete asshole, without a doubt."

I rolled my eyes and motioned for him to open the door.

Tallis

I'D BEEN ON EDGE all day for some unknown reason and by the time I had got home, I was almost vibrating with an rising anger. It was anger. I was sure, and my errant boost the cause.

The sound of her scream haunted my mind. She was moments away from Gaer touching her. I'd taken my eyes off her for a second and she'd wandered away, deliberately breaking the rules I'd set.

I'd messaged Cove on my reader, that it had disappointed me how she intervened with the human. She hadn't replied, and that irked me. The heart crack I expected from Cove's rejection hadn't happened. It confused me more than anything. My perception was irrevocably changed. The ideas I had held onto for so long had disintegrated in the space of days.

I had to endure a call with my dad, who had lambasted me over the injuries the human had suffered and transferred to him. He had to see a healer, the claw marks Nakasha left had been that deep. If not for the binding agreement, the human would have serious wounds and that just made me angrier. I know it wasn't her fault, Nakasha had reacted with jealousy. I knew it was going to happen, and I'd watched with a certain sense of glee. Only after, I didn't understand why the glee seemed to feel heavy and tainted. I wasn't reveling in it today. Instead, it was choking me. It was because she needed disciplining.

I'd tried to track down the author of the insulting comic that had been circulating last night. Nobody seemed to know where it had come from, and that had enraged me even further. It was probably Ambrose having a good laugh at the shambles of my life. Cove rejecting me spectacularly and a human boost to truly rub in how much worse my life could get.

I heard the door open and looked up from where I had been brooding in the window seat. I'd had to rearrange the cushions in their correct order, the human having shifted them into the wrong places again. Fenar heard the door as well, turning on his stool in the kitchen. I'd been ignoring him while stuck in my rage. He'd defied me last night for the human as well.

Wellyn strolled in, looking blissful, and I felt a flash of fury, my fist itching to slam off his face in the bloodiest way possible. I swallowed hard, turning that fire onto its rightful owner. There she was, finally, after a day of checking the feeds obsessively to see if she'd returned. She was still wearing her skimpy human clothes, those shorts showing far too much of her long legs. They were damp, as was her shirt. Her hair had unraveled into tangles about her shoulders and a beguiling pink flushed her cheeks.

"Where have you been?" I asked, standing and folding my arms.

Wellyn sighed and strolled over to the ordering machine, putting in an order for pancakes for two. He gave the human a smile and made to slide the plate over to her. Fenar eyed the plate with hunger.

"That's not part of her diet," I reminded him, rankled by the way he rolled his eyes.

"Really? Is it necessary? She won't be wearing that mask or dressing in the robes any longer. She should eat what she likes," Fenar interjected, a smirk on his face showing me he knew the words would rile me.

I stomped over, gritting my teeth and avoiding my mouthy triad brother. I looked at the human instead. Closer to her now, I noticed her reddened lips, as if she'd been chewing on them. Was she still frightened by her encounter with the Gaer last night?

If I was a kind Legion, I would let her have freedom to wear and eat as she chose. But I wasn't, so I ordered her fluco and placed it in front of her with a grin. This was good. I got a rush watching her nose wrinkle and her face screw up. Wellyn made a noise in the back of his throat, like he disapproved.

"This should be no problem for you, Cami. You have an iron gut," Fenar said with a smile.

"Can I have some water?" she asked and Wellyn rushed to order her a glass, sliding it over with eager fingers. She toyed with the fork in her hand and I knew she was building up the courage to eat the foul meal. Legion despised it all over Melbak, except for a small group of northerners. A rich, brown sauce with meat and vegetables covered in a thick pastry crust. The first time

I had it I spat it out. Crust stuck to the roof of my mouth, the sauce had been salty, the flavors were too strong, and it had burned my tongue.

Cami sliced it open, watching the steam drift out. I could tell she was nervous by the hike of her shoulders. She swallowed a small mouthful and chewed quickly. She turned and covered her mouth, and a husky laugh bubbled out of me.

Wellyn leapt forward with a hiss.

"She must eat it. My rules," I reminded him, and he shot me a wounded look.

"It's okay, Wellyn, I can handle this on my own," she said before taking another bite. This one didn't seem to bother her as much. Wellyn hesitated, pursing his lips, his fingers rapping on the counter until he heaved a sigh and walked off towards his bedroom. When I looked back to Cami—the human, rather—she had almost finished her meal. A feat that had me dropping my jaw. She noticed, a flicker of amusement in her eyes. She sent a wink to Fenar, immobolised by shock.

"Do you lack tastebuds? How do you eat these foul foods so easily?" I sounded like a disgruntled child, which added to my rage. She snorted, swiping a finger through the leftover sauce and popping it in her mouth. Watching her lave the brown sludge off her finger sent a jolt of lust right to my groin. That wasn't right. I shook my head, tearing my eyes from the strangely arousing sight.

"Iron gut, I suppose," she said, her warm voice light and unaffected. I had to stop myself from making a fist. Where were her tears and misery? I grunted and rolled my shoulders back. I would have to use harsher methods.

I pointed to the couch. "It's time for you to be disciplined. Lie over the couch and ready yourself."

Fenar hopped off the stool to hold his hands out in protest. "Now, Tallis—"

Cami gave him a stern look, poking him gently back down wth a finger. "I said I can handle this." She raised an eyebrow, a flicker of unease running over her otherwise shuttered face. "What are you going to do?" she asked, walking over to the couch.

She hesitated in front of it for too long, so I wrapped my hand around her upper arm and bent her over the side of the couch, her ass pointing in the air while her front half pressed into the cushions.

"Is this what I think it is?" She let out a hysterical giggle. She acted like a child, so I would discipline her like one. I swatted her on her ass. The giggle transformed into a surprised yelp. hat was more like it. This would help me assuage some of the strange feelings I had.

"Remove your shorts," I ordered. She stiffened, not moving a muscle.

"What? I can't," she said obstinately. "I won't." Red swam in front of me. I felt a buzzing in my ears.

"Tallis," came Fenar's warning growl, and I shot him a venomous look. He folded his arms, obviously intending to keep watch and make sure I didn't do anything horrible.

"Be quiet if you're going to stay here, Fenar." He shook his head but waved his hand for me to continue. "And you, human, you will...you follow my rules or else. Remember?" I watched with pleasure as she fumbled with the buttons of her shorts, the wet material hugging her skin and making it difficult to peel them down. My fingers itched to rip them off myself.

She revealed a white, creamy bare ass, and I groaned involuntarily at the sight.

"Wh-where is your underwear?" I said through gritted teeth.

"They got wet," her voice small and muffled. "Just get it over with, Bossman."

The term made my hands flare orange, and I had to breathe deeply to control my power.

"What did you call me?" I asked, paranoid, wanting to know who had given her the name used in that stupid comic.

"I don't know," she said, turning her head so that she could look back at me. It was obscene, her wet hair a partial curtain, her white ass sloping over the couch arm, her lips swollen from being chewed on—obviously in fear of what was to come.

My hand cracked over her bare skin and I watched as her eyes widened and shut in quick succession, a second yelp escaping her.

"You have been disobedient," I said, cracking down on the opposite cheek this time. It flushed pink with the print of my hand, a hypnotizing sight my cock responded to.

It meant nothing. I forgave myself as I moved a little closer. It has just been a while since I *sheked* someone.

"I will give you eight more, ten in total for your behavior last night," I informed her, rubbing my palms on my pants, resisting the urge to brush against the hardness that was straining them now. She didn't answer, causing my anger to flare up again.

"Do you understand?" I shouted before bringing my hand down again, thoroughly enjoying the sound it made.

"Yes!" she squeaked. I heard Fenar smother a groan behind me.

"You will stay with one of your triad at all times." My hand stung as I brought it down again.

"OK," she said, her eyes squeezed shut.

"You will never go outside without permission." I spanked her twice, quickly, before she could prepare herself. The sweet inhale of her breath was like a balm to me, the red on her ass deepening.

"Yes," she spat out, and it made me harder. *Shek* I was loving this. That hadn't been my intention, and I was seriously going to deal with my errant cock after, but I had five more to give her.

"You are a bad boost, aren't you?" I was surprised by how silky my voice sounded. She jolted as I slapped her again. Her ass jiggled under the force of it, and I ran my hand over the smooth skin, the warmth from the slaps heating my hands. She turned her head into the cushion, muffling a sound that sounded like a moan. I slapped her again, giving her no reprieve. She turned her head to the side, gasping. Her cheeks were as pink as her ass cheeks now, her eyes glossy.

"Answer me," I ordered.

"Yes."

I heard Fenar's quiet hiss behind me but was too hypnotized by Cami's pert ass to look away.

I swung my hand down again, relishing the way she rocked into the couch, an audible moan escaping her this time.

"Yes what?"

I watched in fascination as she rubbed her thighs together.

"I'm a bad boost," she groaned, the word boost turning into a shriek as I slapped her one last time.

I ran my hand over her again, my fingers splaying over the marks I'd made with a deep sense of possessiveness. My mark on her just looked so right.

"That's ten," she said, pushing back and colliding with my rock-hard cock. I sucked in a breath, pressing her down and grinding into her. Her wide eyes blew open and she froze under my pinning weight.

"It was a punishment human. You sounded like you enjoyed it." I narrowed my eyes at her and grunted as she pushed her ass back.

"I wasn't the only one."

She didn't deny it. She pushed again, making me stumble backwards, and yanked her shorts up. I watched her walk away, my eyes on her ass and my cock crying out for relief. I felt more confused than before.

Fenar's quiet laugh startled me, and I looked back, glaring at him. I'd forgotten he was even there.

"What in all the universe was that, Tallis?" He prowled toward me, raking his hand through his hair. He arched an eyebrow as he spotted the prominent bulge in my pants.

"Nothing, just a reminder of her natural place," I said gruffly, and Fenar chuckled again, his hand coming down to slap my shoulder.

"What? Underneath you? Can't say I blame you. I'll hand out the next discipline if that's the way they're going to play out. That is going to stay in my mind for a long time," he admitted before sauntering out of the room.

I stalked to the kitchen, intending to use the cleaning slot to cleanse my hands. I thrust them into the illuminated space, hesitating over the button for a moment. Humans were filthy creatures, that's why traveling was forbidden to their plane. Every Legion knew of their involvement in the Culling all those years ago. They caused the deaths of scores of Legion because of the diseases that brewed in their skin. But as my hands shook in the crisp light, I found I couldn't do it. I could still feel the decadent heat of her skin under my palm, like it had ingrained itself there.

My hand crept to my pants, palming my hard cock, and before I knew it, I was hurrying to my room. I leaned against the closed door and fumbled with the fastenings of my pants as her faint salty scent drifted around me. It was like a heady perfume, and in that moment I wanted it coated over my cock.

I bit my fist as I stroked my hard length in jerky, frustrated movements. My breath hissed through my teeth as I pictured her bent over the couch, her skin lush and presented just for me. The moans that had escaped her were quiet, but they had been real. She'd liked my hand on her. What would she sound like if she welcomed me truly?

Hot cum cut short my frantic daydreams, exploding out of my cock and coating the floor in front of me. I turned and slammed my fist on the door. Why had I done that? Was I so horny that I pictured Cami—the human—instead of Cove? My chest heaved as I sunk lower into shame. What was I doing thinking of her? She was disgusting, and anyway, she hated me. I'd hear no sounds of pleasure from her. Even if I wanted to.

Cami

I SHUT THE DOOR as quickly as I could, startling Wellyn, who was lounging on my bed.

"I-I figured you didn't want me to come out again," he stuttered. I waved a hand, dismissing him. My cheeks were hot, my ass was stinging and I desperately needed to wash off the sensation of Tallis's hand on me.

"Give me a second," I muttered as I darted into the cleaning room before he could question me further.

"What was that?" I whispered to myself, kicking my shorts off like they held some disease. I was discombobulated.

My knees turned wobbly as I slammed my hand on the button to clean. It didn't remove the invisible sensation of Tallis's fingers smoothing over my curves. It had been in such contrast to the harsh slap of his hand. I felt my cheeks blooming again in parallel with the heat between my legs that I was trying to ignore.

He'd been hard! What did that mean? He got off on causing me pain? He couldn't have known that I was partial to being spanked.

I took a steadying breath and walked from the room, naked and dry. Wellyn gulped as he saw me, sitting up on the bed and blinking rapidly like he was taking a picture with his eyes. I held out my hand.

"Your shirt, please," I asked, and his innocent face furrowed with confusion before it brightened like a sunrise. He scrambled for the hem, tearing it over his head and hurrying to fit it over me. It fell just above my knees and smelled like Wellyn, but that wasn't why I'd wanted it. I remembered what he had said about his creature liking me in his clothes.

I gave him a little twirl. "Does your creature approve?"

He growled and yanked my hand until I was sprawling onto the bed next to him. He hitched up my leg over his thigh and licked his lips.

"He's never been happier. Neither have I," he said. "Can I sleep here tonight?"

I wrapped my arms around him and nodded into his neck.

"I want to show you what I meant before. What I asked you to take care of? I already stored them in your room, under your drawer." Wellyn leapt up and rushed to the door. "It's a little paper bag."

He smiled, opening the door a crack before sneaking out. I flopped on to my pillow, pressing my hand to my stomach to stem the rising wave of nerves that was creeping up. It didn't take long for Wellyn to sneak back in. He closed the door behind him, the photos tucked under his arm, and lowered himself to the bed to stretch out next to me.

"Are these what you wanted?" he asked, passing me the packet.

"I signed a contract saying I wouldn't return home, although I didn't realize that cutting ties meant leaving Earth. So these are all I have left of my family. They don't even really know I'm gone, if the Legion I talked to has done what she said she would." I couldn't help the note of bitterness that came through, and I sighed as I pulled the photos out.

The first was a wedding picture of my ma and dad. She had puffed sleeves on a lace-covered dress. He had a thick mustache and partial mullet. It screamed the eighties, but I loved the way they looked at each other, a glint of amusement in their eyes.

"Your parents?" Wellyn asked, pulling the photo from my hand and looking at it. "You have your dad's hair."

The next one was of my brothers. It had been their birthday and Aaron had a Pokémon plushie squeezed under each arm, of course. Someone had put a party hat on him and it was lopsided. His joy was blinding. Percy was leaning on his chair, a balloon half blown up in his mouth.

"These are my brothers, Aaron and Percy." I pointed to them and Wellyn hummed, bringing the photo close to his face to take in the details.

I went through them with him, explaining what had been happening at each moment. At some point, my voice got strangled in my throat and I tried to shuffle the pictures together and put them away, hoping that if they were gone I could get a handle on my emotions. Wellyn caught my shaking hands and pried the photos from me. He placed them carefully in the sleeve, observing me.

"I promise I will take good care of these, Cami. Thank you for sharing them with me."

I hiccupped on a sob, and he pulled me into his arms, nudging me under the covers and settling my head on his chest.

I knew I was in Eyke's bed by the way his sheets felt on my skin. I was naked and took a moment to enjoy the sensation of the silk against me before I cracked an eye open.

Eyke was sitting on the end of the bed, watching me with his hands in his lap. Somehow, this didn't disturb me. The tingling sensation I associated with him coursed through my body, my limbs heavy and content. I could make out more of his appearance now that the shadows had lessened. He had a thick beard and dark hair, his massive shoulders rolling over like he wanted to make himself look smaller. He gave me a tender smile when he saw I was awake.

"Ah Cami, it's nice to see you again." He spoke politely, and it made a bubble of laughter want to burst out my mouth. This was so absurd.

"Am I going to come here every time I fall asleep?" I asked, pointing my toes and stretching my legs. The familiar buzz settled over my body and made me want to purr like a kitten. I should have been terrified, but when I searched for the emotion, the logical response, I felt only a lazy sense of ease, a sweetness that made my eyelids heavy and limbs languid.

Eyke hummed, his head tilting in consideration. "I am not sure." He shrugged. "This is the first time one of us has escaped the curse, partially, as far as I can tell."

"I tried to do some research. There was no mention of a curse, although there was barely any information from before two hundred years ago. You said there were twelve founding families, didn't you?" I said, rolling up to sit and bringing the sheet.

Eyke shifted, the bed frame creaking under his weight. He sighed as if unsurprised. "Time has passed that quickly? Yes, it was twelve noble families. The peace agreement between us brought Melbak into its greatest power. What do the books say of that?"

"Well, they only mention nine families. A woman I encountered mentioned the cursed Legion and the fact that all boosts deserve destruction. Nobody seemed to take her seriously, though. Do you know anything about that?"

Eyke ignored my question, standing and moving to sit at a table instead. He pulled out a board and set it up with stone pieces. I sat on the bed, watching him with a tilted head, until he leaned back with a blank expression and motioned me to join him.

"Let us play Ratids and Wolves."

"Excuse me?" I said, struggling to keep the shock off my face. "Are you going to answer my questions?"

Eyke cleared his throat, one large shoulder jumping in a nonchalant shrug. "I want to know you better. You may not have long here."

Considering how I'd left abruptly before, I could see what he meant. Looking around the low-lit room, the roughened stone walls and the luxurious but sparse furniture, I wondered suddenly what this place really was. I hobbled over to the chair opposite Eyke. He eyed me with a sparkle as I knotted the sheet so it would sit neatly and not flash him.

"Are you trapped here?" I asked, and he grunted.

"Let us play. If you win, I will answer your questions. If I win, you will answer mine."

He pointed out the pieces, two sets of wolves and ratids, which I learned were those flying rat creatures I despised.

"Wolves are bigger, stronger and more powerful than ratids. But the ratids are clever, cunning and able to fly. This is a game of strategy, to see if you can use both forces to overwhelm your opponent."

He won the first two games swiftly, embarrassingly, and I set the pieces on the board with stiff fingers.

"You dislike losing?" he asked. I flashed him a look, daring him to say something about my game play. But when I saw the stark honesty in his eyes, I relaxed.

"I'm a terrible loser. I can't tell you the number of tantrums I've had," I answered sheepishly, and he smiled. It was a gorgeous smile, enthralling in its fullness. There seemed to be no mask or ulterior motive to it. He wasn't weaponizing his smile like I had seen both Legion and human alike do.

Now that I could see him more clearly, I observed him discretely, looking for horns, scales, a tail or some other marker to show he was Legion, but couldn't see anything.

"You have shared your blood with one of the triad?" he asked.

I sucked in a surprised breath. "How? How did you know that?" I gripped the sides of the chair I was sitting in, examining his face.

"A guess, precious. You seem more whole than the last time I saw you." His eyes shone in the low light. "How was it?" The question sent a lick of warmth through me, remembering the feeling of Wellyn taking my blood for the first time. I had let him feed a second time while we had lain in bed. It was sensual. It had me wanting to climb his body and take my pleasure. I was almost frightened by the pure lust it wrought in me. I hadn't had time to fully process it yet.

"You'll have to win again if you want me to answer that."

He gave me a wry smile and set his pieces back so we could play again. This time, I tried to copy his moves and sacrificed some of my wolves to let my ratids take out the bulk of his. He leaned back in the chair; the surprise was evident on his face as he clapped his hands slowly.

"You are a quick learner."

"I have to be quick, otherwise I'll be having tantrums all the time," I laughed. "Now answer my question from before—the truth of the curse?"

Eyke cracked his neck, his head rolling as he gave himself a few moments to think.

"Legion regularly bred with humans in my age. Some offspring were born unmarked, with nothing to show we were truly Legion. We had powers, but we looked like humans, effectively. Legion considered humans lesser, so to look like one was to be lesser. Eventually, the

Heads exiled humans from Melbak. But the unmarked Legion? We were punished for looking like humans. There were sanctions placed upon us. They denied us access to boosts, rounded us up and sent us to the mountains. Although some of us escaped, taking our human boosts and fleeing to Earth. It wasn't enough for the Heads. They wanted to obliterate us. So, they cursed us to live on the land but never be a part of it, to never die and never be free. All because of the way we looked."

He paused for a moment, a melancholy air settling over him.

"Why would they approve a human boost if they cursed Legion for looking like us? It makes little sense, unless this has more to do with the deaths we supposedly caused? Do you know of that and the role humans played in it?" I asked, more to myself than anything. Eyke hummed under his breath as he pondered the question. Then he arched an eyebrow and nodded to the board.

"Win again and I'll answer." I shook my head, setting the pieces back.

I lost again. Eyke won three more times, wanting to know basic questions about me. He asked me about my most precious possession, and I wondered if I should have been honest and told him about my photos. I told Wellyn, and even though being with Eyke made me feel like I was wrapped in a comfortable blanket, I wasn't sure. Before I could answer, the room bled away. Eyke reached his hand forward and snagged mine as my vision went black. When I woke up, I was tingling all over and alone.

Fenar

SOMETHING WAS GOING ON between Wellyn and Cami. I had my suspicions, but it was hard to get proof with Tallis riding my ass in the training arena. He couldn't understand why I wasn't more motivated now that Head Aydro had us on their team for the Vinko.

He should have been pleased. His latest stunt with Cami was the most successful in terms of what he was trying to achieve. She'd been subdued around him since the spanking. Cove was still disgusted by his juvenile behavior at Ambroses. She was still not speaking to him and insisted on using me as a go-between. His low voice buzzed in my ear as he complained about it. I wasn't listening, too focused on watching Wellyn.

He sat on the couch with a book spread out in front of Cami, pointing out something in it. There was nothing innately suspicious about this, except that his thigh pressed against hers and he had just reached out to tuck a dark curl behind her ear. He had done it tenderly, a secret smile on his face that she'd answered with a blush I could see from across the room.

He'd started locking his bedroom, too. I poked my head in on Cami bedroom, checking she was still in her bed, which she always was. Why would he be locking his door if it wasn't to hide he had our boost in his bed? What was he trying to hide? He'd started taking long morning meals with her, changing his work hours so he was leaving the apartment after us. One morning I'd forgotten my reader and I'd walked in on them. Cami was perched on the bench, looking deliciously rumpled, and Wellyn was tucking his shirt in. It could have been nothing. It didn't mean they were doing anything. She'd just woken up so it might have been sleep that left her looking so *shekable*. I'd been too late to stay and question him, and he'd been avoiding me since.

Even with all this strange behavior, there was something that I couldn't deny. He was bigger. Wellyn had always been on the leaner side, his bones more prominent than his muscles. He was handsome, in a breakable way. Tallis was built like he could push a tree over and I was somewhere in between. But Wellyn had grown. His body was more muscular and he looked taller. Still lean, but his muscles were clearly defined. He had a six-pack for the first time in his life. I saw it when I was testing his door last week. I'd questioned him on it, and he'd gotten defensive with me, asking if it was a crime to work out and focus on his strength.

"Wellyn looks different, don't you think?" I interrupted Tallis, and he narrowed his eyes as he trailed off on whatever complaint he was making. He was miserable company lately. He flicked his dark gaze over to where Wellyn was flipping through the book, landing on a new section and pointing it out to Cami.

"He looks like he's taken my advice, finally," he grumbled, and I resisted the urge to roll my eyes.

I tried again, wanting to bash Tallis over the head with it, but knowing he needed gentler handling right now. "Amazing that he could buff up so quickly." Tallis narrowed his eyes, growing still as he looked at Wellyn closely. "I haven't seen him working out, have you?" I asked, knowing that he'd gone running as usual, but not joined Tallis or me for our intense morning sessions. He worked at the Vault. It wasn't like there were a myriad of opportunities to train there.

"No," Tallis said quietly, and I could all but hear the wheels turning in his brain. "What are you trying to say, Fenar?"

"I'm just pointing it out. No need to take it out on me. Triads bulk up when they're feeding regularly. Isn't that what Ambrose said?" I said my theory out loud for the first time, knowing that it was true even though I couldn't prove it.

"He wouldn't," Tallis said furiously, shaking suddenly beside me.

As if they could feel our intense gaze, Wellyn and Cami looked up. Cami dropped her head immediately, but Wellyn just turned his head to the side quizzically. I motioned him to come over. He whispered in her ear, a startling intimate gesture that made my stomach clench for some reason. He pushed off the couch, loping over to us, and I felt like shaking my head at my stupidity. Of course he was feeding. His thighs looked thick in his pants and his arms bulged as they swung by his side.

Tallis swooped in before I could open my mouth. "You're getting boosts, aren't you?" he hissed under his breath. The venom in his voice made Wellyn flinch, but then he stood tall, shook off the surprise and drew his lips into a thin line. I could see we had missed much more than we realized. We'd always accepted Tallis was the strongest of us, the biggest and roughest, but Wellyn looked like he could take him, and that he would.

"What's it to you if I am?" he replied, a smile tugging at one side of his face. Tallis almost combusted on the spot, shaking with rage so hard I had to put my hand on his shoulder.

"Tallis," I warned, holding onto him until it lessened to a shiver. "We know you are, you look *sheking* jacked, Wellyn." I couldn't help some of the envy leaking into my voice and he raised his eyebrow at us.

"If I was, which I will not confirm or deny, it's none of your business. I always said I wanted a boost, and I don't care that my chance came with a human."

I must have been blind to miss how much he'd changed. He looked content, an unconscious confidence oozed off him through the tilt of his head and the languidness of his stature. It was almost mesmerizing how enhanced he seemed. Still Wellyn, but better.

"I can't believe this. A *sheking* human. I hope you're happy," Tallis spat out and turned on his heel, storming away and out of the apartment. Wellyn watched him go with an amused smirk as he looked back to Cami and made to return to her.

"Is it worth it?" I asked, low enough that he might have missed it. But he stopped and looked over his shoulder. His face melted a little, an expression of pure joy flooding through it.

"It's better than you can imagine, Fenar. She's perfection.

Cami had already invaded my every thought. Her scent seemed to linger everywhere, sending me into a frenzy. I could think of nothing else except the idea of getting a boost. I was hopelessly attuned to Cami and Wellyn. My chest twisted each time they came into each other's orbit.

She smiled at him.

That was the difference. He bloomed under her gaze. He had grown into his skin in a way I had never known he was lacking, but it was stark now, night and day. Everyone else knew it, too. Their eyes skipped me and stuck on him, taking in his undeniable draw now that he was getting regular boosts.

They kept it private. I had never seen him taking one while I was around, but behind closed doors, I heard the culmination. Sounds and noises that made me want to break down the door.

It was jealousy. I knew it but couldn't believe it. I was lost, unsure how to make her see me too when all she seemed to look for was Wellyn. I had become fixated by her veins, blue and many under the paper-thin skin of her wrist. When Tallis provoked her into a temper, there was one that would throb on her forehead. The thick cords of her neck made my mouth water in a way that made me think I was losing my mind.

I couldn't keep doing this. My wolf demanded to be let out to pace the hallway, outside her bedroom, to sniff in her salty scent that permeated the apartment. That was how she found us one morning, the claws clacking along the cold floor. She shrieked, her hand flying to circle her throat. My wolf prowled towards her and nosed her thigh, rubbing along her so hard that she stumbled into the wall.

"Fenar, it's too early for this," she groused. It wasn't early at all, it was almost time for mid-meal, which she seemed to have conveniently forgotten. I had watched Wellyn loiter in the kitchen, his eyes flicking towards the hall as he waited and wilted in her absence. It would have made me laugh if I wasn't so sick with envy. For the first time, someone wasn't moved by my charm or good looks. It was a sobering feeling. Wellyn had the taste of her blood imprinted on him, and he was stronger and better for it. I needed to push more, show her the full force of my desirability. She should want me.

I'd pretended to be sick, resolved to snatch some time with her that wasn't buffered by bickering with Tallis and making moon eyes at Wellyn. I wanted a boost. I had said that at the start, and in my mind, she'd held her own with the tests that Tallis had insisted on. Tallis stormed around in a constant fury lately, his face black as a bruise and his temper shorter than I'd ever known.

I felt a rush of nervous energy. Here she was in front of me, but she didn't want to be. She tip-toed down the hallway, eyeing my wolf with unease. She'd only met him once in passing, despite his insistence on being close to her. I felt the bolt of pleasure that raced through him as her hand fell to the top of his head, giving him an absent-minded scratch as she ordered breakfast. I made him look up, sniffing appreciatively at whatever she'd ordered. The foods she ate for morning meals were interesting and I had become slightly obsessed with pancakes. Coffee tasted horrible, and I'd watched in fixed revulsion as she downed multiple cups a day. She didn't know that I watched her on the feed from my reader. I had become obsessed with every little movement she made. Each bite of food she made seemed to nourish and starve me in the same breath. I nudged my wolf aside, pushing my Legion self through to take a seat beside her. She shot me a narrow-eyed look at my nudity before dismissing me to eat her food.

"What's on the menu today?" I asked, flashing her a smile that I knew made ladies' knees quiver. It seemed to have no effect, which confused me. In fact, she didn't seem fit to fashion me with a reply at all.

Women found me attractive. People could rarely resist me when I turned my attention to them, something I learned the very first time I met Tallis. Albion had dragged him to the Ward Estate when we were about eleven years old. His profile had been haughty, his hands slung behind his back, the very picture of a miniature lord. I don't know how I realized, but the air had seemed charged that day. The looks exchanged between Albion and Hilles had sent lightning down my spine. When they lined us up, I turned on the switch inside me and brought out the unforgettable, brilliant Fenar. My smile was charming, my comments confident, and my wolf shifted and strutted with innate arrogance. Albion had chosen Wellyn and me that day, scoped us out as his son's future triad members.

I didn't realize that at the time, but it had been my charm and confidence that had clinched it. After our tests, he had rigged it so they would place us together. Albion had admitted it to me not long after we became a triad, something I had kept to myself. My ability to charm had irrevocably changed my life. I had spent years honing it, knowing how to smile, laugh and touch to move others.

Cami was no different, so I leaned over and tucked a dark curl behind her ear.

"Can I have a taste?" I was determined to get her to smile at me, but she only glared and sighed. She cut a small mouthful and held it up for me to try.

"It's called eggs Benedict. If I let you try, will you leave me alone?" she asked, waggling the fork at me. I gripped her wrist, feeling her pulse jump under my fingers, and slid the fork into my mouth slowly. The taste was unusual but enjoyable, and I hummed in appreciation. A drop of sauce gathered in the corner of my mouth and I watched her pupils dilate as I gathered it with the point of my tongue. Slow and deliberate. So she wasn't entirely immune to my charms, I smoothed my features, careful not to let her see how pleased I was.

"I thought we could spend some time together today, get to know each other a little better." I flashed her another knee-wobbling smile, deflating minutely when she rolled her eyes, tucking back into her food.

"I have plans," she mumbled through a full mouth.

My shoulders drew tight. "With Wellyn?" I couldn't hold back the bitterness seeping in, and she heard it, clearly. She tilted her head in bemusement.

"No, not with Wellyn," she said finally. "Not sure why it's any business of yours, though."

"You're my boost. Everything you do is my business. You're not even supposed to leave this apartment without one of us, remember?" I knew I sounded unreasonable, and I struggled to tamp down the surge of possessiveness rising in me.

She only scoffed, shaking her head like she knew exactly what was happening. That irked me, that my attention did not charm her and that she dismissed me.

"I'm not your boost," she said.

"We could change that right now. Let me pierce your pretty little veins with my fangs. I'll show you what a wolf can do." I winked at her and leered slightly, my mouth filling with saliva at the thought of it. My cock stirred a little. The two were irrevocably linked.

We'd all seen the aftermath of Nakasha boosting one of her triad. It was a veritable *shekfest* each time. There was an erotic undertone to it, Ambrose had told us once. It makes you want to *shek* until you pass out. That had seemed inconvenient when he had boasted about it, but right now, I was fully on board. Cami was a human, but she was gorgeous. If she had horns, she'd be the perfect package. But I was getting used to her large, empty forehead. She looked sultry and sensual without even trying. Her curves made my hands ache and my body throb with tension.

"Pass," she said, tipping her cup up and emptying it with a swift gulp. Her cutlery clattered to the plate and she slipped off the stool, her hips swaying as she walked to the hall. I sat in stunned silence. She hadn't even hesitated to reject me. What did that mean? Could she truly not find me attractive? I was the most experienced and desired member of the Kerys Triad. Tallis had always gone into physical encounters with a lackluster energy, his fixation on Cove preventing him from wasting time making it good for others. Wellyn wouldn't take a lover until his creature agreed and—

I felt like something had walloped my skull. I leaned on the kitchen table and stared unseeing at the matte white counter. Wellyn's creature had awoken after meeting Cami. Both Tallis and I had noticed how Wellyn had vibrated in her presence. Could his creature have accepted her, found her worthy enough for him to have sex?

Cami launched a shoe at my head. Now I was really seeing stars. I turned in my seat, rubbing the back of my head, shocked.

"What was that for?" I scowled rubbing my head, she had a sheet was wrapped around her and not any of her delicious human clothes. She'd stopped wearing the robes Tallis had given her, and he hadn't argued the point, still sulking about Wellyn's news that he was taking her boost. She threw some tiny shreds of material on the ground.

"Did you shrink my clothes?" she demanded, blowing strands of hair off her forehead with an exasperated growl. I slid off the stool and picked up one, a tiny lavender piece of lace that obviously used to be a scandalous piece of underwear.

"It's a crime that someone has tampered with these. I bet they're gorgeous. Do they come as a set?" I asked with a lascivious wink. She snatched the miniscule scrap from my hand, grumbling under her breath. "This is Tallis. We have a friend who is an accomplished matter manipulator," I said, feeling a rush of anger that Gerad had handled her skimpy panties. What had Tallis been thinking?

"Of course, he's such a childish bully." She pouted down at the pile of clothes. "I have nothing but those stupid robes to wear now."

She walked away, still grumbling under her breath. I collected the items she'd discarded and tucked them into a bag. I could convince Gerad to turn them back to their original size, perhaps with some alterations so that they weren't so daring. That would garner me some goodwill from Cami, surely. I raced to my room and dressed, hoping she didn't leave. She walked out wearing the robes, a frown still marring her stunning face. I sidled up to her, thinking to compliment her, even if there was no praise that could come from wearing that outfit. She held up a hand and stopped me as I opened my mouth.

"Don't feed me some line, Fenar, we both know this outfit has nothing redeeming about it. I feel like I'm about to head off to Hogwarts."

"You enjoy Harry Potter? I'm a Gryffindor." I puffed out my chest in mock strength. She stared google eyed at me.

"You don't know what pancakes are, but you know Harry Potter?"

I chuckled and shrugged. "A friend of ours has a creature who is a giant spider. She insists she was the inspiration for Aragog after sneaking to Earth once."

Cami looked at me, wordless for once, before shaking her head in continued disbelief. "Unbelievable. I need to go visit Dr. Kerys. I know he's not a doctor like he pretended to be. Regardless, I need to speak to him about something."

I stiffened and wrapped my fingers around her elbow. I pulled her against me, stifling my wolf, who was growling inside me in warning. "You can't change triads, no matter what Tallis has told you. Once you bond with one of a triad, there is no switching," I spluttered, my head leaning in close to her. She shook her arm as if to dislodge me, but I held her closer, my free hand catching her luscious hip. She didn't need to know that there was still one more year before our triad was bound. They gave all triads a three-year grace period to build a relationship and brotherhood. If they clashed, there was the option to be moved to a new triad, depending on the Heads' permission. Otherwise, they took a binding oath to be loyal to each other.

"Not true, Wellyn could join a new triad," she argued, and my jaw fell open. Had Wellyn told her our triad hadn't taken the binding oath?

"You can't! You want to break up our triad? He's my brother, he belongs with us."

I was aware my fingers were tightening around her elbow by the way she winced, but I couldn't stop. The rushing in my ears took over every logical thought. Wellyn would leave. I would never have a chance at a boost. We worked well together. Wellyn and Tallis were the only family I knew. I couldn't lose them. I wouldn't. I wouldn't lose her either. Cami was ours.

A voice in my head warned that I was showing too much. I needed to smooth these violent emotions and smile through it. But my stomach clenched as I imagined her with someone else, her and Wellyn ensconced in some other apartment. Her blood in someone else's veins. It was a nightmare. I hadn't considered what a fool I had been, wasting this time indulging Tallis when I should have snatched her blood from the very first moment. She belonged to me; a part of me had known when I first went down on my knees and looked at her stunned face. I knew this down to my very bones and I felt a rush to prove it.

I lowered my head to her neck, my fangs pricking her straining neck. I was close, so close. My wolf demanded I mark her, claim her.

But then she whined, and I came back to myself in a hazy fall. I let her go. Violently, she stumbled, her eyes dark pools in her pale face.

My hands shook as I apologized. "I'm sorry, that was too far. I lost myself for a second," I rasped. "My wolf, he can't bear the thought of you or Wellyn going elsewhere."

"Okay, it's okay," she said in a tense whisper. "I was only teasing. I wouldn't ask to be moved. But I have some questions about Legion history, and I figured Albion could help me."

I rolled my shoulders down, doused in shame. I was a fool. What had driven me to act so rashly? I reached out for her again, a noise of regret sounding in the back of my throat as she flinched back. In a few brief minutes,

I had ruined any headway I'd made. I drew myself up, holding my hands palm up to show her I was backing away.

"I'm sorry, again. That was unacceptable. Of course, I will take you to see Albion. He's been bugging Tallis about bringing you for a check-in."

"Don't worry, I won't tell on Bossman to his daddy," she sneered, her lip twitching with distaste. I couldn't help but laugh. She eyed me carefully, rightly distrusting after my outburst.

"Have you drawn anymore Bossman comics? I would love to see them. Tallis is still furious over the mysterious appearance. He can't understand why no one seems to know who drew it." I laughed again as her eyes widened.

"You took the comic? I wondered what had happened to it," she breathed, still tense. "Why didn't you tell Tallis?"

I motioned her to move towards the door and fell into step beside her. "Are you kidding? It was hilarious and true. He is a childish, petty dictator. Plus, there is nothing more satisfying than teasing him. I made copies and spread them around Ambrose's party. People were enamored by the artist who was brave enough to mock Tallis Kerys. So, if you have anymore can I please share them with your adoring fans? Anonymously, of course, it would do no good to provoke Tallis into scorching your pretty face off."

Cami's lips moved like she was suppressing a smile. "I may have channeled my frustrations into a few more," she admitted sheepishly.

"So what Hogwarts house are you?" I asked her, changing the subject. "You're probably Hufflepuff, right?"

She snorted and looked up at the sky. It was a mild day today. My skin prickled with thick heat and the sky had streaks of blood-red clouds painted across it. The incessant storms of the past week had finally stopped and the silence from lack of lightening made it seem peaceful. Cami's forehead peppered with sweat, the mild heat affecting her more than me. I had a pang of worry for her and had to stop myself from blotting it off and checking her temperature. I had the strangest need to force a glass of water down her throat to stop her from overheating. I had never given much thought to the weather, but now with Cami, all I could think about was how soft and useless she was.

A flock of ratids burst from the trees and screeched into the sky and Cami swore under her breath. "Hate those creepy things. Rats with wings. This is definitely some level of hell." She shivered.

"Hell is for demons," I said, disgruntled at her blatant ignorance. "We are Legion."

"What's the difference?" she asked, sidestepping a pothole spewing yellow gas. I placed my hand on the small of her back, hurrying her forward before she could breathe it in. Could the steam be toxic to humans? What else about Melbak was toxic to humans? I suddenly wished I knew; my body broke out into a cold sweat at the thought of her collapsing at any moment.

"Legion take great offence to being compared to demons, despite our similar features. Demons are creatures of base emotions—fear, anger, despair. They can't function without it. If you think Melbak is a drag, I'll have to take you to the Gates of Hell. What a depressing dump."

"Is Tallis part demon, then?" she joked, and I choked in surprise. "He'd fit right in with them."

"Can you put that in one of your comics? That is hilarious." I imagined his face when he saw something alluding to his heritage being part demon. He wouldn't be able to control his temper, I just knew it.

"Bossman: A Demon at Heart." Cami swept her hands in front of her like a banner and we dissolved into laughter again.

As we entered the building to Albion's place, I wanted to reach out and take her hand but stopped myself. I would win her over, but I had to be more calculated. She was immune to my usual charms, it seemed, and I couldn't smile and wink my way into her good graces. Not after losing my mind earlier. But I knew what I needed to do. Cami would be mine soon, claimed with my fangs to satisfy my wolf. The boost had become secondary.

"Do you have to come in with me?" I raised my eyebrows at her. "Worth a try," she grumbled.

"I have to make sure you don't talk about Bossman," I said, and she sighed, knocking on the heavy door. She didn't put up much of a fight. That was progress, I thought to myself with hope.

"Enter," came Albion's measured voice. I followed in her wake as she pushed the door open. I got a whiff of her salty scent and had to bite my lip to stop groaning. Was it just me, or was it stronger?

Albion sat up as she entered, a pleased smile spreading over his face. He leapt from his chair and rounded the desk, coming to grasp her hands in his. I watched as he leaned over and kissed both her cheeks. A bit much, if you ask me, but he just smiled while I glared daggers at him.

"Ms. Perrin! What a pleasant surprise," he said, urging her to take a seat. There was a sense of déjà vu as I slid into the same seat I had occupied when Tallis had come here. It felt like an age had passed since then.

"What prompts this much happy visit?" he probed, his dark eyebrows bunching in curiosity. Cami shifted uncomfortably in her seat, and I felt a flash of fear that she had lied. She wanted a different triad.

"Your expertise, hopefully. I've tried to research at the Vault, but I couldn't find the answers I need. I thought perhaps you could help." I relaxed a little. She shot me an indecipherable look, her lower lip caught between her teeth. Albion crossed his hands and rested his chin on them, leaning forward so his chair creaked.

"How are you settling in? I would like to discuss how you are faring as a boost," he countered, and Cami scowled momentarily before wiping the expression away.

"Answer my questions first. I'll tell you all the sordid details after," she hedged, and Albion nodded, waving his hand with a stiffness.

"Did you know about the boosts becoming sick?" Cami asked, and I lurched forward in my seat.

"What?" I said, looking between the two of them, waiting for Albion to refute her claim. A grim smile slid across his face, and he shook his head slowly, disbelieving. His tail thumped on the ground, a steady slap while he sat, not saying a word.

"What makes you say that?" Albion says carefully, his tail keeping a steady beat on the ground. She frowned and leaned forward, her little fingers coming to grip the edge of the table.

"Nakasha. She took great delight in the fact that I'd sicken like her. You didn't think it pertinent to mention I might be in the same position after I'd boosted the triad?"

Albion jaw tightened and his eyes narrowed in an assessing way I didn't like, making me edge a little closer to Cami. She looked at me like I was sludge on her shoe and ignored me.

"Nakasha confided in you. That's surprising and concerning. It's not information the Heads want getting out," Albion mused softly, his gaze pinned on the window and the orange sky. Cami made a disgruntled noise in the back of her throat, tapping on the table to get his attention again.

"So, you were aware? She's covered in welts, vomiting and so sick she couldn't move, but she should have kept her mouth shut? It's getting worse."

I choked at her words. Nakasha couldn't be those things. I saw her at Ambrose's and she looked gorgeous. Sharp enough to cut, but gorgeous all the same. She'd retired early, but that was her nature. She used to be wilder before she presented and became a boost. I must have been looking slack-jawed because Cami spared me a pitying glance and patted my knee.

"The four Legion Heads hold the power in Melbak and I work under the Head's direction. Even I, from the

noble house Kerys, am subject to their pleasure. This
trial will be successful, and I will force them to take
action. I want to heal Melbak and our boosts, but that
means playing by rules I don't particularly agree with,"
Albion said. "They are following this trial with a keen
eye."

His eyes were intense, his gaze steadfast on Cami like
he was trying to say something more, a hidden message
in between the words he spoke. I didn't know what
he was trying to say, but it seemed she understood,
slumping a little back in the seat.

"Don't you know of the cursed Legion?" she
whispered. "They still won't accept me if it works, not
after all the trouble they went to purge humans from
your precious founding bloodlines. You know there is
nothing from two hundred years ago in the Vault. Where
did all the knowledge go?"

"The victors always change history. Who have you
been speaking to? Have you managed a successful
boost?" Albion darted a quick look at me but obviously
realized it couldn't have been me she'd given a boost to.
I guess my muscles weren't impressive enough.

"You knew the sentiment towards humans before you
started this. The Heads won't allow human boosts. They
won't allow me to remain here, regardless of if it has
worked, will they?"

Albion's chest rose and fall as his thoughts
percolated. "I hope it won't come to that," he said with
a grimace.

"Will they allow me to leave?" Cami looked around
the room like there were feeds watching her. My fingers
darted forward, curling around her forearm that rested

on the armrest. My heart had hammered my chest at her quiet implication.

"What do you mean by that?" I interjected, wanting to cut through the silent conversation they were having. I looked at Albion, but he was working his jaw, his teeth grinding so hard I could hear it. Cami was stiff, her fingers tapping an irregular beat.

"You made a vow I would come to no harm here," she said, as if she only just remembered.

"If I'm dead, the vow is void." Cami sucked in a horrified breath. I felt like my stomach was going to lose its contents. "I took a gamble, forcing their hand with this trial, and I am hopeful it will pay off. There is only one Head who truly despises humans, Head Lamott. I believe I can convince them. They must if it is for the good of Melbak."

"What about my family? Will the Heads still provide for them if anything happens to me?" I gave her an incredulous look. Did she just gloss over her being killed, so long as her family was still getting paid? Was that truly something that could happen? Humans had triggered the Culling. But hygiene had come a long way in both our worlds and anyone who met Cami could see she was lovely, although featureless.

"I would think—" Albion started when the door swung open and he petered off as an older lady bustled in, a big, bright smile stretching the purple lipstick painted on her lips.

"Ms. Perrin! What a delight. I've been bugging Albion about getting you in here. We were supposed to have a meeting together!" she said, her tone sharpening as she looked at Albion. He had tucked his tail under his thigh, but I could hear the muffled rattle of the head. Cami looked at the visitor with a blank face, her dark eyes drifting up and down in an obvious assessment. The lady looked at me, her eyes narrowing on the brightness of my hair.

"Gloria, how are you?" Cami said breezily. My heart squeezed in my chest. My girl was not about to be intimidated. I saw Gloria's formidable claws as she linked her hands together and notched her hip on the side of the desk.

"Cami popped by to say hello, it wasn't a meeting, Gloria," Albion said, and it shocked me to see how quick he was to give this lady an excuse to placate her. Gloria huffed a dramatic sigh, tossing him a secret smile.

"That's a relief. Head Avanti and I have been giddy with excitement over this trial. I assume this is one of your triad?" Her bright smile turned to me, and I flashed her a grin that I knew was alluring as anything.

"Fenar Leave, at your service," I purred and ran two fingers down the side of my cheek in formal greeting to her. Gloria inclined her head, not stooping to return the gesture to me. Probably a bloodline purist, if her infinitesimal twitch at my last name was any sign. I had grown used to looking for it over the years. It was always helpful to know if someone you're trying to learn more about considered you scum. She turned back to Cami, not introducing herself to me, leaning in close to her instead.

"How is it all going, dear? Have you given any boosts yet?" She spoke like a curious aunt, unassuming and warm.

"I'm still getting to know them. My being a human is a lot for them to overcome, as you can expect."

Gloria tilted her head to side and nodded emphatically, humming in agreement. She darted a quick look at me.

"I understand. Losing Legion from centuries ago cannot be taken lightly, no matter how much time has passed. If you keep yourself well cleansed, then they should overcome their misgivings in time." She sighed, staring intently at Cami. "If you decide you would rather not take on the role, we could always return you to Earth."

"You can't do that."

"She's not leaving."

Albion and I protested at the same time. I scooted over, needing to touch Cami. My fingers curled over her thigh. She looked at me sharply, but thankfully didn't pull away. Gloria laughed, a husky echo in the tense room.

"Well, it seems you've made a positive impression on at least one of your triad." Her voice was laced with disbelief.

"I made a binding agreement. Are you saying you could undo it?" Cami asked, and my fingers tightened involuntarily. She couldn't leave, not after she'd boosted Wellyn, not before I'd had my chance to make her mine.

"You know it's not possible, Gloria, don't sway her from completing the boosts," Albion chastised, visibly distressed. Gloria only chuckled again, leaning to tap a claw in front of him.

"The Heads are capable of much, Albion. I wouldn't discount them so flippantly if I were you. Head Avanti and Head Lamott will do just about anything to ensure the supremacy of Legion." Her round nose sniffed as she tapped once more to ensure he got her message. Albion made a strangled noise of protest, his eyes dismayed.

"I wish we could stay longer, but we promised one of my triad to lunch," Cami said, rising out of the chair before Gloria or Albion could react. She brushed off my hand that I held out to her. Gloria pouted, her lips fleshy like a grape.

"What a shame. You must come and see us soon. I want all the nitty-gritty details! Take care, Ms. Perrin, I'll be seeing you soon," she said.

I planted my hand on the Cami's back, propelling her forward and out the door before anyone could hold us back. I wasn't sure why I was feeling so off-kilter. Perhaps it was the strange conversation Cami had with Albion, the clarity at which she knew things I didn't, that there was danger lurking here. In the space between their stilted words, was a mounting sense of danger. The Heads didn't want Cami here, they didn't want her to be a successful boost, and if they discovered it was true, what would they do then? Would they kill her for it? Did they despise humans that much?

My head eddied with all these thoughts as I shadowed Cami's steps, taking my hand back after she growled at me. I was out of my depth, and I didn't know what step to take next.

Cami

FENAR AND I WERE both lost in thought after the meeting with Albion. I hadn't really received any answers to my questions and my growing fear hadn't abated.

The Heads didn't want this trial to succeed. Albion knew that when he brought me here, so was my death inevitable? Why attach his only son to the cause? Surely, he wouldn't be so flippant with his son's life. I couldn't say if he had the same reservations about mine. The lack of answers made my mind race like ants swarming over a discarded meal, prickling and inescapable.

"We have much to talk about, it seems," Fenar said, sliding me a tense look, his eyebrows obscured by his fringe. I sighed, knowing he wasn't about to let this go. I didn't even know how to explain it to him. I certainly wasn't going to mention Eyke.

"I don't know what to tell you, Fenar," I said finally, a spike of irritation riding through me. These arrogant Legion, thinking they had ownership over my thoughts. And yet none of them cared or wanted to do anything to help me. Except Wellyn. A small part of me protested at lumping him with all legion, and I thought of the way his mouth had latched onto my skin last night. A quick moment in the shadows. And then there was Eyke, the cursed Legion. He'd helped more than Albion wanted to. But I knew I was on my own here. If it came down to it, they would not choose me over their own kind.

"I care for you, no matter that you're a human," he said, as if the admission would sweeten me. He seemed agitated, walking a little closer to me. At least he'd stopped his simpering. Every time he flashed me that megawatt smile, I wanted to scream. It was performative, manipulative, weaponized. But it didn't break me. Each time he turned it my way, expecting me to fall to my knees, I saw someone who was too frightened to show their true self.

"Whoopee for me," I said, looking to the sky for patience. He kept reaching out to me as we walked, offering a hand to steady me around the pulsing geysers or to shield me from a startled animal. His hand seemed to hover mid-air and it made me irrational. All the surging frustration and confusion, the knowledge that I was being used, seemed to channel into the form of his hand trying to guide me with its long, shapely fingers.

It wasn't fair that he had such nice-looking hands. Fenar had painted a few of his nails a dark maroon, and instead of looking silly, it gave him an edge. He looked like a rock star with his stupid painted nails and long fingers that could have plucked the strings of a guitar, his ridiculous bright hair and handsome face. He was sexy as sin.

When he sent me a tentative smile, it was too much. Truthfully, his charm worked on me. I wanted to fall for it, wished for anything that it was true. But I knew his smiles and compliments were all shallow. He didn't truly mean them for me, they were means to an end.

I rounded on him, my simmering temper flaring until it lashed out. My hands hit his hard chest and I shoved him, putting all my frustration in the movement. He toppled backwards. His eyes were comically wide as he teetered on the path.

"I'm sick of you, so sick of this twisted place. I'm a human, so what? You're no better than me. In fact, you need me!" I ranted as his face slowly drained of color. "You need my blood, but you don't want it! You'd rather curse me like the Legion who had the audacity to look like us."

Fenar fell to one of his knees, his opposite foot caught in a sludge-filled hole. He looked paler than I'd ever seen him, beads of sweat popping up on his upper lip. His stupid hand wavered in the air between us, and he looked at it and me in a wide-eyed stupor.

"Cami," he gritted out, and I put up a hand to silence him. My chest was rumbling from the force of the emotions I was finally letting myself feel.

"You would be lucky to have me as a boost. Do you get that? Not that you ever will," I scoffed, cutting off as he fell forward, a sharp whine of pain escaping him. It was then that I noticed the creep of sludge crawling up his pant leg.

He looked up, his bangs covering his eyes. "Cami." He reached his hand out again and this time I grabbed it, yanking on him until I heard a loud, wet *pop* and he toppled me over, his chest half on mine. His lips were turning blue and his forehead was slick with sweat. His eyes were scrunched shut as he tried to lift himself up, faltering and falling back on me.

"You're hurt," I said. "Is the mud dangerous?"

Fenar gave up trying to lift himself, resting his head on my stomach with a pained hitch of his breath. "A glut." He winced, looking towards his foot. "Looks like mud but it's incredibly acidic, enough to melt off..." He didn't finish. I looked at the foot that had been stuck in the glut. His boot was gone and the skin was blistered and red like someone had put a torch to it.

"Oh God," I whispered, and Fenar chuckled hollowly, shivers raking through his body. "Will it spread?" He shrugged, looking decidedly too calm for having a red, bleeding mess for a foot.

"It might. They can release toxins into the bloodstream, which can cause death pretty quickly."

I froze under his considerable weight before scrambling and jostling him onto his back, making him cry out. I opened my mouth to scream for help, but he gripped my shoulder, his fingers digging into the skin.

"Don't bother, there is no one close enough to hear," he said, a deep swallow distorting the words. I looked back to the path we'd taken, not knowing what to do.

"I'll run and get Albion," I said.

Fenar shook his head. "You won't make it back in time." I looked at him, horror etched on every line of his face. He shrugged and opened his mouth to say something, but then closed it again, his lips pressed firmly together.

"What could help? What can I do?" I urged him, not wanting him to die. "What about a boost? Would that help?" I brushed his bangs out of his face. His forehead was hot and it worried me. I pressed my wrist to his lips, urging him to take my blood.

"You're sure?" he asked, pushing my hand away, a strange light in his eyes. "You are choosing to give me a boost?" His fingers tightened around my wrist, and he looked at it like he was starving. I could see the point of his fangs coming down, grazing his bottom lip.

"I don't want you to die." My voice cracked. He fixed me with a heady look. His mouth covered my wrist, the fangs pressing against the delicate skin there. I tensed, expecting pain, but he only pulled away, groaning with his eyes closed.

"What are you doing?" I demanded, leaning over him to press my wrist to his lips. He trembled all over, but his fingers still gripped my forearm as he muscled me back on my haunches. His eyes flashed with guilt as he closed his eyes and breathed deeply. My gaze flickered to his foot, a gasp escaping me as I saw it was healing. The red disappeared from unmarred skin, unfurling and unblemished.

"I can't. I want to but I can't," he spat, seemingly furious at himself.

He propped himself up, his hand still latched around mine.

"You tricked me?" I whispered, trying to understand what I had just seen. I couldn't breathe. My lungs burned for the need of air, but I couldn't, not after what I'd just seen him do. He'd had me just then.

He could have taken my boost, but he decided not to. An attack of a conscience? Too late either way, the damage was done. I glared at him.

"I almost tricked you," he corrected, leaning his face in close to mine.

I took a shuddering breath. "You have healing powers," I said. "You didn't need my boost at all. Why do such a thing?" He pushed himself up and pointed his foot out, assessing. The glut had partially eaten away his pant leg and shoe, but his foot looked perfect.

"I was thinking about the conversation you just had, you know, the one where you insinuated you might die? I can't protect you if I'm not my strongest self, something a boost would give me. I was thinking of protecting you, but then I knew you'd dislike being tricked in such a way."

"You want to help me, so you lied about hurting yourself on purpose?" I scrambled to my feet, my hands hot against the material of my robes.

He frowned. "Who would willingly stick their foot in a glut? You pushed me. I just used the moment to leverage for something that made sense. You need me." He flashed me a full smile, one that I knew he thought would make me forgive him for his lies. He reached out that damned hand to me and I slapped it away.

"I don't need someone who thinks they can manipulate me. Why is it you feel the need to trick everyone into everything? The hair, the nails, the smiles, the flirting? You use it all to get what you want instead of just being honest and asking. You could have talked to me, asked me for my boost instead of defaulting to games. You're no better than Tallis."

His eyes widened in shock, his upper fangs holding his bottom lip hostage. "Would you have said yes?" he asked softly. I could see a glimpse of the real Fenar, the one who thought he had to play these games, who believed that no one would offer him something freely.

"I guess we'll never know," I said, feeling sick to my stomach by the ease with which he had just manipulated me. I walked away from him, my eyes pricking with a surprising show of emotion. Why did it hurt me so much that the tricky charmer acted as I would have expected. I did not differ from any of his other conquests. I could hear his footfalls and panted breaths as he drew up next to me. I ignored him, thankful for the looming apartment building. He tried to grab a hold of my arm but I jerked away from him, almost stumbling over in my haste to get away from him.

"Are you really that mad at me?" he asked, utterly mystified, of course. "I didn't go through with it."

"Your intent was clear, Fenar, and I don't believe you stopped because you didn't want to do anything wrong. You stopped because if I found out, you'd be in even deeper shit," I said, stomping ahead.

I ignored him as he darted a furtive look at me, but he didn't speak to me again. I had enough on my plate as it was. The desire to fall asleep and get back to Eyke rose. What was his connection to Gaer? Why was it taking over everything? I slipped into my room straight away and ducked under my covers, intending to speak with Eyke.

Clothes graced me this time when I awoke in the silk bedsheets. Eyke was playing a game of Ratids and Wolves, his shoulders hunched over like he hadn't moved since I left the last time. His back stiffened as I stretched and sighed.

"You are back sooner than I thought," he said, quiet enough that I had to strain to hear. "Although, time feels different here."

"I feel like we have unfinished business and I don't know who to trust in Melbak."

He turned in the chair, the wood creaking under his bulk. My stomach fluttered as I saw even more details of his face had cleared. It was like an artist worked on him in my absence, scoring out the lines and dips of his face, each individual dark hair of his beard.

"You can trust your triad, surely?" Eyke asked and frowned as I rolled my eyes. "They do not cherish you?" He rose from his chair, not noticing that his knee knocked against the table. His fists clenched at his side as he waited for my reply. I swung my legs over the side of the bed and held out my hands in a placating manner.

"It's complicated, Eyke. I'm a human, remember?" I thought that would make the most sense to him, but he only scoffed, coming to sink into the mattress next to me. His eyes were gray, the smear of a cloudy, stormy sky. I hadn't been able to pin a color on them last time but they were so bright now. I couldn't look away.

"It makes no difference to me," he said, his voice rough and low. "You are perfect as you are. I never thought I would ever have a boost, but with you, it feels right."

I ducked my head at his effusive words. He darted forward, his calloused fingers chucking under my chin and forcing it up to meet his gaze directly. "You think I lie?" His thumb pinched my chin, not to hurt but to chasten.

I rolled my eyes and huffed a breath. "Well, I haven't boosted you and I don't want to talk about my triad. I have been trying to puzzle out what you've told me. With the scraps you've given, I might add." His shoulders shook with a silent chuckle. "The Legion who organized for me to come here basically insinuated that it didn't matter if I was successful, that the Legion Heads would not let this experiment they're doing succeed."

"What do you mean?" Eyke whispered harshly.

"My blood definitely works the way a boost would, but if the Heads know this, I'm worried they'll do anything to silence it. Enough to kill me."

"This is history repeating itself. You must do everything you can to keep it a secret. Also, never let them know you have had contact with me." His fists scrunched the dark, silk sheets and he gave me an unreadable look. "I wish I could be beside you. I hope in the future—" He cut himself off and looked away, his jaw working as he ground his teeth. I leaned over and, without thinking too much about it, grazed my lips over his cheek. He gulped, his head whipping to look at me, lips inches from mine.

His stormy eyes dropped to my mouth, which was tingling from the rough scrape of his beard. Ever since the Gaer touched me, I had noticed the sensation of being around Eyke was that same tingle. It calmed me like a mild sedative. I relaxed in his presence. I inched a little closer, liking the heat he was putting off, wanting to sink down into it like a blanket.

"My head is spinning from all this. I fear what will happen. Thank you for being here for me," I said, wincing at my ridiculously breathy voice. His thick fingers came up tentatively to curl around the back of my neck and slowly, giving me more than enough time to protest, pulled my head into his chest. I didn't want to pull back; I sighed and shuffled my body closer. Eyke and Wellyn had been the only Legion who had helped me make sense of this nightmare. He'd been a gentleman, always making me feel safe, and even cherished. If only I could swap out Tallis with Eyke. Even though I was furious with Fenar, he hadn't gone through with his plans. That was something, at least.

"You brought light to my dark life, Cami. Perhaps you don't realize how much," he whispered into my hair. I wanted to ask him what he meant by that, but the room disintegrated and knew I was going back to Melbak. I clutched Eyke, wanting the feel of him around me until the very last second.

Fenar

I HAD MISCALCULATED.

I wasn't even sure why it was annoying me that Cami was still angry with me after I tricked her into almost boosting me. She should have expected it by now. Legion are at heart devious manipulators. The conversation with Albion had left me off-kilter, and when my foot landed in that glut, it had seemed like the only solution. But as I watched her with Wellyn on the couch, I felt a sharp stab in my chest. My heart was trapped in a vice. I kicked out my legs, deliberately knocking the table leg. The game of Ratids and Wolves they'd been playing toppled and Cami shot me a poisonous look.

I raised an eyebrow, daring her to say something to me, the desperate clawing in my chest getting unbearable. I'd never had to fight so hard for attention before. And from my boost? She should fawn over me, offering me her blood without me having to resort to such petty actions. Still, she didn't take the bait, looking at the board and refusing to interact with me.

Her words echoed in my mind, and they made me feel small and invisible. Her cold eyes cut through to my core, seeing the lonely child that still lived within me. The one I had spent my whole life trying to silence. She asked me why I hadn't just asked her, but what if she'd said no? I don't know that I could handle the finality of that.

Wellyn looked between the two of us slowly. I would have asked him what he'd done to make her so amiable, but it was pretty obvious. He was soft for her, always bringing her drinks and food even though she wasn't supposed to be eating anything except the slop that Tallis had programmed for her. But when he wasn't around, Wellyn was quick to bring her a myriad of her Earth favorites.

I perked up in my seat, fighting the urge to smirk. If the way to Cami was food, then perhaps I could use that to my advantage. I strolled to the kitchen, feeling fluttery and refusing to acknowledge the thought that I was chasing a woman. This was just repairing the misunderstanding. The regular benefits of a boost were what I wanted, so I needed her on my side. At least, I needed her not to hate my guts. I ordered a range of dishes, placing them on the counter, and I pulled out cutlery and laid it to one side. The room filled with a multitude of scents; the counter crowded with a cacophony of Melbak's finest foods. Tallis had given Cami the most disgusting of Melbak's foods, not a representation that I'd want to give anyone. I noticed the pleased tick of her lips when we tried one of her many morning meals. Perhaps she would enjoy being on the other side of the experience.

Wellyn turned, sniffing the air, and letting out an appreciative hum. "What are you doing, Fenar?" he asked, wandering over to the counter to investigate. Cami looked on with interest, but she sank deeper into the couch when I glanced over at her. I resisted the urge to haul her up and drag her over. Curiosity would bring her to me, eventually. Especially when Wellyn pulled out a stool and clapped his hands together. He looked up at me with a boyish grin.

"You ordered my dumplings?" His violet eyes were slightly luminous, a sign that his creature was close to the surface. It was like that often now that Cami was boosting him. I wanted to see the change in his creature but knew better than to ask. I knew he had changed for the first time in years, and I imagined that with a boost, his creature may have grown as well. He was still sensitive about showing him, for which I couldn't blame him.

"I ordered all our favorites, and some well-known Melbak cuisine." Wellyn pursed his lips knowingly and winked at me. Guessing my motive, he swiveled in his chair and beckoned to Cami.

"Pancake, try these." He waved a fork at her. "These dumplings were the only decent dinner we had at the Ward Estate growing up."

Cami came to his side, and he fed her a piece, his hand hovering under her chin to catch any drips. I watched as if caught in a web as her full lips closed over the food and her eyes fluttered shut. I stiffened as a deep moan escaped and her hand shot out to grip Wellyn's shoulder.

It shouldn't be so erotic but *shek* if it wasn't. I looked
about for something else to tempt her. I put a selection
of our favorite dumplings on a plate and slid it over to
her.

"Try these," I said, my voice strangely hoarse. She
didn't acknowledge me but drew the plate closer and
took a bite of Tallis's favorite, the spicy juice dripping
down her chin. Her eyes popped open, and she chewed
faster, hissing as the spice kicked in.

"Oh wow, that's spicy!" she said. Her hand hovered
over her mouth to cover her chewing, I guessed.

"One guess who's favorite that is," I said, and she rolled
her eyes, going to order a glass of milk.

"Tallis," she wrinkled her nose and both Wellyn and I
started laughing.

"You can say you hate him, but you know him well," I
teased, and she waved her hand, wandering back to try
my favorite, a smoky, sweet blend that I was strangely
tense about seeing her chew through. She pointed at her
full cheeks and nodded.

"This is a winner," she hummed, her head tilting as
she directed her gaze on to me. I froze, suddenly getting
what I wanted and not knowing what to do with it. I
gulped, a lump in my throat making me wince.

"My favorite too," I blurted out. I sounded like an
imbecile and wanted to kick myself, but she was moving
on and I felt the absence of her attention like a flower
thrown into shade.

"Feed me something else before Bossman gets home
and throws a fit," she said, clasping her hands together
and rubbing them with glee.

Wellyn swooped in, recommending another of his favorites. And so we went, trying each dish and telling her about the stories behind them. I learned several things. Cami had a definite sweet tooth and watching her eat was becoming an aphrodisiac. She was a very vocal eater, letting out moans and sighs when she bit into something she liked.

Her little tongue swiping up juice from the corner of her mouth was something I wanted to bottle up, and I was already crafting a daydream in which she did the same thing to my cum dripping out of her mouth. I knew I wasn't the only one affected. Wellyn had adjusted himself a few times, and we shared a few looks when Cami was in the throes of ecstasy with another morsel. Right now, I hiding against the counter so she wouldn't see the semi my body was sporting, which would make me lose the small smudge of goodwill I seemed to have earned with her today. She groaned from her seat, rubbing her hand on her soft stomach and narrowing her eyes playfully at me. It didn't help the state of my cock.

"What are we going to do with all this leftover food? I feel terrible about the waste, but I couldn't fit another bite."

Wellyn looked up from where he had dipped his head and blew out a breath, offering her a small shrug. Another idea came to me, one I knew Wellyn would be happy with as well.

"Let's package it up and take it to the Ward Estate. I'm due to go there tomorrow, anyway. They'd love the extra food."

Wellyn slapped the counter and nodded emphatically. "Cami? Would you like to see where we grew up?" He offered a hand to our pretty boost, and she took it without hesitation. The look she gave him was so sweet, and she leaned forward and pressed a kiss to the outer corner of his mouth.

"That sounds perfect. If you think it won't cause any problems if I go, then I'd love to visit."

"Why would it cause any problems?" I said, frowning.

She sighed. "I don't want them accusing me of spreading germs, or some other human-hating idea. Wasn't it obvious from the meeting with Albion? Speaking of that, I need to ask you two something."

I tensed. We hadn't spoken longer than a few words since the meeting with Albion. I had wanted to pump her for information about Albion, Gloria and the Heads, what it all meant. But she'd cut me off since I tricked her, so I braced myself for a tongue-lashing on my actions. Wellyn had already given me his version, his ridiculous violet eyes had glared holes into me and he'd expressed how disappointed he was. I knew he was glad of it now, having two against one with Tallis. He didn't know I'd almost taken Cami's boost, but I didn't want to think about how that was going to be an explosion of epic proportions.

"I need you to keep it a secret, about being able to boost successfully." She fidgeted. Her eyes flicked to me, and I had to hold my wolf on a tight leash. He growled inside me, furious at the nerves on Cami's face. I should be protecting her better, in his opinion.

"You know the boost has made me and my creature stronger, but you're concerned?"

She pursed her lips and hopped off the stool, obviously deciding to keep her cards close to her chest again. But I don't play that way and I wasn't having it. I stepped into her path, enduring her blistering hard gaze.

"I don't want to be blindsided like I was in that meeting. There is something going on that you are keeping to yourself. Trust us. We have a vested interest in keeping you alive." I winked at her, covering the seriousness of my tone. She huffed, more immune to my obvious teasing than I expected. As she chewed her bottom lip, I wanted to pry her mouth open and force the words out.

"I am worried about what will happen if news gets out about me being able to boost you. I don't believe they ever meant this trial to be a success. Right now, we need to keep this a secret," she insisted.

"What are we supposed to do? It's obvious that Wellyn is getting the benefits of a boost," I said as Wellyn smirked, flexing his defined muscles.

"I don't know yet. There is someone I am working with, and I trust them," she said evasively. I felt my throat choking with the need to bark at her, to shake the reticence out of her.

"You can trust *us*," I growled, and she looked at me for a long time before turning a soft smile to Wellyn.

"I trust Wellyn," she said finally. He brightened to a disgusting degree, picking up her hand and kissing the back of it. She blushed like she hadn't just dealt me a brutal slap. My guts churned at the blutness of her statement. They made for the door and I trailed after them, forcing my feet to pick up lest I stumble over them. Why would she trust me? The biggest mistakes I'd made were following Tallis and being dismissive ever since she got here. And I'd tricked her into almost boosting me. I hadn't ever felt regret so thick it slid down my throat, making it hard to swallow and impossible to relax.

It wasn't just the boost I wanted. The truth churned in the acid of my guts. The human in front of me was what I wanted. I ached for her trust.

I looked fine from the outside, carefully handsome and curated to draw the eye, but my heart crushed with every breath I took.

Fenar

THE PORTAL WE TOOK to the Ward Estate spat us out on a pocked path. I dodged deep mud-filled holes and spitting fissures as my stomach settled from the journey. The longer trip seemed to amplify the queasiness. The Ward Estate was tucked in the north of Melbak, surrounded by twisted black woods. It felt peaceful despite the unusual chatter of creatures I didn't recognize in the trees. We trudged down the path, Fenar was steaming ahead, hauling most of the bags while Wellyn and I trailed behind him.

I looked at Wellyn, bemused. He was holding my hand and it felt so cute. My stomach kept fluttering when I looked over at him. It was like we were on a date.

"What is it?" he whispered, his lips twitching with their own amusement

"Fenar has been almost nice today. It's weirding me out," I admitted. Not wanting to draw attention to my giddiness.

"I know he went about it wrong, and he needs to make up for that, but he is a good Legion. Incapable of cleaning up after himself, but he's also the one who protected me when we were growing up. My brother. He had been in the Ward Estate since he was a baby, you know. Never knew who his parents were." He looked away before continuing, he paused for a moment "I was ten when I arrived at the Ward Estate. Not because my parents died, but because they abandoned me. They saw my creature and didn't want to claim such a weak show of power."

I sucked in a horrified breath. His parents had abandoned him because of his creature? I couldn't believe anyone could be so cruel, but I was quickly learning that Legion were brutal when they wanted to be.

Wellyn gave a little shrug. "I was the youngest of four brothers. They could afford to cut off one useless son."

I pressed a kiss to his shoulder. "It's their loss," I said, fiercely protective of my sweet Legion. So, there was a family out there who had rejected this amazing person? I wished I knew who they were. I'd have a few choice words to say to them.

A waft of smoke curled in front of our faces and I batted it away. Wellyn continued, "When I arrived at Ward Estate, it became known pretty quickly why I was there. The kids teased me mercilessly, forcing me to bring my creature out to mock him. Fenar was the only one who stood up for me, fighting anyone who taunted me. He's the first person who ever fought for me, who didn't judge me for my creature."

I hummed, looking at Fenar's wide back as he leapt up the worn steps of a square building and pressed a button on the entry. It looked rundown, the material on the outside patchy, with flakes hanging off where it had peeled. The door looked like it was one stiff breeze away from falling in. It creaked as it slid open.

A thick-waisted woman bustled out, squealed, and enveloped Fenar in a hug. His arms struggled to hold the bags as she wrapped her arms around his waist.

"Fen! We weren't expecting you today!" She pulled back, not quite relinquishing him. She had short, graying hair and ears that drooped like a mini elephant's, wide and wrinkled.

"Wellyn and I thought we'd surprise you and the children," he replied, clear warmth in his voice, no trace of his usual snarky tone. The woman poked her head around and, seeing Wellyn, her eyes watered, and she waved her hands at him. He obliged her, pulling me with him.

"Get up here, my little one!" It was a laughable nickname, given that Wellyn towered over her and, in his boosted state. She must have realized it too, as she squeezed his arms with a salacious grin.

"What have we here? You've filled out, finally!"

Wellyn ducked his head, stepping out of her reach.

"Hilles, can I introduce my boost, Cami?" He turned, and the pride in his expression took my breath away. Hilles saw it too. I waited for the judgement and disgust, but she only smiled, catching me in a bone-crushing hug that had me gasping for air.

"Hilles! Don't hurt the poor girl. I've got bags of food for the children. Let's share that around, shall we?" Fenar said and she finally released me to wander inside.

"They'll be so pleased. The food orderer has been broken for months, not that we've had spare coin to indulge in much. I heard that there was a human boost. I thought they mentioned your triad, but I couldn't believe it was true!" Hilles said, leading them forward with a steady stride.

"I was going to fill you in when I came in two days, but didn't think you'd mind meeting her in person," Fenar teased, elbowing her gently.

Hilles laughed a husky chuckle while she wagged her finger at him. "The ladies at cards will vomit when they know I have the inside scoop. Tell me everything." The last part she directed at me, and I had the uncomfortable sensation of realizing that this was essentially a meet-the-parents lunch.

"Don't worry, she's harmless," Wellyn whispered, his arm wrapping around my waist and pulling me to him. I leaned into his calming cold, thankful as ever for his presence.

The Ward Estate was plain, tidy but lacking, worn furniture from overuse by rowdy children I assumed, a stream of which came racing through the door and collided with Fenar. A hoard of wriggling, laughing children surrounded him like playful puppies. It was surreal seeing their Legion features—tiny horns and tails that looked almost cute. They bounded around Fenar, yanking on his sleeve, trying to get his attention.

The noise reached the point where I was about to clamp my hands over my ears when Hilles clapped her hands together and boomed, "Enough, little ones! Fenar has brought food, so I want you to set it up in the dining hall." She directed the children to take the myriad of bags from Fenar and shooed them out the doorway.

"But, but, but will you stay? I want to show you the fireball I've been working on!" a small girl begged, ignoring the look of reproach Hilles gave her. Fenar crouched down until he was on the same level as the girl. She was thinner than she should have been, but her cheeks were rosy,

"Of course, I will. I'm sure you'll be as strong as Tallis one day, Allee!" He tousled her hair and sent her off with the others. It confused me watching Fenar in this way. He seemed so different, so at ease.

"Are you still insisting on this?" Hilles scowled, reaching out and plucking Fenar's bright hair. He darted a look at me, looking almost embarrassed. He batted Hilles' hand away and shrugged.

"Leave it," he begged.

But Hilles continued, "You don't need these bright colors to make yourself noticed anymore; those bloodline purists will never see you the way you want them to. Besides, you have a boost now. I bet half of them are beyond envious."

Fenar grimaced, looking like he wanted the ground to swallow him up. He changed the subject. "Can we go to the blue room? I want to heal before I see the other children." Hilles looked at him like he'd offered her a million dollars.

"You think so? Because of—" she cast a furtive look back to me, "Randell has struggled this week."

Fenar looked pained and put his hand on Hilles' arm, narrowing his eyes. "I haven't been lucky enough to be boosted yet. But besides that, as far as anyone knows, Cami hasn't boosted anyone yet. Please, it's important that no one knows."

Hilles widened her eyes before covering her surprise quickly by winking at me.

"Your secret is safe with me. How is Tallis enjoying boosted life?"

Fenar grimaced as I snorted while we walked down another faded hallway.

"He's not happy to be boosted by a human," I couldn't help saying.

Hilles frowned. "See, those pure bloodlines have always had a tizzy about silly things like that. Melbak needs more boosts. Who cares where they come from?"

I hadn't expected her to be so accepting, but I guess she housed so many children that were seemingly unwanted anywhere else. She had seen the worth in Fenar and Wellyn, and it had helped them grow up knowing that they were safe somewhere.

We walked up a set of faded wooden stairs. The bannister cracked and split in one place.

"That's new," Wellyn said mildly, his fingers tracing it as he walked past. Hilles clucked her tongue, shaking her head.

"Some youngsters were testing their strength, little troublemakers. Like two others I might know!"

"Were you a bad boy growing up, Wellyn?" I whispered in his ear, enjoying the way his breath hitched.

"Fenar led me astray, but if you need a bad boy, I can channel that for you." He winked and pinched my butt.

I almost barreled into Fenar as we came to the blue room, and I realized, my stomach sinking, where the inspiration for the name came from. The room itself was white, one wall adorned with a mural of a thick jungle with yellow eyes hidden in the dark shadows. It looked creepy, but I suppose for Legion it was on par. They were all little psychopaths. The blue came from the feeling of the room. Beds lined each wall in regular intervals, each one housing a child who looked like they were wasting away. It was deathly quiet, a sound one should not associate with the young.

Fenar crossed over to a bed in the middle. Randell, I assumed. He pulled the chair next to the bed closer and sat down. Randell had shorn blonde hair, his skin milky white with veins like rivers underneath. One hand lay on the simple bedspread and I sucked in a horrified breath at what I saw. His tiny hand was black, as if covered in tattoos, but the skin looked like it was moving. It seemed to bubble, tiny tendrils snaking up his skeletal arm. I recognized it as the touch of the dark substance that terrorized Melbak.

"Gaer? How? I thought it killed those who it touched," I whispered as Fenar picked up the hand of the catatonic boy and closed his eyes. Wellyn watched Fenar as he bowed in on himself, his own face pinched with pain.

"Some survive. They send the children that do here. The Heads deemed those Gaer touched a lost cause because we haven't healed any from the coma they are under. The Gaer eventually spreads until it is too much for the body to cope with."

My hand covered my mouth, but I couldn't look away from the wan form in the bed. He had tiny dark claws on each hand, but other than that, he looked like a boy. Like he could be one of my brothers. I imagined one of them laying here, being told there was nothing to help them and that it was only a waiting game until the black substance ate them alive. Gaer had taken me to Eyke after I touched it. I wondered if the curse was reversed, whether the Gaer would be so lethal. Whether it would disappear.

"Fenar comes every month to heal the children. He does what he can to stave off the Gaer from taking them."

I was thankful for Wellyn beside me because my legs trembled and threatened to buckle. The Gaer on Randell's arms shifted back, brushed away by an invisible blast of wind until it resettled on his wrist. Such a small amount had moved, and yet Fenar's forehead prickled with sweat already. How could he heal this entire room without harming himself? A need swelled inside me and I sank to my knees in front of him.

He looked at me, a vulnerability in his face and an intensity that I felt I was seeing for the first time.

"Your healing power will grow stronger if I boost you, right?" I heard Hilles' startled gasp behind me.

"That and more. If you boost me now, Cami, I think I could heal the room with no trouble." He looked at Randell, laying his hand back on the bed gently. "This was another reason I wanted a boost. The real reason. I know I'm an ass. I wasn't kind to you, and I betrayed your trust, but my healing powers can make a difference here."

I couldn't reply, except to nod once and join Fenar as he moved to the next bed. I held my wrist out, a

silent invitation, trying to ignore the swirling disbelief
and awe on his face. I didn't forgive him, but I felt some
of the sharp ire against him fade. He cared for these
kids, more than their Heads who had forgotten them,
and with my boost he could really make a difference in
their Gaer-touched lives.

"You're sure," he breathed.

I frowned. "These kids need your help, and we can
give them a better chance."

He gulped and took my wrist as gently as he had
Randell's, his warm breath coasting over the skin for
a second before the sharp pierce of his fangs jolted
through me. The pull of his mouth lessened the pain, the
swipe of his tongue sending a wave of dizziness down
my spine. I sagged against his side, letting his arm slide
around my waist and anchor me to him.

Wellyn took my boost with reverence, sweet and
constant, but this was different. Fenar took from my
veins like he was starving. His fangs, imbedded into my
skin, should have hurt. But it was scorching, like the
heart of a fever. It had only been moments, but when
he pulled away, waving a hand over the small puncture
wounds, I felt the loss. He pressed his head against my
stomach, his arm clenching.

"Thank you." His voice was thick with emotion and I
let my fingers come and run through his hair, comforting
him. It was like he couldn't believe I had said yes, and I
wondered how many times Fenar had anything in his life
that he hadn't tricked or seduced out of someone else.

"Come, heal the others," I encouraged softly, staying
by his side as he picked up the hand of the next
bed-bound child.

Cami

HILLES AND I WATCHED Fenar and Wellyn play with the children from the steps of the Ward Estate. Fenar had finished healing as much as he could. My wrist still tingled with the feeling of his fangs sliding into me. There were no wounds, but the sensation remained.

"Take good care of my boys now, won't you?" Hilles said. Her eyes crinkled as Wellyn tackled Fenar to the ground. I grimaced.

"Well, I wouldn't call them my boys," I said, even though it sounded nice on my tongue. I wondered what it would be like if Tallis wasn't such an asshole. Would he be here too?

My thoughts flittered to Eyke and how he might fit in with the triad. My stomach flipped at the idea of them all together. It made sense, somehow.

The two boys wandered over to us, escaping the racing children. Fenar was covered in mud and Wellyn had a streak down the side of his jaw.

"You're filthy," I laughed, pushing Wellyn away when he tried to cuddle me. He looked down in dismay, then grinned.

"You like dirty Legion though, don't you, Pancake?" I felt my cheeks heat and whacked him in the arm.

"It's a shame the Gaer has overtaken the temple, I used to love using the hot springs to wash," Hilles said, eyeing the mud with a wrinkle of her nose. "I would have liked one more dip before they move us out of here."

Fenar's muddy head whipped up, and he frowned. "What do you mean, move you?"

Hilles shrugged, her eyes heavy as she squinted over to the horizon. "The Heads want to use this land for more apartments. It's prime land that could be used better, or so I'm told." She sounded bitter, and I didn't blame her. Wellyn placed his hand on her shoulder, looking concerned.

"Where are they sending you and the children?" he pressed. She sighed.

"They're clearing out a floor at Rillia," she admitted and Fenar cursed, whirling away with his hands clutching his hair. Wellyn's face drained of color and he shook his head.

"They can't do that. Rillia is full already. How would they fit you and the children?"

"Not to mention it's a breeding ground for the worst kind of Legion. What are the Heads thinking? Rillia is not a place for children. Who is spearheading this move?"

Hilles darted a look at Wellyn, her lips thin and white as she pressed them together. Wellyn cast a look at the sky, laughing colorlessly.

"Of course, he would do this. It's not enough to ruin my life. He must destroy the only home I ever knew."

Hilles turned to comfort him instead, none of them explaining the outburst of information. Fenar came to stand beside me, his jaw gritted.

"We will put a stop to this. Somehow, we will destroy that bastard," he said fervently.

Wellyn wrapped Hilles up in a tight hug, murmuring a promise in her ear. Hilles untangled herself and shrugged.

"Don't concern yourselves, boys. I always knew this land would be snatched back eventually. I've made my own contingencies and they do not involve moving these children to Rillia."

"However, if we can help, let us know," I interjected, despite not knowing what was going on. I knew Hilles deserved to be protected, not least for having given Wellyn and Fenar a safe place to grow up. She gave me a soft smile.

"We had best say goodbye now. I don't want you tramping through the house with those filthy clothes."

She engulfed me in a hug before I could say anything, squeezing my ribs so hard I squeaked. She blew a kiss to Wellyn and Fenar, waving for the children to follow her inside.

"Come back soon, my sweet ones. With Tallis next time, perhaps?" she said.

"Unlikely," I said under my breath.

"Now, now, you never know," Fenar said, recovered from his earlier outburst, his hip bumping mine. "That discipline session he had with you? That is some serious sexual tension you guys have."

He smiled at me smugly and I punched his arm, bounding down the steps to get away from him.

"Fucking perv," I snarled, not wanting to think about that time a second longer. I certainly would not tell Fenar how the feeling of Tallis's fingers soothing the sting on my flaming ass had imprinted in my brain like some twisted porno. Wellyn jogged the steps, leaning down to murmur in my ear.

"Do you think we could remove the Gaer from the temple like we did the springs?"

I stopped walking, looking at Wellyn in surprise.

"You think we could?" I chewed my lip and looked back at the Ward Estate. "I'd like to do something nice for Hilles. She was so kind and didn't judge me at all for being human."

"She's the best. We'll make sure Head Lamott doesn't touch this place. What are we doing for her?" Fenar asked as he pushed between us.

A slow smile slid over Wellyn's face, and he shrugged.

"Oh, it's nothing. Cami and I may have a way to rid the temple of Gaer. We've done it before at the springs."

Fenar's jaw dropped, and he gasped out loud. "That was you? How?"

The springs had remained free of Gaer since I had boosted Wellyn there, and Legion had been ecstatic, flocking there to make use of the beautiful water. Wellyn grabbed my hand, tugging me from the path and across the muddy field. We pushed past into the trees. I looked ahead to see small cracks in the ground with steam coming from them. A screech came from the straggly branches, and a flock of ratids exploded from a hollow

trunk and scattered into the sky. I swore, lurching into
Fenar in surprise.

"God, I hate those things!" I said, not protesting when
he threw a heavy arm around my shoulder. He looked
down at me in bemusement.

"Ratids can be tame, you know. Quite sweet little
things, very loyal and social." I shuddered. "Ambrose has
a heap he bought after Nakasha said she desired one."

"Disgusting," I said, moving closer to Fenar despite
myself. His broad chest was comfortable to lean against
and I felt safer walking through the trees with him close
to me. "If you ever treat me like an actual boost, just
know that the way to my heart is not with small, hairy
creatures that can fly."

I meant it as a joke, but Fenar stiffened and caught me
in his intense gaze.

"Have no fear, Cami. I am committed to making things
right between us."

I tore my eyes down from his intense gaze, trying to
pull away, but his arm clamped around me. He would
not treat me like Wellyn did, like how a triad should
treat their boost, if all historical accounts were true. I
still hadn't forgotten how easily he'd almost manipulated
me. I certainly would entertain nothing else about our
relationship. But after seeing him at the Ward Estate, I
felt like I'd seen a side of Fenar that he kept hidden from
everyone else. Something that other Legion might not
consider positive—helping others and honoring where
he grew up—but to me it went a long way to thawing the
chill between us.

The longer I walked pressed up against his hard side,
the more my thoughts drifted to what he considered his

most deadly weapon. His body. Fenar was arrogant and cocky. I wondered if he'd be like that in the bedroom. I'd slept with guys like that before and it was always a letdown. They thought their cocks did the work for them, never realizing that it wasn't about looks, but passion. They used tricks they'd done a hundred times before, thinking it would unlock a woman's body like a cheat code.

A shambling stone structure rising out of the thick brush interrupted my sordid thoughts. It had been abandoned for a long time, it seemed. The outer walls cracked and oozed with Gaer, the dark substance bursting through like blood. It seemed more solid in places, rope-like vines wrapped around and through the walls like they were a living part of them.

"This temple has seen better days. You really think you can shift the Gaer from here?" Fenar didn't relinquish his hold on me, and Wellyn came to stand next to me, shrugging.

"It's worth a try, if you're still willing, Cami?" His cool fingers ran down my arm, tangling with my own and turning my wrist so it faced him. I had boosted Fenar at the Ward Estate, but I felt strong enough to go again. My blood thrummed in my veins. I couldn't quite look away from the temple. There was something about this place that spoke to me, a whisper in a language I couldn't understand spoken on the wind, but my blood heard it and understood the call. It wanted me to do this.

"We must." I nodded, looking at Fenar. "Can you?" I lifted my wrist and gestured to his fangs, hoping he would make the puncture hole. His eyed flared as he lowered his head, his lips soft before the sharp bite of his teeth. I hissed, my hips jerking back into his body. But not for long. Wellyn took over, lifting my wrist to his mouth and sucking. His tongue laved at the shallow wound and the sensation made my knees wobble. I was suddenly glad for Fenar as his arm banded around my chest, taking most of my weight as Wellyn continued to drink from me.

It felt different, dangerously charged. My skin felt hot, like my blood was bubbling in my veins, dancing to a tune I couldn't comprehend. I twisted in Fenar's hold, my focus zeroed in on the sensation of Wellyn's mouth on my skin. I ground my ass against a hard length, almost sobbing at the throb it wrung from my pussy.

"*Shek*," Fenar choked out, his fingers spasming under my breasts. "Is this what you did last time?"

Wellyn looked up at me, his violet eyes luminous and his mouth curving against my skin. I knew he was feeling the strange heat as well, his cock pressing against the material of his pants. I ground against Fenar, knowing I'd likely regret it later but needing the delicious hardness and touch. My eyes flitted to the temple where the Gaer seemed to react to the charged boost. It was shuddering, slowly folding back into itself, but I could sense the need for more. It needed something else.

"Bite me, Fenar," I panted, arching my neck. "I think you need to boost as well."

Fenar shook his head, looking torn.

"I don't want to take too much. You already boosted me."

Wellyn scraped his blunt teeth on the wound, and I cried out, the sensation sending a spark of pleasure through my body. I needed more. If Fenar wouldn't take my boost, he had to help me find release in some other way.

"Please, touch me, then," I whined, writhing against his body. I could feel how much he wanted me, but he just held me tighter, trying to stop my movement.

"Baby, you don't want me like this. It's a boost haze." He sounded like he was talking through gritted teeth, and I wanted to cry at his rejection, even though part of me was thankful. Wellyn laid his tongue flat on the puncture holes, dropping to his knees in front of me.

"Are you needing? You taste so incredible. I could taste you all over. If Fenar doesn't want to take care of you, I will."

Fenar groaned behind me as I slowly nodded. My head was buzzing with that strange conversation with the Gaer, and I knew I needed this release. Embarrassment didn't cross my mind as Wellyn tugged down my pants and lifted one leg on his shoulder. He looked at my pussy, marveling at my slick folds. He looked up at me, eyes wide with adoration and his cool breath making my throbbing clit pulse.

"You are the most beautiful thing I've ever seen. My creature is riding me hard right now. Can I try something?" He said it like he expected me to turn him down, as if I would ever turn him away.

"Yes, I need you. I love y--, I love your tongue on me." I swallowed, my whole body flushed red. What was I thinking? I had almost said I loved Wellyn.

I couldn't stew in my almost-blurted declaration of love for long, as Wellyn dove in, his tongue slowly tasting me. His languid strokes made me crazy. I threw my head back onto Fenar. Around my legs was a cool sensation, and I looked back down to see that instead of arms, Wellyn had wrapped me in two tentacles.

"You can partial shift?" Fenar said behind me, his voice hoarse. Wellyn looked up.

"Since I boosted, I have been able to. My creature adores Cami, just like me." I groaned as the suckers on the tentacles pulsed against my skin, sending a wave of pleasure to my pussy.

"God, that feels good," I moaned, writhing my head on Fenar's shoulder. I turned and caught his gaze. If I could burn up from one look, it would have been at this moment. He was showing remarkable restraint, having turned me down, but right now it looked like he was about to snap. I trembled against his hard chest as Wellyn circled his cool tongue around my clit.

"Kiss me," I said, straining towards Fenar. "Just once, please," I begged. I was so close I could feel the hot pants coming through his gritted teeth.

"This is crazy, I've never felt like this before."

"Please." I scrunched my eyes closed as the tentacles swiped the inside of my thigh. Goosebumps erupted on my skin. Fenar's lips fell on mine, and I opened my mouth immediately, welcoming the demanding swipe of his tongue. We moaned together, the vibration of it sending my hand flying up to grapple the back of his head while the other pressed Wellyn further into my pussy. I wrapped my fingers around their hair like they were an anchor. My blood was scalding under my skin, my pussy throbbed like it was about to explode. Wellyn thrust his tongue inside my hot channel, making me wish it was his cock. Fenar's hands came to grab my breasts, pawing at them in desperation.

"Under, under, I need your touch," I babbled against his lips, urging him to touch my bare skin. My nipples felt so hard, and they rubbed against the material in a way that only built my frustration. I needed his hands on them.

"Baby," he groaned, strained as my lips chased his again. That delicious edge was so close. I grabbed my shirt, hoisting it up before guiding his hand to my breast. I sobbed into his mouth as his fingers rolled my nipple.

"Yes! More!" I couldn't think of anything but the sensation of both of them touching me. My thighs shook around Wellyn's head as he placed his mouth over my clit and sucked. I came with a cry, flooding Wellyn with juices as pleasure made me spasm and jolt. My hand tightened around Fenar's hair again, so tight that he hissed. His teeth scraped my lip as I pulled him down to kiss me through the fading orgasm. We continued making out, our tongues tangling while obscene noises escaped us.

Wellyn extricated himself from my legs, and as he lowered my thigh, I turned and pressed against Fenar fully, hoisting my leg up to grind against him. There was something indecent about the friction of his hardness on my wet folds. A thought cut through the mind-altering madness that I'd be leaving a wet patch on his leg. Wellyn dug his fingers into my shoulders.

"As much as I don't want to be a cockblock, look at this."

He pulled me firmly away from Fenar, who growled, his fingers reaching to snag on my shirt, not willing to let go of me yet. I looked to where Wellyn was pointing.

The walls were moving like it was coming alive. I realized it was the Gaer folding in on itself to reveal the temple in its decrepit glory. It moved quickly, the whisper that had wormed its way into my brain seeming to fade as it drew away from the structure.

I shimmied my pants up and raced over to the door. It was a few warped boards, the rest long destroyed.

"Woah, wait!" Fenar said, grabbing my arm before I walked in. "You don't know if it's really gone."

I looked at him, his lips swollen from our voracious kissing and hair mussed from my machinations. I shrugged. I don't know how I knew, but I was certain the Gaer had given up its hold on this place and would not return. Wellyn sidled past me, poking his head through the gap in the rotting wood, looking back at me with a boyish grin that made me tingle all over.

"It's gone, and the spring is clear." That cherubic smile turned devious. "Who's ready for a dip?"

Fenar took my hand and guided me through the door and into the temple itself. The spring was at the center, with steps leading down to clear turquoise water. The inside was smooth gray stone, seemingly untouched by time, unlike the wood. The builders carved symbols into the columns that bordered the spring, which glowed as though lit with a red backlight.

Wellyn hastened over to the spring, stripping off his clothes as he went. I eyed his tight behind as he waded into the water and groaned with pleasure.

"It's the perfect temperature," he confirmed, wasting no time in diving under, his lithe form changing into his creature. I watched in fascination as the tentacles spread out, one sliding up as if to beckon me closer. An eerie red glow filled the spring, the heat making it comfortable and intimate.

"Wellyn's creature," Fenar breathed from beside me, following me as I walked toward the edge. I cut him a dark look, daring him to say something degrading about his beautiful creature.

"He's grown so much. The last time I saw him was years ago. Your boost did this?"

I bristled a little at his tone. Did he not believe it was possible? Dangling my fingers in the water, a tentacle came up immediately, dancing over my knuckles. I leaned down and brushed it with my lips.

"After what we just did, you're still surprised?" My cheek flushed slightly, clarity seeping into my boost-addled brain. Boost haze, Fenar had called it, and I think I was only just escaping it. I didn't regret it, but I didn't really understand. I was waiting for a cutting remark from Fenar which didn't come. Instead, he sunk into a squat at my side, his hand landing on my knee and giving it a quick squeeze.

"Look, I don't want you to hate me more, especially after what just happened." His eyes heated, and I felt the prickle on my skin. I licked my lips nervously. Fenar dragged his fingers off my knee, leaning back on his heels, a hesitancy rounding his shoulders. "I am committed to earning your trust. I know I don't have a right to that, but I will. Just give me time to prove it to you."

I hummed under my breath. His intensity was unnerving. This morning, things had made sense. Fenar was a prick I couldn't trust. Now he was a manipulative

Legion who used his powers for good and could kiss the pants off me.

I got to my feet and wandered deeper into the temple, past the spring. If I was honest, I wanted to put some space between us, but I wasn't about to admit it. I followed the dim red glow until I came to the source, a smooth black plate with an etching that shone red. My fingers moved towards it, unbidden, tracing the sharp edges of the picture.

It was me.

Or rather, it was a depiction of a boost. The version in this picture had human features, her arms slightly outstretched from her naked body. There were two men on their knees at her feet, latching onto her wrists. Stranger still was behind her, two more men with their heads lowered to the junctures of her neck and shoulders. They had the features I was becoming more used to, the horns, tails, and claws. Except for one, who was tall and broad, like Eyke, looking like an ordinary human giant.

This wasn't a triad like I had been constantly told about. This was its true form, what Eyke had spoken of. The need for a fourth, one of the cursed, dark Legion. Before the Heads wiped everything clean from the history books and replaced it with the idea of a triad. Looking at this etching, I couldn't help the feeling of peace that swept through me, a knowing that this was right.

"What is this temple for?" I called out, curious why this depiction could remain when everything else seemed to be scrubbed clean, a different version of history in its place. I traced the scored lines of the picture, not looking up as I felt Wellyn and Fenar come up beside me. Wellyn reached out a dripping hand, touching the picture with a slight frown wrinkling his face.

"It's a boost," he confirmed, but he sounded unsure. I looked to Fenar, who was rubbing his jaw, looking disturbed.

"They've drawn it wrong, there is an extra guy getting in on the action." His lip twisted half-heartedly as he tried to joke, but I could see that the picture was affecting him somehow.

"Have there ever been cases of boosts having four?" I asked.

"No, it doesn't work that way," Fenar said, fear jerking his lip up in a sneer. He tugged at my elbow, pulling me away. "Forget the picture, it's nothing but a relic."

I cast one look back at the glowing red light, thinking of Eyke in his dark prison, and the Gaer, how it had swarmed this place. This was all connected. I just didn't know how.

Tallis

THE APARTMENT WAS EMPTY when I got home. I had lingered in the middle of it for a short time. I had never noticed before how cold and bare the apartment was and how my room lacked warmth. I knew where it came from, but I wasn't about to admit it to myself. My thoughts skirted around the absence of the other two points of my triad and where they were. The apartment itself smelled like a buffet of all our favorite foods, and it made my hackles rise that they had been feeding the human, introducing her to Melbak's different dishes. I wondered if she liked any of the same foods I did.

Where are you?

I messaged Wellyn on his reader, more reliable than Fenar in replying.

Is the human with you?

The tension crept through my entire upper body. My hands warmed with excess energy, tingeing red as my thoughts crept back to my missing triad and the interloper. My reader chimed with a reply, and I hastily unlocked it to read.

We took Cami to see the Ward Estate. Fenar is doing some healing.

They'd taken her to the Ward Estate? For what reason? I knew Wellyn was nursing a ridiculous crush on the human, but it surprised me Fenar would want her there. They were wards of the Heads, something that had been a sore point for me when I was younger. I loved Fenar and Wellyn like brothers, but as a Kerys, I had thought my triad would be one of significance, a joining of the most elite bloodlines like Ambrose's. He'd been a close friend when we were younger, but after his tests and his triad was announced it was like I didn't exist anymore. It only worsened when I completed my tests, and they made my triad with two no-names with questionable bloodlines.

Fenar was powerful, his fighting prowess and his creature were universally respected. But Wellyn? It had taken me many years to get over my own prejudices and several more of constant bloody knuckles to make everyone else know better than to challenge me on the strength of my triad. I was fiercely proud of my brothers because that's what they were now. There was still time to challenge the Heads decision and move to another Triad, but I knew we were meant to be together.

But even I had only been to the Ward Estate a handful of times. It had been a long time since I had felt so adrift, so out of place, even in my own home. I ground my teeth, wanting to know what I could do to the human to break her. Everything else had failed.

I searched the ground out the window for a sight of them, a flash of dark curls and delectable curves. I growled, launching away from the window seat. The cushions were perfect, and it made my anger rise for some reason. It drove me mad when the human moved them about for her pleasure, but to know she hadn't even sat here, that she had not been in my space? It made my guts clench in a way I couldn't recognize.

I intended to storm down to my room and stay there until they returned, but the lingering scent of food made my fury mount. I don't know why I paused at Wellyn's door, or why I turned the handle. It didn't open, just as Fenar had pointed out to me a while ago. I let my fingers curls around the handle, my forehead coming to rest on the door. Wellyn often slept in Cami's room, although he was discrete about it, so why the obsessive need to lock his door? Unless he had something in there that he didn't want me to find?

I pulled out my reader and made a call. It would require some apologizing, but if the tingling down my spine was correct, it would be worth it. Wellyn was hiding something, and I would swallow ten bowls of seffe if it wasn't something to do with that knife in my side, the human.

I sat in the window seat, my skin buzzing with a frenetic, dark excitement. My imagination had been going crazy with ideas of what Wellyn might have been hiding for the human. I'd gone through her things already, but she'd brought nothing but her unsuitable human clothes and I'd already messed around with them. Fenar had been unhappy about me enlisting Gerad to ruin them, and after he'd explained what the tiny triangles were for, I had felt a flush of heat. I'd asked Gerad to fix them, watching over his shoulder obsessively and snatching the scraps of silky material as soon as he had finished. It seemed wrong that he touched things that were so intimately hers. So, I had nothing else I could ruin. I had contemplated cutting her hair, but I didn't know if that would count as physical harm and displease my dad, with his admittedly handsome mop being trifled with. A quiet part of me protested at the thought of messing with her dark tresses purely because I liked the way they framed her face. I needed something else, hence I called Cove.

She didn't take long to arrive, sweeping through the door with a raised eyebrow. We hadn't been speaking, me licking my wounds after saying I loved her and she annoyed I was squandering my chance at a boost. Her hands gripped her hips as she waited, her opal sheath looking chic and delicate.

"I wanted to apologize," I said, unfolding myself and making my way over to her. Time to give an impressive performance. "I admit I haven't been myself and have a lot to make up for." I turned my head, sighing quietly. Cove leapt forward, her big heart not allowing her to stay still while she thought I was in pain. Her slight form crushed into me, snaking her arms around my waist.

I waited for the pulse of passion, of lust at having her close. I put my hands on her back, pressing her close to me, but all I felt was the warmth of her small body. Nice but not titillating. I couldn't help but think about the time the human had pressed back against me and the ravenous wave that crashed over me. The warring rage and disgusting lust that my hand on her skin hadn't tempered. It had only grown, my cock not getting the message that I did not mean to desire her. It was Cove I loved, right? But in this hug, I could feel the difference. It was fuzzy and muted. Sweet. I searched for the longing that had kept a hold over my heart for so long and found the space empty.

"Oh, Tallis, I knew you'd come around eventually." Cove squeezed me one last time before letting go. Her big, blue eyes stared up at me with utter bliss. Before the human, this would have sent me dumb. My tongue thickened at the sight, but it didn't happen, and I couldn't quite wrap my head around it. I ran my fingers down Cove's arm to comfort her, but also to test the sensation. There was no flare, zing or anything inside me. My body didn't react to her anymore. Her skin tone was too light, her forehead too crowded with her horns, her hair too short and blonde. It was wrong. I wanted—

No! Before they betrayed me, I cut my thoughts off. I cleared my throat and gave Cove a tight smile.

"I'm not there yet, but I also don't want to fight anymore," I explained. That was the truth, I wanted things to go back to how they used to be before the human burst into my life and put this wedge between me and everyone I cared about. The rest of my triad were off showing her around like she'd earned the right to know anything about them, like they wanted to share things about themselves. It made me sick. I wanted her gone, even if the foolish I idea I had about Cove had imploded. I wanted freedom from the twisting in my guts when I saw the human. It was like an addiction to see her eyes flash with rage at me. I was sick of dancing around my house, feeling uncomfortable in my space. I'd caught myself sniffing the cushions! I had to get control of myself again.

Cove narrowed her eyes at me. She knew me too well and could see right through me.

"I never thought I'd be here. I just want to mend ours and the boys' friendship."

"You're fighting with the other two? Wellyn hates fighting, though!" Cove said, her lips falling open in surprise. I nodded slowly, slumping my shoulders like it was really weighing on me.

"He's head over heels for the hu—I mean, Cami." Cove pursed her lips as I continued, "and I think Fenar might head in the same direction."

"I'm glad for them. Please treat her kindly. I like her for you. Your bloodline does not impress her, and she doesn't seem to back down when you act all pompous and controlling."

I curled my lip at her words, but quickly smoothed it over. "She has proven herself strong. Nothing I do seems to shake her," I admitted, but perhaps after Cove helped me, I would find the key to cracking her unbreakable facade. After clearing my throat, I gestured to the hall.

"I was hoping you could help me with something. I want to make it up to Cami, but I need your help."

Cove followed me with her hands clasped together with excitement. "If I can't be a boost, I'm going to make damn sure you take care of yours, Tallis! What can I do to help you sort this out?" I rapped my knuckles on Wellyn's door and gave her what I hoped was a sweet smile.

"I want to make a grand gesture, a big apology, but I need something that Wellyn has locked in his room. I can't ask him if I can borrow it as he couldn't keep a secret from Cami if he tried."

Her name on my tongue sounded illicit. Cove leaned on the wall, her arms crossed, waiting for more information. *Shek*, I hadn't thought that far ahead. I thought she'd open the door without even realizing I was being vague.

"I want to apologize in front of our fellow Legion, to prove that I am serious about committing to her," I hedged, and Cove's face transformed. Her dangling earring shook as she bounced on her toes.

"Good idea. Humbling yourself in front of everyone would make her see you are truly sorry. So what do you need from Wellyn's room?"

"Well, after that I want to bring her back here and have the apartment set up, ready for a romantic dinner and hopefully a boost at the end of it. I need something from Wellyn's room to make it memorable."

The thought of tasting her blood sent a jolt straight to my groin, and the answering nausea in my gut made me lean against the door. This reaction I was having to the human was tearing me apart. I had to get rid of her before I did something I knew I would regret. Like fall for her and drink her blood like a fool. I shuddered. My father might sacrifice everything for this human, but I wasn't going to. She could find someone else's triad to ruin.

Cove walked to the door and hovered her hand over the lock. She cut me a bright smile while she manipulated the air into the small area to force the lock open.

"Good for you. I'm proud of you, Tallis. You deserve happiness, and even though you've struggled with the idea of a human as a boost, it could be an exciting new future for us. If she's boosted Wellyn and Fenar, it's only a matter of time, anyway."

I froze, struggling not to react how I wanted to, to turn the hallway into an inferno and burn everything to a crisp. I sucked in a deep breath, the smell of ash thick in the cool air.

"The human hasn't boosted Fenar. H-he wouldn't just, not after Wellyn—" I cursed, thinking of how he'd taken her to the Ward Estate. He wouldn't do that unless he was serious, or if he'd already tied himself to the human. Cove tilted her head in confusion as the sound of the lock releasing echoed in the tense hallway.

"I think he has, Tallis," Cove said softly, her hand curling in the air towards me. I pulled back, focusing on putting a lid on the fire that was crackling inside me. If she had boosted them both, how could I get rid of her when she was a proper boost to them now?

"Meri heard them fighting outside a week ago. It didn't sound like she was happy with him. He'd tricked her into agreeing, somehow."

I sagged against the wall, my breathing shallow. All my plans were for naught. The bleakness of the reality slammed into me. I would have to take her as a boost or abandon my triad, a weakness that the Heads would judge me for. I knew my dad would push for me to be punished if I took it that far. Perhaps he'd even compel me to be boosted with a vow, like he'd threatened.

"This has come as a shock," Cove stated, hovering by me, her forehead creased.

"It's no matter," I lied. "So I will be last to be boosted. When she sees how sincere my apology is, she will consent, I'm sure. I won't need to trick her like Fenar did."

I managed a weak smile, wondering if I looked as I felt, Cove hesitated, her fingers brushing my arm in a tender touch.

"I'll help you organize it, shall I? I could have everyone meet tomorrow night on the rooftop, if the weather holds?"

I nodded, not trusting myself to speak over the knot in my throat. Cove had to be removed before I lost it.

"She'll forgive you, Tallis, and everything will be perfect," Cove said, and I nodded again, giving her another unconvincing smile. She patted my cheek gently, realizing I was not in a state to converse, for which I was thankful.

"I'll get in touch with you tomorrow, we'll make this an apology to remember." She didn't wait for me to reply before she left the apartment. I breathed in for ten beats before letting go, sinking to the floor as the flames hurtled out of my body in a violent rush. The heat didn't burn me, but I felt like it torched me anyway. The betrayal by my triad hurt. When I closed my eyes, I saw that damned human. Her dark curls, expressive eyes, full lips, curves and snark. This was killing me. If I took her as a boost, I wouldn't survive. I knew it. I would turn into a mindless follower, desperate for a hint of her warmth. She had wicked magic. She had worked a spell on me, tricked me into wanting her, somehow.

I reared back from the want, staggered to my feet and leaned against the wall. My fingers scrabbled at the handle to Wellyn's room and I almost sobbed as it opened. I was not thinking clearly as I searched his room. I was driven by a sharpness that bled through my body. My hands tore through Wellyn's dresser, the pressure riding my back.

I wanted to mark Cami. She was taking everything from me, ruining everything. No one else could see it, how her mere presence had changed everything. Now my brothers were being pried away from me, loyal to her instead of me, keeping secrets from me, spurning me!

I pulled a drawer out and saw a white packet lying on the ground. My heart thumped in my ears as I sat back, slowly sliding out the contents, air constricting my throat as I realized what I held. I knew what these were called on Earth. Photos. As I flipped through them, seeing the frozen images of Cami at different ages, joy clear on her face. The other humans in the photos must have been her family. I recognized the likeness in the older ones, and the children must have been her brothers. This was who she cared about. This was who the money was going to. She didn't care what I did to her, but her family? They meant everything to her.

I stopped myself from scrunching up the photos, sliding them reverently back into the envelope. They couldn't be ruined yet. I'd found the key, the thing I knew would break her. That was why she'd hidden them; she wanted them protected. Well, tomorrow I'd show her how well she knew me. She was right to hide them, because now that I had them?

I was going to use them to destroy her.

Wellyn

"You're going to apologize?" I couldn't help the distrust that leaked into my voice. Tallis nodded, his shoulders drooping where he sat by the window. He ran a hand through his dark hair, the strands unkempt. His tail slashed the air as he looked between Fenar and me. Cami was still asleep, and I was hoping she would stay there until I could slip back in with her before work. Tallis has insisted on setting this meeting before the sun rose, well before anyone should rightly be up.

"I want things to be as they were. I don't like the division between us," he said, his dark eyes looking sincere. But I couldn't quite believe him. There was something about the way he was sitting, like he couldn't be still, jerking his knee up and down.

"You know they can't go back to the way they were, right?" Fenar arched a bright yellow brow, his hands tucked behind his head as he reclined beside me.

"Obviously not, especially since you've both boosted now." Fenar stiffened, and his eyes widened as Tallis gave him a dark smile. "Yes, I know about your little secret."

His teasing tone was at odds with the whistle his tail made as it swiped through the air, like it wished it was connecting to Fenar's face. Fenar cleared his throat, darting me a look. How could he have found out so soon?

"I never meant for it to be a secret, Tallis, it's still so new. I didn't go about it right the first time and I've been trying to smooth things over with Cami."

"I understand," Tallis answered magnanimously "I am trying to do the same thing, so I'm sure you see why I need all the help I can get."

Fenar chuckled at that, his head nodding readily. We all knew what it felt like to be on the receiving end of Cami's sharp tongue. Still, I didn't quite believe Tallis. It seemed too abrupt a change.

"What has made you change your mind?" I asked, wanting desperately for this to be real. I had imagined it so many times, all three of us in this room, talking and laughing like we had a million times in the past. But with Cami here as well, nestled into my side with her feet curled up under a cozy blanket.

Tallis looked toward the window, his jaw ticking. If he was pretending, he wouldn't be able to keep a lid on his emotions so well. He seemed contrite and, more than anything, sad. I felt my creature roll under my skin, and I shared in his excitement. It would be the greatest gift to have Cami as our boost in the proper sense of the role. All of us together as our best selves. It seemed like it was too good to be true.

"To be honest, it was Cove rejecting me." He flinched, closing his eyes as if remembering. "You know my feelings towards her. But I realized after that what everyone had said had been true. I didn't truly love her, just the idea of her. Now I can cling to that idea, pretend I was right, but I would lose you. My brothers. We are a triad, and those bonds are unbreakable. No matter what, we should be together."

His dark eyes turned back to us, pools of earnestness. My heartbeat surged in my chest, and I couldn't stop the gleeful smile bursting across my face.

"Of course, brother, our triad means everything to me as well," I assured him. "How can we help? Direct us as you need."

"So, you intend to take Cami as a boost?" Fenar pressed, a glint in his eye I didn't recognize. Tallis huffed a sigh and smiled ruefully.

"One step at a time. I have to earn her forgiveness first." That seemed to convince Fenar. He was in the same situation, after all. Although, after yesterday, I knew Cami had taken steps towards forgiving Fenar, at least a little. The memory of her pressed between us had kept me up late into the night. I couldn't wait to repeat the experience, perhaps with Tallis involved as well. I wondered if she would welcome that? Cami wasn't shy about expressing herself, but three Legion was a gigantic leap for a human who might not be used to it. I bounced in my seat, the idea of it filling me with an excitement that I could hardly contain.

"She's worth it, Tallis. Once you taste her, you will wonder why you fought it so long," Fenar drawled, getting to his feet. Tallis didn't reply, just nodded to each of us.

"I'll send you the details on your readers. This will be a night the human never forgets."

My creature stilled at the toothy smile that spread across his face, but I was leaping up from the couch, already eager for tonight. We would finally be a family.

Cami

IT WAS MY BROTHERS' birthday today. I had kept a tally since I'd arrived in Melbak. The scribbled calendar had seemed like a good idea, a reminder of why I was here, of why I wouldn't give up. But looking at the date, September third, I was engulfed by a gaping hollowness.

On Earth, Percy and Aaron would have pancakes at Dilly's, a tradition for our family. Dad would put a candle on the stacks of fluffy circles, dripping with maple syrup, and we would sing Happy Birthday, not caring that the café was full of patrons. They'd open gifts, usually something Pokémon themed, given the boys' obsession with the cartoon. I wonder what they would think if they knew horns, tails, and claws surrounded me, albeit not as cute and fluffy as most Pokémon were.

Rolling out of bed, I wanted to distract myself from my sinking thoughts. I sat on the side of the bed, my head hanging down, a curtain of hair covering my face. Tears threatened behind my eyes, hot and pressing. It had been my job to light the candles. Ever since they were born, it had been my role. Who would light the candles this year? It seemed like such a silly thing to focus on, but I couldn't picture anything else. Would they pause and shake their heads, feeling like someone was missing?

I knew they wouldn't. Gloria had made sure of that. They would go on not knowing I wasn't there and would never be there again.

I forced myself to move, to shed my clothes and enter the cleaning room. My limbs felt heavy as the laser swept over me, the sensation not affecting my energy, unfortunately. It didn't take away the ache in my chest and the stone in my stomach. I bit my lip when it trembled. I couldn't allow the weakness. This was penance, after all. I didn't deserve my brothers' sweet smiles, parents' warm embrace. Being here, sacrificing myself, gave them more than my tainted presence ever could.

One errant tear blazed a path down my cheek before I dashed it away, squeezing my eyes shut before any others had the same idea.

"Cami?" Wellyn's muffled voice came through the door, and I tensed. I needed to get a hold of myself, so I wrestled with the emotions, forcing them down, hoping I was stronger than them. I was.

"What's up?" I answered, my fingernails digging tiny red half-moons into my palms.

"Morning, Pancake. Technically, it's midmeal, but I thought you'd like pancakes. From Dilly's, of course." His voice was sure, and I was glad he couldn't see me because his comment had me crumpling to the ground. I kneeled, my fists pressed to my eyes as I swallowed past the lump in my throat.

"No," I choked out finally. "No pancakes, please, no pancakes. Just scrambled eggs, if you can."

"Ok." Wellyn sounded worried as I bit down on my fist again. "From Dilly's?" he clarified, and I contemplated calling him in. I knew he'd bundle me up in his arms and lavish me with care if I told him how I was feeling. But I knew I needed to get through this on my own, to prove that I was strong and that I could handle this on my own. Only I didn't know how I could function. How could I pretend I was fine when I felt my insides were being torn from my body, a hot, throbbing slash that stole oxygen from my lungs?

"It doesn't matter," I said, knowing I sounded robotic but unable to pretend otherwise. I heard him shuffle outside and I knew he was worried. My tender Legion. I had let him get too far under my skin. He could tell when I wasn't myself already.

Eventually he left. I let myself linger, wasting time in the wardrobe even though the selection of clothes I had was limited. I noticed a sheath I hadn't seen before, like one Cove had worn the first time I'd seen her. The color was a burnished red though, shimmering with lines of black like it was threaded with Gaer. I took it off the hanger and held it against my body. It looked like someone had made it for me. Desperate to feel detached from my Earth home, I slipped it over my head. Melbak was my home now. I had to get used to wearing their clothes eventually.

When I walked out into the lounge room, I froze. It was the middle of the day from what Wellyn had said, so why were Tallis and Fenar leaning on the bench while Wellyn fussed with a plate that was obviously for me. His russet curls jostled as his head jerked up, a brilliant smile lighting up his face. He patted the seat, showing I should come and sit down.

"I knew the color would suit you," Tallis said, leaning back with his arms crossed. I stumbled, looking at him like an owl as I righted myself and slipped onto the stool.

"This is from you?" I said, incredulous. He tilted his head, one dark lock falling over his forehead. He gave me a little shrug and a smile that made my stomach wriggle. What was he up to?

"I am the fashionable one of this triad. That is well-known," he said, as if that explained anything. He prowled forward, looking down at the eggs Wellyn had organized for me. They looked fluffy and delicious, a vibrant yellow that spoke to their quality. Unfortunately, there was nothing else on the plate, just a mountain of eggs.

"Humans eat such intriguing morning meals," Tallis said, his voice low and hypnotic. He wasn't even looking at me and I felt my body erupt in goosebumps from his sultry voice alone.

"I liked the eggs Benefrick," Fenar chimed in from across the table. He was spinning a fork in his hand, clearly readying himself to help himself to my breakfast. I narrowed my eyes at him until he froze, looking sheepish.

"It's eggs Benedict," I corrected. "Normally this comes with more." I toyed with the eggs. I had really wanted pancakes, my tastes running towards the sweet, but I couldn't. Not today.

"Oh, I'm sorry," Wellyn said. "I can order them for you." His eyes were wide like a puppy dog's. I slanted a look at Tallis, waiting for him to butt in and disagree, to recommend I eat something from his approved list. Instead, he nodded, moving towards the ordering machine with raised eyebrows.

"Tell us what else comes with this meal. I am curious to try human fare. I have yet to have any."

I must be dreaming. Fenar gave me a smirk and shrugged when I looked at him. Who was this Tallis and where was the sulky, nasty one I knew?

"Come now, human." He rolled his eyes, motioning for me to hurry.

Ah, not so different.

"Toast, bacon and hash browns," I said, thinking what might soothe the ache for pancakes. Greasy, crispy potatoes should do it. Tallis did as I asked and brought the plates over. Wellyn laid out four plates, and I dished up enough for all of us, all the while waiting for this bizarre dream to end. Instead, Fenar complained about the rough treatment he'd received from one of his trainers and Tallis laughed, teasing him about being weak despite having a boost. My head felt like it was about to spin off. Tallis knew I'd boosted Fenar and hadn't killed him?

"You look so beautiful," Wellyn whispered in my ear, the faint brush of his lips making my cheeks flood. He was sitting almost on top of me, his thigh pressing against mine. It was like an anchor. Even though he didn't realize it, he was keeping me from dissolving right now.

The food was fine, but it tasted sour in my mouth. It wasn't pancakes and it wasn't with my family, but I passed the meal without having to speak too much, for which I was thankful. It felt too nice, the banter flying around me and the ease at which the triad interacted with each other. This was how it must have been before I arrived, and I felt a brief pang of guilt that I'd disrupted their close relationship so thoroughly.

"We are to attend a Legion gathering tonight, but until then, will you join me at my work?" Wellyn asked, pushing his empty plate away from him. I hummed thoughtfully. I could bury myself in books again, perhaps find some mention of the cursed Legion to compare with Eyke next time. I was still in knots over the thought of it all. It seemed such an enormous task.

"Will Seb be there?" I asked, grimacing at the thought of fending off his slimy advances again. Fenar and Tallis stiffened, the latter's cutlery clattering down onto his plate.

"Seb Decker?" they growled. "What did he do?" Fenar added, a tightness in his body as he waited for me to answer. I looked at Wellyn, pleading with my eyes, but he didn't take any notice.

"He tried to convince Cami to join his triad. Apparently two Wards of the Heads are undeserving of a boost, human or not."

Tallis's hands fired red on the bench. I waited for the material to sizzle before I remembered. Everything was fireproof in here to cater to the hot-tempered Legion.

Fenar's fangs peeked through his lips as he snarled, looking at me with a wild, possessive air.

"Not happening," he said through those fierce teeth, and I couldn't control the urge to roll my eyes.

"Calm down. I want nothing to do with him. He thought I'd fall over myself at his offer. Wellyn warned him off. He was stunned that I wasn't more receptive to his offer."

"The gall," Tallis sniffed, sharing a look with Fenar. "We will accompany you to the Vault. I won't have Seb thinking he can approach what doesn't belong to him."

I might have snorted if I had been in a better frame of mind, but I was stretched thin today. My thoughts were preoccupied with memories that had always made me smile in the past, now felt like a knife in the gut. Wellyn ducked down to look into my eyes.

"Would that be alright with you?" he asked me. I shrugged. I knew Tallis would do what he wanted to, anyway. I didn't have it in me to fight.

When we arrived at the Vault, Wellyn set me up in the alcove I had before, bypassing Madam Reason and her pinched face. She'd opened her mouth to say something disparaging, but it had morphed into an insincere smile when she noticed Tallis entering behind us. He'd sniffed down his sharp nose at her, like the perfect aristocratic snob, and spared her a curt nod. Both Fenar and Tallis squeezed in beside me, boxing me in like I needed protection.

"What are we going to do to pass the time?" Fenar asked, the leer on his face telling me where his thoughts were headed. I rolled my eyes as Tallis made a noise of disgust.

"This is a place of refinement and knowledge, Fenar. Try to contain yourself," he chastised as I stood, attempting to squeeze past them. Tallis held out a hand to stop me. He wasn't even looking at me, just raising his eyebrow in challenge to Fenar. My healer only laughed.

When had I started thinking of him as mine? My body shook with a wave of cold tingles. I didn't know how I felt about that. We'd shared a moment of intense passion and I could admit that I would have been happy to take it further. But now, with some distance, I needed to put a pin in it. I still felt unsteady around the wily wolf. He'd proven how easily he could trick me and use me to get what he wanted. One amazing make-out session would not make me change my mind.

"Oh, don't pretend you didn't take Ryleen back into the stacks when she still worked here." Fenar tucked his hands behind his head, reclining back like he was totally relaxed.

"Move," I said, pushing against Tallis's muscular arm. He looked me over lazily, a hint of a sneer like he couldn't believe I'd interrupted him.

"What are you looking for?" he probed.

"I am educating myself on how to be a perfect, obedient boost." I clasped my hands to my chest and fluttered my eyelashes at him. His lips quirked as if he was holding in a smile, and he eased his arm away.

"Obedient?" he drawled. "You don't know the meaning of the word." My mind filled with images of when he'd disciplined me for my previous inability to follow his rules. I felt my cheeks heat and hurriedly pushed against his arm, wanting to scurry away before he pushed me further, as I knew he would. To my surprise, he relented, sending me teetering off-balance as I walked away from the small alcove and into the stacks.

I wandered through the stacks with no real aim in mind. I knew I would not find the knowledge I needed in these open shelves, despite most of the books looking ancient with thick pressed spines and yellowing pages. Eyke knew things that the average Legion didn't because he was from an age long ago, before time and busy hands had stripped away the footprints of the cursed Legion.

I ran my finger down a maroon tome, appreciating the decorative etches that adorned it. I leaned in until my nose almost touched the book, letting my shoulders slump and some of the banked pain to trickle in. It was a fine balance, allowing myself to feel the agony of missing my family while still maintain my composure. It would not be this bad ever again, I comforted myself. In time, I would forget the sound of my brothers' laughs, like a water trickling over stone. The aches and pains would smooth over and be forgotten. I just had to get through today.

"Are you interested in the raising and care of ratids?" came a voice from behind me. I pushed back from the maroon book with a noise of disgust. Seb Decker stood at the end of the stack, an expression of amusement twisting his golden lips.

"Absolutely not, those things are disgusting." I grimaced.

"Are you looking for more information about boosts?" Seb raised his eyebrows. His hands were linked behind his back and it made some of the tension leave my shoulders. During our last encounter, he had crossed a line, but it seemed he had taken Wellyn's advice and was treating me professionally.

"I am just looking around," I admitted lamely, and Seb nodded his head like he understood. He took a step back from the stack entrance, as if realizing I might feel unsafe with him blocking it. He pointed. Further away from alcove where I assumed Tallis and Fenar were still holed up.

"If you like the craftmanship on that book, there is a section of ancient tomes I can show you."

I hesitated, not knowing whether I could trust the golden-scaled man, and he seemed to read my indecision, ducking his head with a sigh.

"I must apologize, Cami. The way I acted when I saw you last was unconscionable." Regret steeped his voice, yet I remained unmoved. He saw my reticence and winced. "I deserve your ire. I was—I was jealous, if I'm honest. But that excuses nothing. If you would prefer, say the word and I'll go."

I didn't have it in me to fight today, so against my better judgement, I walked towards him. He looked forlorn, shuffling on his feet as he waited for the anvil of my judgement to strike him down.

"Let's see those pretty books, shall we?" I said instead, wanting to put the awkwardness behind me. Seb sucked in a breath, his scales flashing as his hand gripped his chin, covering his gaping mouth. He nodded, reinvigorated, and rushed ahead, throwing me a smile over his shoulder.

"Oh, this way, this way," he said, leading me towards a glass-encased room. There were shelves of books, some with pages laid out for inspection. Seb produced a round metal disc and inserted it into a slot in the wall. The door slid open with a hum, a blast of cool air hitting me as he ushered me through. He turned and inserted the disc again until the door closed. A prickle of unease swept up my neck, but Seb seemed desperate to redeem himself, keeping a concerted space between us.

"This one is three hundred years old, one of the oldest in the Vault," Seb said, pulling down a huge tome and placing it on a stand. I perked up at his words, wondering if there would be any mention of the things Eyke had spoken to me about. Seb opened it carefully, waving a hand at the illustrations.

"Niroe Soet, a legendary Legion and one of the most well-known academics who documented much of the early years of Legion, did these drawings." I peered over Seb's shoulder, noting that the writing was unreadable except for a few words I recognized. I reached for the page but hesitated.

"This area is pressurized to allow for handling. It's not advisable to stay in here for too long, as it locks moisture inside of the body so as not to allow any secretions to damage the books while handling. But I thought you might enjoy them."

I reached forward, flicking through the pages and devouring the images. I paused as I saw a depiction that was eerily like the picture in the temple, only this one was more detailed and in color. The boost was clearly Legion, with tall horns jutting up from a head of curly hair. She was reclining on a couch, four men sprawled about, leaning towards her as if unable to resist her. Their mouths were rimmed red, and I could see a line of red drawn on her throat as though she'd just been boosted them. I looked closely at the men, each with a tail, wings or some other feature that made them clearly Legion, not anything like a human.

"What does this page say?" I turned to Seb, who had moved to give me room. He took in the picture and flashed me a considering look. "Don't be a creep and make me regret coming here with you," I warned him, and he whipped his head down to look at the page.

"It talks of a boost needing balance. Four must support a boost." His tone took on one of confusion as he read further his lips moving as he read the page. "It says boosts are living links of Melbak and deserve respect and protection. The twelve founding families agreed with the land when they brought Melbak into peace. A quartet protects their boost, and in return, grants them increased power and connection to Melbak."

Shivers ran down my body at his words, my skin erupting in goosebumps. I ran my hands down my arms, attempting to soothe the feeling. I had found proof of what Eyke had been talking to me about.

Seb scoffed. "A quartet? I've heard nothing so preposterous. The fourth is the boost, hence the triad." He shook his head, talking more to himself. I flicked the page over and tried to see if the illustrations showed more of a boost, but it was a landscape, one that looked like a forested area on Earth. Seb reached over and closed the book, hoisting it up on the shelf with careful ease.

"Also, there are only nine founding families. My own ancestors are from the Hibis family. Some of these tomes were filled with nonsense. Times have changed after all," he said with a shrug. "Unless there was something else you wanted to look at?" He reached past me, his body uncomfortably close as he pulled a small, golden book from the shelf.

"This is a diary of a boost from several hundred years ago. It might interest you."

A slam on the glass startled us both. Seb dropped the book into my hands as he whirled around. I looked past his shoulder and saw the murderous faces of Fenar and Tallis. The former had his clenched fists resting on the glass and his fangs bared in anger.

"Why is this door closed?" Tallis snarled, banging on the glass. I tucked the small book in my dress pocket, slipping it in easily. Seb rushed over to the door and inserted the disc. The door slid open and Tallis stalked in, muscling Seb back until he was pressed up against the shelf.

"Why are you here, Seb, so very close to my boost?" Tallis leaned forward, glaring. Seb only swallowed thickly and turned his head.

"Leave off, Tallis, he was just doing his job," I interrupted, feeling sorry for Seb when Fenar crowded in on his other side, his fangs close to the tendons in the Legion's neck. Tallis flashed a furious look at me, jerking his finger in warning.

"Be quiet, human. For once, be quiet and obedient," he growled.

"I did nothing, I promise, I didn't—" Seb stuttered. His hands shook as he gripped the shelves as if they were holding him up. I rolled my eyes and stalked over to Tallis, trying to catch Fenar's eye, but he was fixated on Seb, a low warning rumbling from his curled lips.

"I can't deal with this today," I grumbled, moving towards the door, intending on finding Wellyn and seeing if I could return to the apartment. Wallowing in my bed hadn't seemed inviting earlier but having to shoulder the exhausting weight of my pain and grief was too hard. Longing for space hit me. Perhaps I would find sleep and visit Eyke.

"Stay away from my boost. Don't even look at her again, understood?" Tallis said, his voice gravelly like he was trying hard to rein in his power. Fenar gave Seb a little shove before plastering himself to my side.

"Why were you alone with him?" he snapped under his breath, shooting me a wounded look.

"Yes, human, I'd like to know why as well. You can't switch triads now." Tallis took up my other side, and I stopped walking, folding my arms over my chest, raising an eyebrow at them both.

"I could always replace you, though. Right?" I deadpanned towards Tallis, who stiffened, his face growing thunderous as I held his gaze.

"Don't rile Tallis. It's too easy and you're changing the subject," Fenar scolded, sharing a placating look towards Tallis, which surprised me. He tugged on one of my dark curls, pressing closer until his nose grazed my neck.

"You smell faintly of him. It offends me," he said.

"Seb was much better mannered than last time. He apologized, even. More than I can say for some others I know," I sighed, disgruntled.

Tallis wrapped his fingers around my wrist and tugged me forward, not bothering to answer me.

Fenar jeered. "I don't trust the little prick, and you shouldn't be going anywhere without one of us anyway, remember?" He conveyed a lot in his heavy look as Tallis continued to drag me back to the alcove. There was a heavy undercurrent of tension, the clench of his jaw as he pulled me along in his wake was off-putting.

He manhandled me until I was sitting in the middle chair in the alcove again. He slid into his with a huff, his eyes narrowed like he expected me to argue with him. I felt the spark of passion flare inside me, but it spluttered and wavered as though used to drawing on my unending ire for the fiery Legion. Normally, I couldn't stop my mouth from spouting some argumentative comment, but when I waited for the words to come, they didn't. The spark was snuffed out. My insides felt too raw to deal with Tallis today. I slumped into my chair, fingering the outline of the book in my pocket. I don't suppose I should have taken it out of its special air-pressured room, but I couldn't find it in me to feel guilty. It was more useful to me than wasting away in a glass cage.

"You don't have any impertinent words for me?" Tallis prodded, his dark eyes hungry for a fight I couldn't give him. Fenar clapped a hand on Tallis's shoulder, giving him one of those heavy looks again, his eyebrows raised in a secret code.

"Let's not fight today," he said, his finger tapping the table as if once to punctuate his words.

"I am not feeling well, would one of you take me ho—to the apartment?" I choked on my request, the word home sticking in my throat. I couldn't say it or my precariously built protections would implode, crumbling down around me. This place was not my home, but I couldn't let myself dwell on the place my heart truly considered home. My vision blurred, the colors swirling like a kaleidoscope as a sheen of tears covered my eyes.

"You cannot be ill today, we have an important event to attend tonight," Tallis said coldly. I tipped my chin up, hoping to stop any of the tears from falling down my chin.

"Well," I said, through gritted teeth, "sorry to disappoint you, Bossman." The tears mercifully dissipated, and I stood, wanting to get out of here before they returned.

"Where are you feeling sick?" Fenar asked, reaching down to swipe Tallis's legs out of my way. I moved past before he put them back, knowing he would do anything to irritate me.

"I'm tired and my stomach hurts," I said, thinking it was vague enough to satisfy them. Fenar made a clucking noise, entangling his arm with mine.

"You can rest for a few hours before the event, right?" He looked over my shoulder for confirmation from Tallis and it galled me to wait for his assent. He grunted, sounding perturbed by the idea.

"Cove is coming to make you presentable in a few hours, so if rest is required to make you suitable for that, so be it."

I took a deep breath to stop myself from snapping at the bane of my existence. Wellyn came up the stairs, his freckles a stark smatter over his button nose, his cheeks lightly flushed from his work. His face fell when he saw me. He rushed to my side, casting a worried look at Fenar.

"What is it?" he asked. "Pancake, are you alright?" I winced at the nickname, the memories that came with it too sharp. Fenar fended him off when he tried to take me in his arms, making a noise under his breath.

"Don't you start. She's a little unwell, nothing a rest won't fix right up."

"I knew it," he breathed, anxiously twisting his hands. "You haven't been yourself today."

That did it. His words, and his face, twisted with genuine concern. For me. I rushed into his chest, crushing my arms around him, and squeezing tight. He didn't hesitate, wrapping his cool arms around me and pulling me deeper into his chilly embrace. It countered the flush of my cheeks, the rush of tears that I had tried so hard to squelch down since I'd awoken.

"Hey, hey now," he soothed me, brushing his hand down my back as I tried in vain to stifle the wet sobs that choked my throat.

"What is wrong with her?" Tallis asked, mystified and a little disgusted. I cringed into Wellyn, my head tucked against his chest.

"T-take me out of here, please," I whispered, my voice cracking.

"Let me take her, you have to work," Fenar insisted, his fingers settling on my waist. But I wanted Wellyn. I had denied myself this morning, but I admitted to myself I needed him. I was desperate for his gentle heart, the man I had shared with before, who had been at my side since the very first day. I refused to let go of him. My darling. A Legion who I was happy to call mine, I realized.

"I need you, Wellyn, just us," I whispered, pressing up into him, trying to communicate what I wanted. He didn't hesitate, hoisting my legs around his waist and carrying me like a child.

"I'll take her to the higher stacks. They need sorting and she can rest near me."

I cried again, incoherently thanking him as he started moving. He pressed a kiss to my forehead.

"We'll ensure someone organizes things properly for tonight," Fenar said, his fingers squeezing my hips like he was reluctant to relinquish me.

"I have you, you are safe with me," Wellyn murmured.

He carried me up another flight of stairs, my weight not even straining him as he took each step with ease. There were walls full of shelves and a wide-open area that looked out into the Gaer-infected woods. It might have been nice if Melbak wasn't like the inspiration for every post-apocalyptic world ever. Wellyn lowered me onto a chaise and sat next to me, my body curling around his. He seemed content to stay silent, his fingers running through my hair in a methodical, relaxing pattern. My outburst seemed to dry up, the tears turning to a trickle. I sniffed, looking at the mess I'd made of his shirt.

"I'm sorry," I said, plucking at the wet patch. "I've made a mess of you."

He looked down on me and his expression made me want to bawl again, for a different reason. It was pure adoration in those violet eyes, luminous like his creature was trying to be close to me as well.

"Never apologize for that. I'm yours to make a mess of," he whispered, brushing a curl back from my head. "Just tell me, was it something Tallis did, something he said?"

I snorted and shook my head. "He has actually been less annoying than usual today," I said, which seemed to please Wellyn. He hummed his approval and pulled me closer to him.

"Good, he has much to make up for. But if it wasn't him, then what has upset you? You don't have to tell me if you don't feel comfortable."

My heart thumped at his words as I sighed. I wanted to tell him, I realized. I needed to. The ache was simply too large to carry alone. Even though I wanted to be strong enough on my own, sometimes asking for help and leaning on others was true strength.

"Today, it's—" I cleared my throat, laying my head on his chest so I didn't have to look at his face while I spoke. "The twins' birthday. The day they were born, it's a big thing to celebrate on Earth. In our family we would go out for breakfast and always we'd have—" I cut off, turning to muffle a sob into Wellyn's chest.

"Pancakes from Dilly's," Wellyn breathed, understanding immediately. "Oh, my sweet, I wish you had told me this morning. That was why you didn't want them?" I nodded wordlessly, and that seemed to be enough. Wellyn resumed brushing his fingers through my hair, my scalp tingling with pleasure. It was enough, that one confession and his acceptance of it. I felt cocooned in his embrace like something precious and protected.

Eyke

I REARRANGED THE PIECES of the Ratids and Wolves board, idly toying with one of the ratids. I looked toward my bed, longing rampant in my veins, a habit I had long given up on breaking. There was something wrong. It needed a Cami-sized shape in it, the silken sheets wrapped around her beautiful body. It was agony to sleep there, her scent on my pillow a balm and a curse. I wanted it gone and multiplied simultaneously. I owed my boost everything, her shining light having awoken me from a centuries-long curse.

The Gaer had fulfilled its purpose. It suspended my mind in madness, my body reduced to semi-sentient matter that apparently terrorized Melbak. Two hundred years had passed with me trapped in a prison of my own making. The Heads had been clever to deal with us, but they didn't understand the Gaer. Only I knew it's true purpose.

I looked to my bed again, a small pinch in my chest that it remained empty. I couldn't control when she came to me. When she slept, she was more susceptible, and I would feel the change in the air. The hairs on my arms would stand on end, a prickle running over them I could focus on and reel in like a fishing line. There was none of that now and yet I couldn't stop looking at the bed, hoping for her to come again.

Two hundred years ago, the idea of a boost would have sent me into a rage. That I would debase myself in the archaic practice would have been inconceivable. It was the ultimate irony. I needed to take a boost from Cami to be free. I bet the Heads laughed at the absurdity of it. But time can change any mind. The knowledge that I'd been trapped for so long and that Melbak was struggling to contain the deadly substance filled me with a guilt that ate away at me.

I had been slipping into my old routines, morning practices that took me deep in my mind and strengthened my powers. They felt warped in this strange place, and I wondered if it was all a figment of my imagination. Whether I was making all this up after all, and Cami was just the desperate longing of a mind descending into madness.

I sucked in a thick breath, feeling my heart surge with worry. I couldn't think too much like that or I would spin out and lose myself even more. Cami did not find a record of my time in the books, which had relieved me. As soon as she had first appeared, I knew the meaning of being boost-bound. Everything I'd mocked other Legion for chasing had slapped me in the face. If I ever got out of this place, I would see the Gaer destroyed to allow the boosts to present again.

My chest throbbed at the horrors it had wrought but I couldn't focus on it. I was a changed man. If I was careful, Cami would never know the hand I had in any of this. Thinking of those who had wrought this horrible curse on me, the features wavered, except for minor details. They would be long dead now. I remember the tapping of claws, blood red, impatient and unfeeling while I and those like me were condemned.

I wondered about the group that had escaped Melbak, who had ventured to Earth to find a new world to live in. With human features, they had hoped to fit in without the prejudice against them. Most had creatures of their own but had been banned from being able to bring them forth. All cursed Legion had restrictions put on their powers. Thankfully, mine had been mental power, one they couldn't control unless I wasn't careful enough, and I was always careful.

I looked to the bed again. There was no Cami, but if I closed my eyes, I thought I heard her sigh, sweet and quiet. She'd be here soon.

Cami

"CAMI," WELLYN WHISPERED IN my ear. I protested, trying to snuggle back into his warm chest. "It's time to get ready now."

I cracked open one eye, a frown at the ready. I was surprised to realize I was back in my room in the apartment. Cove was leaning in the doorway looking bemused. I pushed up on my arms.

"How did we get here?" I asked, rubbing my eyes from the short sleep I must have had. Wellyn swooped up and pulled on my arms, trying to encourage me to get up.

"You conked out at the Vault, so I brought you back. I'm on my break, so I can't stay long. I only wanted to see you settled and let you know I'll see you tonight."

I scrambled to the edge of the bed, casting a quick look at Cove before pitching my voice low.

"Please, can I skip this thing tonight? I don't think I could stand it, especially given my last experience."

Wellyn perched on the edge of the bed and motioned me to come closer, cupping his cool hands around my face. His rusty lashes fluttered as he looked me over, an earnest expression deepening the violet in his eyes.

"I wish we could, but tonight is important. It's the night of a new beginning. By the end of the night you will smile, I promise you."

He leaned in and brushed my lips with a sweet kiss. His lips were soft and I chased them as he pulled away, pouting when he bounded toward the door.

"Cove will look after you." He paused next to her, giving her a serious look. "Won't you? Cami needs the best tonight."

They shared a look while she gleefully rubbed her hands together.

"Of course! Leave your precious boost with me and I'll return her to you in a few hours."

I wanted to protest. The last thing I wanted to do was to be left in Cove's presence. As nice as she had been to me so far, I didn't really know her, and I wasn't in the mood to be made over. I slumped back down on the bed as Wellyn left and Cove turned her narrowed gaze on me.

"Don't get comfortable," she warned me, a glint in her eye. "We have much work to do."

Some time later, I was convinced Cove was not to be messed with. I was riddled with exhaustion but I didn't look like it. She'd bullied me into the cleaning room, wanting to stay in the room and inspect me, which I didn't allow. She'd made me try on a dozen outfits before deciding on another red sheath, not unlike the one I wore this morning. This one had two cutouts at my waist, and I liked how sensuous the material felt on my skin.

Cove tackled my hair next, gathering my dark curls into a series of intricate plaits that wove in and out of some loosened locks. After that, she'd painted my face, using what looked like a literal paint set. Tubs of different colored gels were mixed and dabbed on my face. It had felt a little like a toddler playing with finger paints. The color choices made no sense, but when I saw the finished product, my jaw fell open. There was no sign of the distinct bags under my eyes, persisting despite using the cleaning room. My skin looked glossy and clear, a shimmering highlight made my cheekbones look sharp. She'd painted my eyelids ochre, rimming them with white liner. It looked part tribal, part alien and entirely Legion. Around my upper right arm, she'd tied a red ribbon to show my status. Her fingers toyed with the ends a little longer than she needed, and I could see the longing shimmer in her eyes.

"Are there men boosts?" I asked. Cove's head snapped up to smile at me, a little sharp edged.

"There hasn't been a male boost in over a hundred years," she shrugged. "I know my chance of being a boost are unlikely, but I can still dream of being part of a true triad. I know it seems like a silly thing to wish for."

"They'd be lucky to have you," I said sincerely, and she reached up and squeezed my shoulder.

"I'll keep dreaming. Maybe one day." Her voice was so sad it made me want to bundle her up in a hug.

I wondered what would happen if Nakasha touched the Gaer? What would it do for Melbak to have two complete quartets? I would have to boost Tallis, though, and that made my stomach turn. Him agreeing was unlikely. And then there was Eyke, my shadow, who still wouldn't tell me everything. I had been leaning towards boosting him, to see if it would truly free him. He deserved to be free.

Cove squeezed my shoulder again and nodded to the door. "Let's head to the roof and show you off to your boys."

"Let's not get ahead of ourselves. Fenar and Tallis still have a lot of improving to do," I said with a sigh, getting to my feet. I felt strangely buoyant. The time with Cove had kept my mind busy, and I hadn't focused on my brothers at all. Perhaps the party wouldn't be so bad. Anything would be an improvement over the last one.

"Let's see if you think that way by the end of the night," Cove countered, bouncing down the hall with a squeal.

She linked her arm with mine and took me to the portal, where it transported us to the rooftop of the building. The doors slid open with a hiss, showing off the throng of Legion and an unencumbered view of Melbak. Cove didn't release me, ushering me through the groups scattered around instead.

It was mood, with a dark red glow coming from hidden lights that matched the bleeding sky scattered with thick, dark clouds. It felt like a cocktail party with everyone standing and Legion with trays mingling through the crowd with tall glasses filled with an oily, green substance. A slight whisper of steam rose from the top of the drinks like they were boiling.

"You can try that later, but baak is a tad sour. I heard you prefer sweet." She gave me a sidelong glance, and I managed a lopsided smile.

"What can I say? Sugar is my jam."

Cove gave me a confused look, patting my hand. "Try to keep the humanisms to a minimum, dear."

The crowd seemed to part for us, and I saw my triad watching us approach. They had dressed up, each wearing dark, form-fitting shirts, slacks and flowing black robes. It seemed to suit each of them, Wellyn looking like a fire spark, Fenar looking like a modern painting, his fangs flashing with a smug smile. And Tallis, well, dark suited his soul, but this made him look every inch the demon I knew him to be.

"Cami," he purred, stepping forward to snag my hands in a firm grip. "Don't you look divine. Cove, you've worked a miracle." He was doing so well until then.

I tugged at my hands, shooting him a glare. I looked to Wellyn to intervene, but both he and Fenar seemed dopey with wobbly smiles melting across their faces. Fenar's eyes were hazy as he roved over my figure, taking in the cutouts with interest.

"You look good enough to eat." He gnashed his teeth. I rolled my eyes, still trying to extricate myself from Tallis's grip.

"Cami has naturally beautiful features. It was a pleasure to help pamper her." To me she said, "I'll let your triad have their fill of you and speak with you soon." She rose on her toes and brushed a peck on my cheek before slipping off into the thick crowd. Wellyn nuzzled my neck, sucking in a deep breath and letting it out with a sigh. He perched his chin on my shoulder and blinked slowly.

"Cami has beautiful everything. She is beauty, beauty is her," he murmured, and Fenar clapped his hands and tugged Wellyn into a rough embrace.

I realized, slower than I should have.

"You're both trashed," I said, doing little to disguise the horror in my voice. I had hoped Wellyn would keep me from Tallis's cruel clutches, the ones he had yet to let up on. He was drawing me in closer until I was inches away from his gorgeous, haughty face. His dark eyes danced with amusement.

"They may have gotten a little excited. I have to say, I encouraged them a little. Tonight is a special night, you know. It's a celebration." His low voice was seductive, and it was unfair how it made me shiver. "It's a new beginning, the way it should have been." His dark eyes licked over me like flames, and I felt his fingers curl around the bare skin of my hips. I flinched as he stroked the skin, staring at me like he wanted to devour me.

"You look utterly terrified," he remarked lightly, his fingers brushing a scorching, slow path up and down my exposed skin. I felt the tickle of something on my calf and looked down to see his tail was caressing me. I gave a squeak and tried to pull away, but his fingers clamped down on me, unrelenting. "Your fear is intoxicating. The scent of it is almost as good as your arousal."

My cheeks flushed at his crass words, and it made a smirk fly across his face. What game was he playing? I knew he was toying with me, but I couldn't think what he would gain for it. Was he trying to mollify me now that he'd seen the benefits of my blood in boosting the rest of his triad? My stomach dropped and I struggled in his hold again. That was the last thing I wanted to deal with, especially considering nosy Legion surrounded us and were eating up this little performance. Still, his fingers dug into my skin, hard enough to bruise. His closeness made me feel dizzy.

Fenar slung an arm over Tallis's shoulder, jostling his hold enough for me to slip free. I didn't wait around, turning to dart through the crowd, tripping as his tail attempted to keep me next to him. My head spun as I looked around, trying to find somewhere dark to slink into and hide. Just for a moment, I needed space. I needed to be as far away from Tallis as possible.

My throat was thick, air struggling to get through as I pressed up against the wall near the portal. I ignored the curious looks I'd gotten from those around me. I couldn't blend in here, not when I looked so entirely human.

I swallowed a groan when I saw someone I definitely didn't want to speak to approach me. Ziggie. Her hands clenched into fists by her side, so at least she didn't have a drink to throw at me this time.

"Were you invited to this one, or did you sneak in again?" I couldn't help goading her, but the flash of ire she couldn't smother made me regret it. I should remember not to provoke unstable Legion. Ziggie was their poster child. She pinched her dress between her fingers, drawing the material tight across her thighs. I hadn't gotten a close look at her last time, but as I looked at her, I realized her gaze was wholly black. Her pupils took up her entire eyes, with only the smallest sliver of white around them. If she wasn't so crazy, I might have likened her to an owl. She sneered,

"A reckoning is coming," she taunted, and her haughty tone made something snap in me. I was sluggish from grief, my nerves already raw and frayed, so I stepped up to her, satisfied that she was a good deal shorter than me.

"You think I care? I've already lost everything. What more do you want, my life and soul?"

She blinked rapidly, jaw tightening as she thrust her head back, trying to look unbothered by my proximity. Her nostrils flared and I knew she was scenting me, something various Legion had done since I'd arrived. They smelled the ability to boost in my blood.

"Demons steal souls. Legion would never stoop so low," she said, as if that was the most important part of what I'd said. I sighed in exasperation.

"I'm truly not in the mood for your special brand of doom and gloom. Can we just assume you spewed some prejudice at me, and I'm suitably cowed and desperately frightened?" I gritted my teeth.

My throat ached for a drink. I knew things were getting bad. Even if I was thinking about drinking, I wouldn't do it. I had not taken a drop of anything mood altering since dad's accident.

Confusion smashed her eyebrows together and her mouth gaped before she recovered. "You will fear us. Legion will rid Melbak of your kind, returning us to the gloried days of—"

An elegant, clawed hand reached out and swatted at Ziggie's arm, silencing her fevered words. She stumbled to the side and I looked to see who had saved me from another lecture. Nakasha. Her triad was streaming through the portal and milled around their boost with a mixture of responses. Pyke sniffed at me, his eyes sliding off me distastefully before he stalked off, leaving her with the other two.

"They'll let anyone into these things, won't they?" Nakasha mused to Ambrose, her lip curling. "Be a dear and *shek* off, Ziggie. I think the human gets the general idea."

Ziggie speared me with a glare, those wide eyes narrowing, her mouth sour. She whirled on Nakasha, raising a trembling finger.

"You will fear me by the time we're finished," she threatened, but Nakasha only rolled her eyes and made a shooing motion in Ziggie's direction. Ambrose raised a sculpted eyebrow and Kevin gave me a sheepish nod of his head, a slight blush dusting his cheeks.

"*Shek. Off.*" She repeated slowly and Ziggie finally whirled on her heel and stomped toward the portal. She slipped into the whirling blue, confirming my thought that she hadn't been on the invitation list.

"Does she always turn up with something nasty to say?" I asked, slumping against the wall. This day was turning into one long, drawn-out nightmare. Nakasha raised a shoulder, making it look somehow elegant. She'd dressed in red again, but it was dark, almost black, like dried blood.

"Ziggie is harmless. She finds me wherever I go, so I guess she's targeting the weaker boost now."

I didn't take offense to the statement. Nakasha wasn't trying to hurt me. I was human, and that meant inherent weakness to Legion. She slid in front of me, unconsciously barring me from most of the crowd, and I relaxed a little as she tilted her head and regarded me. Ambrose and Kevin hovered a brief space away, creating a further buffer.

"Are you well?" She cast her voice low, obviously wanting only me to hear her question. This wasn't a social catch up. Nakasha wanted to know if I'd fallen ill like she had. She thought I was weak, but I remembered her trembling limbs and damaged skin. Tonight, she'd covered her body with long sleeves so only part of her legs and head were visible. I wondered if welts covered her underneath the beautiful garment.

"I am," I answered, hesitating before continuing. "I believe I have a way to help, with what we talked about previously."

Instead of looking relieved or grateful, her mouth tightened in a snarl, and she snapped, "How arrogant of you to think you could find a solution when I've all the resources and the support from the Heads."

My chest stung at her accusation, but I let it spread and fade. It wasn't me she was truly angry at. They had trapped her in agony; the Heads knowingly deceived her. Underneath her bluster and sharp exterior, fear drove through her. I wasn't about to change her mind during one conversation, especially since I didn't know if it was entirely true, as I hadn't boosted Tallis yet. I only shrugged, keeping my points to myself.

"If you would like help, you know where I am." I saw Cove over her shoulder, who was beckoning me, so I finished, "Just know that the Legion advising you may not have your best interest as a boost at heart."

I moved around her without waiting for a response from her or her triad. I don't know what it was about today, but I would not give another Legion a chance to take a bite of me today.

Cove gave an excited squeal, latching on to my hand and pulling me back towards where I'd left Tallis and the drunken fools.

"It's time!" she whispered in my ear, her fingers moving to my shoulders to propel me faster.

Legion parted before me like they knew something was happening. I stiffened, noticing for the first time the intense curiosity, the sneers and unmasked glee at whatever it was Cove was pushing me towards.

"W-what is going on?" I asked her, trying to stop. But despite her small stature, she was strong, and she maneuvered me forward easily.

"Tallis has something he wants to say, something that's been a long time coming," Cove said. She was trying to reassure me, but her words only sent a frisson of terror through me. Nothing good came of Tallis wanting to say something, especially given his strange behavior today.

Tallis stood where I'd left him, with his hands clasped behind his back. I looked for Wellyn and Fenar and saw them seated behind him, eyes glassy and heads lolling to the side. Wellyn looked like he was half asleep. I would not get any help there. My heartbeat hitched, and I choked on the irregular rhythm, struggling to fill my lungs with the foreboding pressing on my chest. Cove stood behind me, her hands gently rounded on my shoulders. The implication was clear. She was holding me still. Should I try to run, she would thwart me.

Tallis cleared his throat. That was enough for the hush to fall over the gathered Legion. I was stiff as a board, waiting for him to speak, knowing implicitly that it would not bode well for me.

Yet there was a small part of me that thought perhaps he was going to make amends. He'd despised me from the first, but we'd bounced around each other like magnets, sometimes repelling and sometimes inexplicitly drawn to one another. Even now, he was standing there, the very picture of a gentleman. A tortured, broody gentleman, with his indolent dark curls falling to partially obscure his shadowed eyes which were sparked with excitement. I didn't care for it, despite how painfully handsome he was.

Even the rattlesnake tail stood to attention behind him. I was used to seeing these oddities now, those Legion features that made him unique. It was another way to read him, as it seemed to broadcast his true feelings, swinging wildly in anger and still when he was calculating.

"I gather us here today to celebrate a very special boost. The first human boost Melbak has had."

His confident voice carried over the heads of the gathering and I only had a second to think before he spoke again.

"She has successfully boosted two of my triad. All but me."

I hissed as he boomed, the knowledge that Eyke had warned me to keep a secret in the ears of everyone here. I looked about the crowd, not sure what I expected. Was Gloria to come and hoist me off to a dark dungeon? The crowd looked unsurprised, and that chilled me further. Was it so obvious that I had boosted Wellyn and Fenar?

"Relax, Cami, trust in Tallis," Cove whispered in my ear, feeling the slight tremors that were coursing through my body. A surge of adrenaline had crashed out when

Tallis started speaking and it was zapping my entire body.

"We haven't been great friends. It's known that I haven't accepted the human. I wanted her tested as all Legion are as children. I admit," he chuckled and raised an eyebrow, "She has spoiled every effort I made to break her, short of physically harming her. The human has prevailed."

I was so tense I thought my chest creaked when I sucked in a quick breath. Tallis seemed languid. He scratched at his brow and shot me a wry smile.

"I didn't want a human boost, despite seeing what boons it has given my brothers." He sighed, the crowd caught in his charming story. I could feel the pinch of the silk as he trussed me up in the careful web he was spinning. "She has maligned me from my triad. I was pushed to the side in favor of a boost, but the human is undeniable. She lacks horns, a tail or even fangs, and yet she has tormented me. I didn't want to want a human."

I must have looked hilarious. The strange mixture of insults and compliments confused me. What was he trying to accomplish? For a moment, I don't think he knew either, as he snapped his head up and shook it, his locks mussed.

He took a deep steadying breath, and a slow sinister smile tilted on his shapely lips. He took a step forward and withdrew his arms from behind his back, brandishing an envelope. One that I knew the second it became visible, the one I had entrusted to Wellyn for safety for this very reason.

Tallis stared at me like the view of me crumbling was the most delicious meal he could have. A strangled cry fell from my parted lips. I looked to Wellyn, who was curled up in the chair, his head resting on his chin, his eyes at half-mast as he listlessly watched Tallis brandish the only traces I had of my family. I jerked in Cove's hold, but she dug in her fingers.

"Just wait. He has a plan. It's all going to be fixed," she muttered, but even she sounded unbelieving as Tallis extracted the photos of my family. The envelope fluttered to the ground as he smiled even wider. There was not a sound from the crowd. Each Legion's curiosity piqued, knowing that Tallis was about to do something spectacular.

"But I found it," he said, triumphant. "The means to dismantle my formidable human."

Tallis held the photographs up, and before I could protest, he tore them in two. The sound it made was etched in me forever. I couldn't school my face, not with this most personal dagger to my heart. Everything that he had done to me before I could shut down, put in a box. But this was too much. My knees buckled and I slid to the ground, Cove releasing me finally.

Dark satisfaction flashed over Tallis's face, and he bellowed out a laugh. Victorious. The surrounding crowd echoed his laughter. I could see the mirth on their faces, but I could no longer hear it. My ears were roaring their own fury, blocking out every other noise. I looked at Wellyn and Fenar, but they hadn't even reacted. Fenar looked bored and Wellyn still had a lopsided smile on his face.

"You still want them?" I saw Tallis mouth mockingly. He waved the ripped pieces at me, and I nodded, a spark of hope flaring in me. He must have seen it too, because his smile grew wider, more demonic. As if in slow motion, the photos started smoking, the first spark from his fingers lighting a bonfire inside of me too.

As I watched the last remnants I had of my family turn to ash, I became gray, hollowed out and numb. Drained of color. Tallis was still chuckling, his fingers stained black as his heart. The faces of those around him blurred, my vision swimming with tears. Somehow, I pushed myself to my feet, following some unconscious order while caught in the throes of flames. Tallis's revenge and the pure joy he was experiencing at causing me pain was agony.

I found my way back to the room, thankful that they had added my handprint to open it, and fell into bed. My heart sent out pulses of pain with each beat, so much that I gasped, muffled by the pillow. Hysterical sobs echoed in the room as I burrowed under the covers, desperate to escape the agony in my soul. I had already been so close to breaking and this last betrayal was the key to launching me over the edge. I couldn't stop picturing it, the smug satisfaction on Tallis's face while Wellyn and Fenar stood by and did nothing.

How had Tallis gotten the photos? Did Wellyn give them to him? The hurt I felt at his duplicity made me want to tear my heart out, to let Tallis set fire to that as well. I swallowed down the nausea I felt. I'd let those monsters touch me, I'd let get them so close without protecting myself.

What a fool I was, filled with naivete to think that this place was anything except a punishment. I deserved it for being too trusting, for falling for the scraps of affection they'd given me. I groaned, thinking of how they must have laughed at me, how stupid I was to have fallen for their lies.

The tremulous huff of my breath heated my cheeks and the covers encasing me had me feeling like I was less of an open, gaping wound. I curled up and focused on forgetting, thankful for the darkness over my head.

I imagined I was in my childhood home. Dad was calling me down to breakfast. He had the morning paper flicked up in front of him. Ma was sipping her coffee, her eyes slits from lingering fatigue. The twins were finishing their cereal. I could go down to them, but I wanted to sleep a little longer. The bed was so warm and safe. I could stay there. Just a little longer. I was safe here, surrounded by people who loved me.

"Pancake?"

I could hear a voice calling me. But I was in the backyard with Aaron now. We were kicking a ball to each other.

"Baby? *Shek*, it's like she's not even there!"

I kicked the ball again, Aaron scoffing and stopping it easily.

"We were out of our minds. Cami, talk to us," Aaron said, his little lopsided grin flashing.

Wait.

No, that wasn't right.

I buried deeper until the voices became buzzing bees in my ears. It was spring, after all, and there were plenty of them hovering over the sweetly scented blooms in the garden.

I heaved in a deep breath, enjoying the feel of the sun prickling over my skin. I raised an eyebrow at Aaron.

"Gimme all you got," I taunted him.

The End

Want all the sneak peaks for the next book? Join my facebook group for all the behind the scenes and extras!

Epilogue

WELLYN

My mouth was dry as I attempted to open my crusty eyes. I swiped a hand over them, the lids protesting as I forced them to open to slits. My body was slumped like a contortionist in the chair and I groaned at the ache that spread through my limbs. I looked over to Fenar, still asleep with his mouth open and an obnoxious rattle coming from his mouth. It was my second night in the lounge area of our apartment, ever since Tallis had pulled his last prank. Although that was too light a word for what he'd done. It arrested my heart in an endlessly rushed pattern, the aftermath of Tallis' actions. I perched on the couch in the misguided belief that I could convince Cami I wasn't a part of his ridiculous games. I took up place as a sentry, determined to talk to her when she emerged from her room. When the *Baak* had worn off, it had left only patches of hazy memories. But each one was a brand on my brain, looped a thousand times and seared with agony and guilt. Cami had looked at Fenar and me with the same expression of betrayal, and in our obliterated state, we had played right into Tallis's plans. I shifted on the lumpy couch, uncomfortable with my stupidity, rather than the cushions. I should not have trusted him. He'd never wanted to reconcile with us. He'd wanted a last-ditch attempt to slice through Cami's resolve, to hit her where it hurt the most.

He'd succeeded.

Cami loved her family more than anything. She'd given them up to ensure they had a future without stress and fear of financial ruin. She'd chosen to say goodbye to the life she knew and sacrifice her own happiness to ensure they would have their own in spades. I knew how deep her self loathing went, how she blamed herself for her family's struggles.

"Nothing?" Fenar said softly, and I shook my head. He cursed under his breath, running his hand through his bright yellow hair. Deep bruises framed his under eyes and his fangs had nibbled his bottom lip until it was raw. I knew he was just as torn as I was. Our boost devastated and we couldn't do a thing about it. It had been two days since Tallis destroyed the photographs and she'd stayed in her coma like state. Fenar and I had raced to her bedside as soon as we were cognizant of what had happened, intending to comfort her and instead found her unresponsive. She breathed, if shallowly, seeming to be suspended in a sleep that no amount of pleading could bring her out of. Cami just curled herself tighter, her eyes shut tight and all our words rolling off her like she couldn't hear them. She'd completely shut down. Tallis had finally won. I couldn't stop myself from aiming a glare at him, his arms cradled around a cushion on the window seat. His dark hair had fallen over his head and his nose nudged against the material as he stared listlessly out at the stormy expanse of the Melbak sky. His neck was darkening with the marks my tentacles had throttled out of him. When I'd realized what he'd done, I couldn't stop myself from partially shifting and letting my tentacles wrap around his neck. He'd been at my knees, face puce and cheeks puffed out as he tried to steal oxygen. My creature had demanded retribution. There was no coming back in his mind. But I saw the depths of Tallis's eyes, dark and unfathomable. His body struggled, but he begged me to do it without words. He'd wanted to die. So I let him go, let him slump to the floor so he could feel the depth of regret we all did. I wouldn't let him have an easy out. Whatever he thought he'd feel after destroying Cami hadn't eventuated. He was in agony and not only that, he'd ruined the relationship between himself and us.

"She has to come out soon," Fenar said, feverishly tugging on his hair again. Our readers chimed in unison and I whipped mine out to see who was intruding now. I expected it was Cove, who had visited daily, dripping in mortification for her role in Tallis's betrayal. At least now I knew how he'd gotten the photos and Cove had rained down apologies at how she'd used her powers to help Tallis gain entry into my room. She refused to even look at Tallis, who had taken to hovering on the surrounding outskirts, cowed by a boost who was a cocoon in her covers. I wish Cami could see it, that ruining her had destroyed Tallis in turn. But it wasn't Cove. It was from a number I didn't recognize.

Kerys Triad to present themselves at Heads tower in three days' time.

I looked at Tallis, the force of habit to turn to the leader of our triad for instructions.

"This must be to do with the Vinko, but I don't know why they insist on all of us being there."

I felt a shiver slink down my spine at the thought of being in a room occupied by *him.*

"I'm not leaving Cami," I said, jutting out my chin, expecting Tallis to argue with me, but he only gave me a slow nod.

"Neither am I," Fenar said through gritted teeth. "You can go in our place"

Tallis's jaw ticked, and I knew he wanted to argue, to assert himself as he normally did. Instead, he swallowed and let a frustrated hiss escape him, his tail rattle shaking jerkily.

"I will do my best to postpone it. Cami is in no state to be interrogated by the Heads"

"Who's fault is that?" Fenar snarled, his fragile state snapping at the reminder of why we were in the position. Tallis tore his gaze away, glaring out the window. He'd seemed as affected by Cami's self-inflicted coma as the both of us.

"I'll take care of this," Tallis replied stiltedly, pulling his reader out and stalking out of the apartment. He looked like a ghost, the bags under his eyes dark and haunting. Fenar flashed his fangs at him as he walked by.

"It's the least you can do," he spat out, a parting shot. I cradled my head in my hands, overwhelmed by the nausea sloshing around in my gut. I didn't know how to fix this. I didn't know what to do to make it right.

FENAR

I fussed through a pile of my softest blankets, pulling out the one Cami had used to cover herself, when Tallis had first started his cruel games. She'd curled up underneath it with that blasted mask covering her face and napped on the couch. I lifted it to my nose and took the meagre comfort that her faded scent offered me. She tucked herself in her bedroom still, so very close but still so far away. I didn't want to violate her privacy, to force myself into her space, not when she was still in her broken stasis. I wrapped the blanket around my body, uncaring that I looked like a swaddled baby, not when Cami's salty scent surrounded me. It was so faint and yet even my wolf stopped his raging to settle. Wellyn had his head in his hands, unmoving for the past hours that we'd held up vigil in the main room. The despair was pouring off him and he shook softly, likely his creature was reacting strongly to what had occurred. The door creaked open, Tallis returning from his dad's I thought.

"Tell me you postponed it" I sighed, but it wasn't Tallis, it was Cove. She darted a quick look around the room, seeing that there were no Cami or Tallis.

"It's just me," she said, walking over to wrap me in a hug. Wellyn looked up briefly, hopelessness swirling in the violet depths.

"Hi Cove," he said, and she went to him, dragging her fingers down the side of his face. She fussed over his collar, pressing out a non-existent wrinkle.

"Cami is still---?" she paused, unsure of how to describe Cami. Her endless slumber was disturbing and hard to imagine. My top fang pierced my lip as I bit down to stem the wave of agony that flooded my body. The impotence I felt made me want to smash something. Preferably Tallis's face, but it wasn't satisfying as he seemed to want it.

"No change," I told her, and she grimaced, her hand resting on Wellyn's curls as he sank his head into his hands again.

"You're sure there isn't more to this? Could she be suffering from an illness, something human related?"

Was it possible? Wellyn's head whipped up, and we stared at each other in abject horror. We'd left her in her room, thinking it destroyed her what Tallis had done, but what if it was just a catalyst to cause some other illness that we didn't recognize? What could cause a human to strike down and sleep for days on end? I scrambled to my feet and moved to her bedroom, my hand twisting the door open before I could think it through. The door swung open slightly and through the gap, I could hear light sobs.

"No," Wellyn gasped, pushing past me to race to her side. Cove sidled up beside me, eyeing me with concern. I stepped into the room like my shoes weighed like lead, gaze pinned to the small, shaking figure on the bed.

My boost.

She'd twisted in the sheets, her limbs wrapped in swaths of the material. The low light of the outside filtered in, but I didn't need the extra light, seeing her in excruciating detail with my wolf's increased eyesight. Wellyn perched on the bed and leaned over Cami, his hand hovering above her head. I sunk to my knees opposite, staring at her face with a whimper. Cami's face scrunched tight, her forehead furrowed and her lips muttered wordless entreaties. Water streaked her cheeks, wet with the tracks of tears that squeezed out from her swollen eyelids.

"Is she hot with fever?" I whispered to Wellyn, unable to check for myself. My chest ached with sudden fear Cove was right, that Cami was sick and we'd let her suffer not realizing. Wellyn lay the back of his hand over her skin and the wrinkles on her brow immediately smoothed. Her lips parted and a soft hiccup escaped them. Wellyn's glowing eyes flitted to me.

"She's cool. I don't think she's sick."

"What is it then?" Cove asked softly from the door. She hadn't come in, which I was grateful for.

"Tallis broke her, but from her point of view, it was all of us. She thinks we took the last link she had to her family. She thinks we betrayed her." I said.

Cami let out a little cry, a plaintive sound that made me want to howl with despair. It was killing me to see her like this, trapped in a coma of agony. I couldn't dwell on the idea that she thought Wellyn and I may have played a part in Tallis' deception. Wellyn snatched his hand from her forehead, hovering it over her hair instead, as if wondering if he should touch her again. Cami twisted in the bed, her chest rising as she sucked in stuttering breaths.

"Do it," I urged, somehow knowing that even though Cami had spurned us, that his touch would settle her. Wellyn plunged his fingers into her hair and ran them gently through the strands, carefully navigating the knots.

"I'm here Pancake, Cami. I've got you," Wellyn crooned, methodically brushing his fingers through her dark locks. My lungs burned as I watched her settle, eyes pinned on every inch of her face. I sucked in a breath as she seemed to slump, her restless turmoil slipping into actual sleep. Wellyn kept his hands on her, softly coaxing the tension from her body.

"What are we going to do?" Wellyn whispered, his voice cracking with emotion.

"We don't give up," I reply fiercely. "We fight however we can to fix her"

Seeing Cami so utterly stripped of her usual brightness was jarring to me. I only wished I had fought for her sooner, had realized like Wellyn did how special this girl was. I made a promise to myself that when Cami came back to us, I was going to come at her with more determination than anything I had ever done before. If it meant I had to wrench my chest open and hand her my beating heart? I'd do it.

This girl was going to be mine.

———————

TALLIS

I sat on the bench overlooking the springs, struck dumb by the sight of the crystal clear water. I had often visited this place when troubled or needing space. Sometimes my feet brought me here without me consciously realizing. I can't remember the last time I was here, and the water was clear. It was usually thick with Gaer, looking more like a wasteland than my mother's favorite place.

I missed her.

I rubbed my chest as it ached, my throat feeling thick with the words I wished I could say. I wanted to speak to my mother, to get her counsel. I imagined her soft embrace melting into her arms and spilling my guts with the regret and darkness that consumed me. My memories of her had faded with time, but the longing for her never seemed to diminish. I felt desperately lost in this moment.

What would she have thought of Cami? She would be disappointed in me. Somehow, I knew this to my bones. My insides felt like they were coated in gaer, a poisonous hell.

"Mother" I whispered, miserably. I couldn't call my dad. He would tear me apart for what I'd done to Cami. My triad brothers wanted nothing to do with me. I considered calling my other triad fathers, but they had melted out of my life years ago. Consumed by the grief of losing my mother, their boost. They'd forgotten about me, and I'd never let go of the fact that they weren't there for me. I had never felt so alone. In my head was a building pressure. All the ideas and beliefs I had were burning me to pieces on the inside. I lifted my hands, trying to bring the spark of my power to light them up, but there was nothing. It was like hurting Cami had sliced my powers from me. Seeing her face after I used them to destroy her had unlocked something deep inside me. Regret had crashed over me immediately. My reader rumbled in my pocket and I pulled it out reluctantly.

"Tallis," My dad's voice was reproachful. I sighed, staying silent for the lecture I knew was about to occur. "Are you alright my son?" he added, and I almost dropped my phone, surprise causing my mouth to gape open.

"I heard what happened. The head tower is teeming with gossip about a human successfully boosting a triad. I didn't believe it, especially after I saw the recording."

My heart sank. He'd seen the video. Now the tongue lashing would occur. I gritted my teeth in readiness for his disappointment.

"I know you better than them son, I know a hurting soul when I see it"

I made a noise of regret, of pain, of utter desolation. I cracked open at the honesty in his words, a hand of support through the line.

"Talk to me," dad said, a whisper and plaintive plea.

"I ruined everything," I admitted, my voice breaking as I spoke the truth for the first time. A wave of misery crashed over me as I looked out at the clear spring. I was here alone, with no-one to share this beautiful place. And it was my fault.

"She didn't boost you did she" it was a statement. The rattling sigh that followed told me that. I imagined my dad in his office, shoulders slumped and tail limp.

"No," I said, and she never would. Not after what I did. "I should have listened to you, dad. In my mind, I thought I knew what I wanted, but you were right. It was a farce. I've been working so hard to keep everything the same, to keep it safe and comfortable. I didn't want to end up like—" I cut off, not wanting to offend my dad. But he didn't let me shy away from the harsh words.

"Like me? Like your triad fathers?" his voice echoed in my ear and I was stiff as the silence drew out. I didn't know what to say. I'd seen him whittle away the years as if they didn't matter now that she was gone. I'd taken that knowledge and digested it, proof that love was dangerous, all-consuming and that it was better to make a safe choice.

"You think I regret loving your mother? Her loss was the hardest thing I have ever had to endure, Tallis. I won't lie to you. But if I had the choice to go back, I would do it a thousand times over. Because you see the aftermath of the pain, the agony of losing her, but my heart is still overflowing with years of passion and love that keep me moving. I can't speak for your triad fathers. If they knew you held yourself back out of fear, it would devastate them."

My throat tickled as I drew in careful breaths, balancing my shame and suffering like a knifes edge. One wrong word and I would slice myself through, no coming back.

"It's too late. I didn't know why I was fighting so hard against her pull until I threw us both over the cliff of no return." What could I have had if I'd listened to my body, that knew it wanted her before I did? I thought I wanted the fight, the spark that flared in her eyes that seemed to feed my fire. When she bled out on that rooftop, the agony in her gaze smothered my fires. I'd thrown the killing blow to her, not realizing it was my own demise I was wielding.

"It's never too late, there is always a way," dad soothed, and I bit my tongue with a sharp retort. You can't paste together ash. The minuscule remnants of the photos long since carried away on the wind. I jolted, an idea forming in my mind. My breath froze in my lungs and I felt the burn in my chest as a plan formed. I couldn't bring back the photos, but what if I could replace them? It wouldn't fix what I'd broken, but I'd do anything to see the life breathed back into Cami, to see her fire burn me again. I'd let her flay me gladly, let her whip strips off with her tongue, anything to atone.

"Dad, I need to postpone the meeting the heads have requested. Cami is still recovering. She's in no state to face them." I said, my eyes unseeing as I plotted.

"Of course, I'll call in a favor," he hummed. "But how do you mean to make this right with her?"

I stared out at the springs, mist rising off the top of the warm water. It looked so inviting, the water like liquid diamonds sparkling in the filtered sunlight. I set my jaw, rising to my feet. I wouldn't dip my feet in this water, not until I could bring Cami with me willingly. Not until she'd forgiven me. I had amends to make. My knees were about to hit the ground and stay there for a long time. But I imagined bringing Cami here, her sweet curves against mine in the water, laughing with Wellyn and Fenar. It would be worth it.

"Another thing," I said, feeling resolved, "I need to find a way to Earth."

Glossary

Legion: closest comparison on Earth are demons. Can take on different forms, have powers as well as tails, claws, horns and fangs.

Melbak: The small plane on which Legion live

Triad: A group of three Legion that are bound together.

Boost: Person that has special qualities in their blood that gives their triad increased power and strength. Their power feeds back to Melbak and helps strengthen the land.

Plane: The world they live in, e.g. Earth or Hell

Gaer: black, tar like substance that has taken over Melbak. Somewhat sentient.

Legion Heads: Chosen leaders of the Legion.

Noble Legion Houses:
Lamott – sub-house: Hoppe and Filay
Aydro – subhouse: Kerys and Trellys
Avanti – sub-house: Custray and Hibbis
Kindale – sub house: Lea and Canoste (these houses were erased from history)

The Vinko: Legion olympics, help every four years. Teams are compiled by the noble houses and the fourth head is chosen from the winning House.

Reader: Similar to a smart phone.

Shek: A curse word, interchangeable with 'fuck'

Binding Agreement: A promise that cannot be broken.

The Culling: Mysterious plague that wiped out scores of Legion which was supposedly spread by humans. It is the reason humans were banned from Melbak.

Cleaning room: bathing with a kind of laser beam without the need for water or soaps/shampoo

Ratid: flying rat-like creatures. Like a Chinchilla with wings.

Glut: acidic mud hole capable of burning clothing and flesh.

Afterword

BIG THANK YOU

If you are reading this, you have my endless gratitude. This book popped into my head, with the scene of Tallis destroying the photos and wrecking Cami. It just would not leave until I put it into words. From there it evolved into a wild book that I'm so happy to finally share with you.

To my wonderful husband, James. My biggest fan and endless supporter. Thank you for always having my back and believing in me.

My best friends Chantelle, Kirsty, Rachel and Sarah.

My editor Casey, thank you for your invaluable criticism and suggestions.

If you want to join me and see lots of behind the scenes, artwork and future works, scan this to join my readers group on facebook!

About Author

Mae Pierce fell in love with reading ever since she was a little girl. She loves fantasy, romance and redeeming her irredeemable male characters. She is a creative creature and loves curling up on the couch with whatever new hobby she's taken on that month like embroidery or paint by numbers.

Mae lives in Melbourne, Australia with her two wild boys and her ever patient husband, who enables her book buying obsession.

Made in United States
North Haven, CT
15 June 2024

53688428R00202